Early Praise for Killing Her Sharply

Killing Her Sharply is a gripping mystery from attorney-author Katherine Burnette that blends psychological depth, sharp procedural detail, and heart-pounding suspense. Set in Oxford, North Carolina, the novel offers a vivid picture of the social contradictions and dread realities of contemporary life in the postindustrial South gleaned, no doubt, from Burnette's experience as a prosecutor. Detective protagonists Bob and Tony are fascinating, relatable, and contradictory in exactly the right ways. Readers will love following their investigation into this small-town serial killer. If you're like me, you won't be able to put it down!

—Taylor Black, author of *Style: A Queer Cosmology*

Also by Katherine Burnette

Judge's Waltz

In the Judge's Waltz, author Kat Burnette reinvents the notion of the Hanging Judge with a twist and a vengeance, taking readers on a rollicking mystery ride through small town South as achingly familiar as Maycomb or Mayberry, one where the ancient monsters have left the woods and taken up residence in the corridors of power.

—David Payne author of *Barefoot to Avalon and Ruin Creek*

KILLING
HER SHARPLY

KATHERINE BURNETTE

ISBNs
Hardcover 978-1-960346-68-1
Paperback 978-1-960346-69-8
eBook 978-1-960346-70-4

Authorsunite.com

For my siblings:
Julia Ann, Mary Brooks, and David

CHAPTER ONE

The lighting was perfect—dim and diffused through the mists of fog that swirled on the intermittent puffs of wind. The few shoppers clutched their raincoats closer and hurried to their cars. A young woman, Cassie, hurried to her Honda Accord with two bags of groceries, one in each arm. Her car had seen better days with its rusty bumper and peeling stickers. *Coexist* was now only *exist*, and *Black Lives Matter* was reduced to just *Black Lives*. Cassie clicked open her driver's door and shoved aside her briefcase full of depositions and trial briefs to set the bags down. She pushed aside her curly hair, turned auburn by the streetlights.

Cassie stopped to put up her hand and admire her new engagement ring in the car's muted light. Two carats from her fiancé's grandmother's ring were mounted in the center of the platinum band and surrounded by small diamonds just big enough not to be called pavé. She sighed in contentment.

Before she could slide into the front seat, he pressed himself and the knife against her. She whimpered when he whispered, "Do as I say. Don't make a sound."

Trembling against him, she awkwardly eased out her wallet from the purse she'd slung across the front of her body. She pulled out the cash and cards. He took them with the hand that wasn't holding the knife. She prayed he'd let her go.

The knife's blade was cold and sharp where her shirt had ridden up over her stomach. He whispered again to her. "I want that ring. Give it to me," he said. His voice had risen an octave in his excitement during this last command.

Tears poured down her face. Cassie slid her new ring off her finger. At the last minute, she took a steadying breath and swallowed it. The knife pressed into her side, cutting her, and she cried out.

"Goddamnit!" he growled.

She tried to jerk away, but he held her tight.

"You'll have to cut it out of me now," she cried in defiance.

"With pleasure," he said and smiled.

CHAPTER TWO

*H*is fiancée *is missing, but he seems mighty cool about it,* mused Bob, the older of the two detectives seated in the den of the sleek gray and white condominium owned by Dr. Mark Graham and his fiancée, Cassie. For the last hour, they'd been going over and over the same ground.

The good doc's irritated by Tony's questions more than anything, the detective thought while he continued to stare at Mark. Periodically, Bob scribbled in his small flip notepad. A stocky Boston transplant from solid blue-collar stock observed the doctor's body language—his fidgeting hands, his facial tics, his posture.

"For the love of God," Mark said, "I haven't seen Cassie since dinner time last night. I haven't heard from her, and you just sit there and keep questioning me." He ran his fingers through his dark hair and started the story again for the detectives.

"We had an early dinner here in the condo. We got takeout, and then Cassie headed to the grocery store, and I headed into work. I went to check on my patients at the hospital. When I got back, I turned on the TV and fell asleep on the sofa. I took a sleeping pill before I turned on the TV and woke up with a crick in my neck and a sore back. All I know is that I didn't hear her last night or see her this morning, and there were no groceries in the fridge. With that sleeping pill I took, though, Sasquatch could have come in and I wouldn't have heard him."

"Aren't you worried?" asked Antoine Duval, the younger of the two detectives, "You can call me Tony."

"I was worried. That's why I called 911. Cassie is the most responsible person I know. I'm scared out of my mind," Mark said. Tears glistened in his blue eyes. He offered the detectives coffee again, which they refused again. To give himself time to compose himself, he started the espresso machine.

The condo had an open floor plan, so the detectives could see Mark in the tiny kitchen. White and blue tiles filled in the backsplash, and small pots of herbs sat on the wide windowsill. Tony stood up and called out to him.

"So, Doc, where had you been before dinner?" Tony asked.

"We were out of town celebrating our engagement with her parents. We forgot there was nothing in the fridge for us to eat for dinner. We usually do the shopping on the weekend. She goes to the same grocery store every week. Haven't you guys checked the cameras out there? Don't all stores have cameras now?"

The detectives looked at each other. Bob answered after shifting his toothpick from the right side of his mouth to the left. A former smoker, Bob needed something in or near his mouth most waking minutes. His shoes were scuffed, and his pants were shiny at the knees. He'd been doing this a long time, and something felt off with Mark. "Look, I know you're anxious, but our patrolmen are out there now looking for her. They are systematically searching all of the places you told us she went or might have gone. We just need to get as much information as you have," Bob said.

Tony looked around the small den. Decorated in hues of gray, the only splash of color was an oddly shaped tangerine pillow. "It's a pretty small place for a doctor and his lawyer fiancée," he said.

"What's that supposed to mean?" Mark snapped. "We have to live close to the hospital because I'm on call and I spend a lot of hours there. As if that's any of your damn business."

"Okay, okay. So, you had dinner here in the den, and that's the last time you saw her?" Tony asked. Tony was six feet tall and slender, with skin the color of café au lait. He'd come up from New Orleans a few months ago and was trying to settle into the Oxford Police Department.

Mark brought his coffee over, placed it on the glass coffee table, and stared at it. Mark was slightly taller and a lot wider than the young detective. He took up most of the quilt-covered couch. He scrubbed a hand over his face. The stubble on his chin was so dark it was almost blue. "What am I going to tell Cassie's parents?" Mark moaned.

"Look," Tony said, "Let's hold off on upsetting anyone, unless her folks are nearby and could help support you while you're waiting?"

"They live over in Chapel Hill, just under an hour from here. They're cool people. I know they'd want to know. I should've already called them. Oh God, what am I going to say to them? I've lost your daughter?"

Closing his small notebook, Tony stood up and put his hand on Mark's shoulder. "C'mon, let's give Cassie's folks a call. Do you want me to do it?"

"I'll do it," Mark said. "Just give me a minute." He wiped his eyes with the sleeve of his green scrubs. He stood up, went back to the kitchen, and grabbed his cell phone.

Tony looked over at Bob. "You got the text?"

Bob nodded and took his toothpick out. He'd been closely observing Mark while he answered Tony's probing questions. Bob didn't want to rush to judgment.

"Yeah, poor bastard. Let's give him a minute before we tell him our guys have found a body," Bob said.

"Agreed," Tony said.

After Mark confirmed that Cassie's parents were on the way, Bob told him about the text. Mark broke down and sobbed inconsolably on the couch. Bob called in another police officer to sit with Mark until Cassie's parents arrived.

"Look, Doc. We don't know for sure who it is over at the grocery store parking lot, but one of us will get back to you once we know anything more," Bob said.

Mark didn't respond. His shoulders shook while he sobbed in the open doorway.

The two detectives left in the department's older model dark sedan. Based on its age and style, the car fairly screamed "unmarked police vehicle." Bob drove cautiously.

Tony nagged at him to hurry up. "You drive worse than my sainted grandmother, God rest her soul. Where'd you learn to drive, Sears?" Tony asked.

"When you're a senior detective, if you live that long, you can drive however you want. Until then, shut up."

Tony said something in French, then snorted with laughter.

"Whatever, man," Bob said. "You wanna keep up the Creole shit, be my guest. You ain't in Louisiana or anywhere close to it anymore. You'd better cool it around the crime scene techs. You know they hate your guts. We won't get the scene processed until next week if you keep up this stupid feud with them."

Tony threw back his head and laughed. He'd riled up all the techs with his derogatory sneers toward them at his first official crime scene. Unfortunately, their superior officer, Clementine Laforte, had spent summers near the bayous with his grandparents and knew enough of what Tony said to translate it. The techs refused to speak to Tony now unless directed to do so. Even his high cheekbones and wide, boyish smile failed to earn him a glance from one of the team. "*Cherchez la femme*," Tony said to himself.

Bob parked the unmarked car so close to the crime scene that it nudged the yellow caution tape inward. The patrolman glared at the car until he saw who was driving. Bob pulled Cassie's photo out of his jacket pocket, a jacket that looked like it belonged in the dumpster. '

Clementine grunted at Bob and Tony's arrival but stayed bent over a portion of the crime scene. The yellow caution tape surrounded the rusted dark metal dumpster in the far corner of the grocery store parking lot. The neighborhood store had been in business for over twenty years and was patronized by the residents who lived nearby, hospital employees, and local community college students.

The midday sun beat down on officers standing knee deep in garbage. The sanitation workers had already mucked up the crime scene by shifting the heavy bags around by hand to redistribute the container's weight. One bag had split open, revealing a gruesome sight: one arm, one leg, and one head spilled out.

"Ever hear of dry cleaning?" Tony snarled as he shoved his car door open. Bob grunted, pushing himself upright with the aid of the steering wheel.

Tony always became snarky at crime scenes. Bob was used to it now, but it didn't make things any easier. He had to run interference between Tony and the techs, the medical examiner, the patrolmen—damn near everybody. The techs in their outer space-looking white suits scattered when they spotted Tony. Bob pulled his antacids out of his pants pocket and shoved two in his mouth. *Gonna be a bastard of a day*. Seeing the head on the tarmac confirmed it. Its dark brown curls were matted with a substance he did not want to examine too closely, but he went over anyway. He put his linen handkerchief up to his mouth and then slicked his upper lip with VapoRub to dull the foul odor emanating from the head and the dumpster. His ex-wife, Gloria, had bought a bunch of the handkerchiefs with his monogram on them. Sometimes the things came in handy, like today.

The medical examiner had stayed in his huge Lincoln with the engine and air conditioning running until the detectives arrived. A big white-headed man, formerly from Texas, Dr. Cameron Patterson was gruff but good at what he did—quick and methodical exams. Plus, he was a beast on the stand at trial. The District Attorney's office loved him. Cool and calm, he never appeared rattled or anything other than at ease, whether at a crime scene or in the witness box.

Tony got on Patterson's nerves every time, or that's how it seemed at first. Lately, though, Bob had caught Dr. Patterson looking at Tony with something other than disgust. Tony seemed impervious to his barbs. Sadly, Tony seemed impervious to most insults.

Tony, the newest detective on the force, was assigned to Bob straight out of his transfer in from New Orleans. Tony was enthusiastic, irritable, caustic, annoying, and smart—way more seasoned than most detectives Bob had known at the age of thirty. When Bob complained to the Chief about the partnership, the Chief just looked at Bob for a few minutes, then said, "Bob, I'm going to be honest with you. You've been in a rut for two years. I don't know what else to do with you. I've tried to be patient and think I have been, but Gloria's been gone two years now. You're a good detective, but you need to turn your focus back on the job. This young guy from The Big Easy, Tony, will shake you out of your depression. Tony will either have you laughing or fighting every asshole he insults. Either way, I'm betting you'll quit coasting, and you'll smooth off his rough edges in no time. You're too young to retire and too old to bust down to patrolman."

Tony hunched down beside the head and impatiently motioned Bob over. Bob shook himself out of his daydream and walked over to Tony. Snatching Cassie's photo out of Bob's hand, Tony said, "It's her."

A long shadow darkened the taped area.

"Got an ID, looks like," drawled the old Texan.

"Yeah, Doc Holliday. Got us a positive ID. Where's your horse? The boots are a good look," Tony said.

Dr. Patterson looked down at his shiny hand-tooled leather boots. "They're pretty swanky, but I like to dress to impress. Wouldn't be too hard to impress a scruffy ol' Cajun like yourself, would it?"

Tony straightened up to his full height and pushed his chest out.

Oh, boy, thought Bob. He wedged himself between the two men.

"Unlike my friend Bob here, I like some nice threads," Patterson said.

"What the fuck is it with you two?" Bob asked, stung. "What have you got against my clothes?"

"Everything," Dr. Patterson and Tony said in unison, then started laughing. Bob left them discussing Dr. Patterson's year-long wait for boots designed by Charlie Dunn. Dunn's death delayed their construction, but his successor promised to fabricate them for him.

"Jesus," Bob said, and started to walk over to talk to the two sanitation workers. He stopped and turned around. "There's not a damn thing wrong with this suit," he complained. He'd bought it ten years ago at Joseph Banks and it still looked good. Well, maybe a little worn at the hem and cuffs, but not so shabby." Switching gears, he asked, "What about it, Patterson? Was this poor girl alive when, you know…"

Patterson shrugged. "I can't tell if the cuts were made prior to or after death. I also don't see any cuts that were started and then aborted. Looks like no hesitation on the part of the killer. I'd say that he or she knew just what they were doing."

Getting the times of the discovery of the body parts from the terrified sanitation workers and getting the store to pull up its tapes for the outside cameras took more than an hour. Tony canvassed the employees in the other stores in the strip mall, but no one had seen anything. Most of the stores were not open past six in the evening, so all the employees could give him were their security tapes. Unfortunately, a lot of the businesses had cameras but no tapes in them. Tony directed three of the uniformed patrolmen to stand by and pull tape for the relevant times.

When Tony returned to the crime scene, Bob was talking quietly to Dr. Patterson over by his Lincoln. "Should we wait on more information to make a positive ID, you know, before we get Mark, Cassie's fiancé, down to the morgue?" Tony asked. "I'd hate for him to have to see her like that, if it is her. This is going to be rough."

"I'd like to spare him this too," Bob said, "but she has the same hair color and facial features in the photo. I think we've got to bring him in and talk to him again anyway. And we need to contact her employer—some lawyer's office—and one of us should go through her personal office. To corroborate any ID, we're gonna need to get the lady's dental records. You got a time of death, Doc?" Bob asked, turning to Dr. Patterson.

Patterson had crouched back down over the body parts, holding a flashlight and a small camera. "No, nothing I feel comfortable with until I can get the body, um, parts to the morgue. I'll tell you, though, whoever did this had some skill."

"How do you figure that?" Tony asked.

"These parts were severed with some professional type of equipment and not your everyday kitchen knife," Patterson replied.

"What about a medical doctor? Would most of them have that skill?" Tony asked.

"Yeah, they would," Patterson said. "What a mess. Have you guys located the rest of the poor lady?"

"Nah," Bob said, "but they're looking. We'll keep searching until the dumpster's empty."

"I don't envy your officers that," Patterson said. The big Texan stopped to wipe his forehead. The sun warmed the contents of the dumpster and the body parts. The scent of decaying lettuce and stale beer mingled with the smell of human decay.

"Me neither," Bob said. "Hey, you guys want to get a sandwich? I'm going to bring some lunch back for the poor guys in the dumpster. They're going to be here awhile."

"I could go for something. Sure. What have you got in mind?" Dr. Patterson asked.

"Don't worry, Doc," Tony said. "Bob's taste in food is superior to his taste in clothes. He always knows the best places."

"Now, let's see. There's the Chinese over on Broad, or some good sushi on Main. And, there's the new soul food place that just opened around the corner. Heard they got some ribs that are mighty fine," Bob said.

Dr. Patterson smiled and rubbed his big hands together. "Boy, that sounds good," he said. "I'll meet y'all over there." To the techs he said, "See you guys over at the morgue in about an hour."

The three men piled into the Lincoln, which purred down the street and floated into the gravel lot of the Soul Food Diner.

The front door opened to the tinkle of bells. The hostess smiled at Bob. "You back again, honey?" she asked him and collected three menus on the way to a big booth. "We got cornbread, pork chops, and turnip greens on special today."

"I'll take four to-go orders of the special when we leave," Bob said. "With sweet teas," he added.

She left the menus on the table and winked at Bob.

The other two men looked at Bob in silence.

"What?" Bob asked. "Someone enjoys my company, and that's a shock to you?"

Tony played with the saltshaker. "No, no shock. How many times you been in here to eat?"

Bob counted on his fingers. "Well, about three times this week. I hate cooking for myself, and they do it up right in here."

Examining the menus, Tony and Dr. Patterson got Bob's advice on dishes that he'd already tried. On her return, the hostess, Corrine, brought three unsweetened teas, sugar packets, and a bowl of lemons. She pegged Tony's accent, and they were off and running on the best restaurants in New Orleans. Bob finally interrupted their patter so they could order. He and Tony got the catfish plate, and Dr. Patterson ordered the ribs after making sure that they would be almost as good as the ones back home in Texas.

Every bite of the golden fish and cold coleslaw was delicious. Even Tony had nothing but good things to say. Dr. Patterson cleaned every rib bone. Sheepishly, he asked Corrine if he could buy some extra ribs to take home to his dog. The hostess laughed and put a small bag in his hand when he left.

"Let me guess what kind of dog you have," Tony said. "Give me three guesses. I bet it's a big dumb Lab?"

Dr. Patterson smiled but shook his head.

"Okay. I got two more. It's a sheep herding dog—what do they call those? I know, a Border Collie?"

Dr. Patterson shook his head. "Give up?" he asked.

"Hell, no," Tony said. He snapped his fingers. "I got it. It's a big ol' thickheaded Bloodhound. Just sits on your porch beside your rocker while you strum the banjo."

Dr. Patterson threw back his head and laughed. "Nope. Okay, Bob. You want three guesses?"

"I'm guessing it's a German Shepherd," Bob said. "One of those fancy monastery-bred dogs."

"Now, how the hell did you guess it?" Dr. Patterson asked.

"I'm a seasoned detective. I detect. And, you left the Skete monastery brochure in the backseat," Bob said.

"That's cheating," Tony said.

"Quit whining. You started it," Dr. Patterson grumbled.

"I'd love to see your dog sometime when you have a free hour. Those are beautiful shepherds. My son always wanted one—a German shepherd. We just never got around to getting a dog. I wish we had," Bob said, lost in thought and walking ahead of the other two.

Tony started to say something, but Dr. Patterson caught his eye and shook his head. "I'd love for you both to meet Franz sometime. He's still a puppy, but give him a couple of weeks and he'll have some training behind him. Guess we need to head over to the morgue now. I'll drop y'all at your car so you can drop the food for the guys, and then you can follow me over," Dr. Patterson said.

* * * * *

They sat in silence while Tony drove back to the crime scene. Bob resolved to spend more time with the young detective. He reflected back on how it had been when he first joined the police department. Even though he had some experience, it had been rough being a *transplant*, and one from Boston at that, one that didn't "talk right."

The first week, someone left him a note to follow up on some car breaking-and-entering cases. They'd put the name "Mr. Raymar" and a cell number on a pink message slip. Dutifully, he'd called the number and asked for Mr. Raymar. A brief pause ensued, then the speaker repeated the name. "You want to speak to Mr. Raymar?" the man on the other end of the call asked.

"Yes, this is uh, Robert, I mean Bob Kelly," Bob responded impatiently. "I'm a detective with the Oxford Police Department. I'm following up on a tip involving some breaking and entering of cars here."

A longer pause ensued.

"Well, I don't think it was Raymar," the bodiless voice drawled.

"I'll be the judge of that, sir. I'm the detective after all. Put him on."

"I gotcha," the man responded, "but, you see, Mr. Raymar hasn't left here for about twenty years."

"For God's sakes, just put him on the phone," Bob thundered.

"Well, Mr. Raymar's having his breakfast, so he can't come to the phone."

Bob pulled the black handset from his desk phone away from his ear and stared at it. He cursed under his breath. "I'm coming down there. Now give me the address," Bob said.

"Okay, boss. Up to you. But we're not open until ten o'clock in the morning. And Mr. Raymar ain't too keen on mornings anyway."

"Give me the address," Bob barked, fumbling for pen and paper. He knocked over his coffee cup and narrowly missed putting his tie in the mess.

"Asheboro Zoo. Can't miss us. Just head down I-85 and follow the signs."

"The zoo?" Bob asked.

"Yeah. Mr. Raymar, as you call him, is our oldest silverback gorilla. I just don't see him breaking into cars, but what do I know? You're the detective."

CHAPTER THREE

Mr. Bruno Lamberti, birth name Billy Joe Currin, sharpened his kitchen knives by the light of the streetlamps. He didn't want anyone to know he was working so late. The snick of sharpening blades soothed his frayed nerves. The cool of the steel felt comfortable in his calloused hands. The kitchen was redolent of onions and the not unpleasant smell of grease.

Lamberti had overcome his origins in the Hurricanes part of the county and his high school reputation as a shambling, mullet-wearing slacker whose only talent was wrestling.

For the past five years, he'd enjoyed regional acclaim as Lamberti for his beef medallions and various succulent Sunday roasts. Lately, however, he'd been in a creative slump. His weekend clientele petered out. No one came to the Oak Room for Sunday lunch. No one asked to meet the chef.

Part of the problem started six months ago when a group of lady lawyers met for their yearly get-together. They'd laughed, talked about who would likely be engaged by summer, had a few drinks, and stayed past closing, but one of them posted photos of the food and wrote a scathing review of his newest medallions dish. The photos featured graying and congealing meat. Other people chimed in on the social media conversation with increasingly brutal and negative reviews. Dinner reservations started to fall off.

The staff gave him a wide berth these days. His temper flared up at the smallest of things. He was finding it harder and harder to hold it together, but he had to. He needed the job to support his mom in the Beechwood Assisted Living Center's dementia unit. He was her only child. Some days she remembered him, but most days she did not. Thankfully, she would not see or understand the terrible posts about the restaurant and about him.

He wasn't a young man anymore. There was more gray than dark in his hair and beard. It would be hard to start over in another kitchen. Starting at the bottom again would be the final blow to his fragile ego. The fear of failure pressed down on his chest like a physical weight.

Tears scored his face, and he used his shoulder to wipe them away. "Get a hold of yourself," he muttered.

Sharpening each knife brought him peace. The motion's rhythm was hypnotic, and the feel of the wooden handles soothed his nerves. Satisfied with his work, he placed the knives back into the drawer and into the knife block.

All but one knife went back into its holder. The sharpest and largest he continued to hold, running his fingers lightly up and down the cool steel.

Shaking himself out of the daydream, he hung his chef's jacket on the hook by the back door and slipped the knife into his backpack.

* * * * *

The morgue visit was every bit as gruesome as Bob had expected. Tony kept up his nervous talking until Bob wanted to take a swipe at him to shut him up.

That'd suit the Chief down to the ground, Bob thought. *Taking his rookie out for talking like a chatterbox.* Tony was up and pacing in the small, sterile space, and Bob was seated on a metal folding chair that he'd hauled into the room. After Dr. Patterson checked the dental records he received from patrol against the head's teeth, he was prepared to say that at least that part was Cassie. He would do DNA testing on the arm and the leg to confirm whether they belonged to her too.

The thorough search of the dumpster revealed a lot of things, but no more body parts. Handbags, shoes, money, wallets, food wrappers, hats, rugs, drugs, condoms, just about everything had been shoved into the receptacle.

One thing the patrol had not found in abundance was blood. The medical examiner concluded that Cassie had been killed or dismembered somewhere else and brought to the dumpster later.

Dr. Mark Graham was on his way to make the identification. Cassie's parents had offered, but Mark felt responsible for Cassie and wanted to do this for them.

"What kind of doctor is Mark anyway?" Tony asked.

"A general surgeon, why?" Bob answered.

"A general surgeon would know his way around a knife."

"Yep. And, a few blocks from their condo was a whole floor of surgeons. What's your point?"

"You don't like him for it? Isn't it always the boyfriend or the husband?" Tony asked.

"Not always. I don't know about here. We're going to have to check out Dr. Graham's alibi. See if it matches up to his story. Talk to the takeaway restaurant, run everything down."

"Yeah, okay."

Bob yawned and rubbed his eyes. He had not gotten much sleep the past few days. Tony looked over at him and said, "I can handle this part. Why don't you go home and get some sleep? We can meet early tomorrow at the hospital and start checking."

"Okay," Bob said and tossed Tony the keys to the car. "I'll grab a cab outside and meet you at 8:00 a.m. at the hospital cafeteria. How's that?"

"Sounds good to me. I'll call you from here if he doesn't ID her. Okay?"

"Yeah, thanks. See ya, Doc."

"I'll get my draft report over to you and the DA tomorrow afternoon. I need to spend some more time running some tests," Dr. Patterson said.

* * * * *

Bob let himself in the front door of the one-and-a-half-story brick home, the one that he, Gloria, and their son, Matthew, had shared. Now, it was just him. He only used the den, his bedroom, and, less often now, the kitchen. Planted beside his recliner, the dingy TV tray held his most cherished possessions—his remote, reading glasses, and his stubby and none-too-clean glass.

Almost two years ago, Gloria had packed up her car and headed to Myrtle Beach. She'd bought a condo and started taking classes: cooking, salsa, tango, watercolor, line dancing, the list went on and on. She'd gotten a part-time job selling real estate and had done pretty well for herself. He followed her on Facebook every now and then.

They hadn't fought. They'd just quit talking to each other. The silence in the house was killing them both. Bob dealt with it by

25

working long hours and falling into bed exhausted each night. Gloria had turned to wine, then mixed drinks, then straight vodka, then whatever was on hand. Sometimes she'd be fully dressed, spread-eagle in bed, dead to the world when he got home, and other times on the sofa, passed out. The ghastly hangovers made her irritable, angry, and weepy. Finally, she'd packed a small bag and checked herself into rehab a few states away. She'd stayed there for ninety days.

Bob never told her how proud he was of her for sticking with the program. She hadn't fallen off the wagon afterwards, but she'd fallen out of love with him. When she finally moved out, she didn't have much to say to him. She left behind a piece of paper with her new address and her new phone number, and that was it. Twenty years of marriage tied up in a U-Haul box.

Bob avoided thinking of the real reason their marriage didn't last. He worked until he was dog tired, came home, and did crossword puzzles until his eyes glazed over. He refused to look at the family photographs on the mantle. He wouldn't or couldn't move. He kept the room dim. Except for the light of the television and the reader's lamp beside him, the room was dark. The curtains were kept closed over the white shutters. No plant had ever survived that environment.

When he couldn't keep himself busy or exhausted, the memories crowded in, almost destroying what little equanimity he had left. Whole weeks could go by, but then he'd hear a song on the radio and turn to talk to his son and realize he wasn't there. Those were the days Bob wanted to eat his gun and be done with it, but he didn't have the courage to do it. Too many years of his mother drilling Catholic rules, the Ten Commandments, and her own moral code into his head stopped him from pulling the trigger.

One soft spring night, with a sky filled with sparkling stars, Matthew had died of a drug overdose. Their straight-A student varsity athlete who'd just been accepted to his dream college had taken heroin and died. Unknown to Matthew and his friends, the heroin had been laced with fentanyl. Their beautiful boy, their tow-headed toddler, had quit breathing on someone's dirty sticky basement floor surrounded by needles, wax bindles, tin foil, and beer bottles. When his friends couldn't get Matthew to wake up, they picked him up, threw him in the cargo area of the SUV, and sped to the hospital. Scared of what would happen to them, they rolled him out onto the concrete in front of the hospital and pulled off. If they'd only had Naloxone or run in and asked for help, Matthew might still be here with him and Gloria.

Almost equally as devastating was excavating their son's secret life. Once they'd found out the lies, they couldn't forget them, and they didn't have him to talk to about what they'd found out. According to his friends, Matthew had been depressed since Madeline, his steady girlfriend, told him she was pregnant. Matthew didn't know it, but Madeline had lied. She'd only been "testing his love for her," she said to them, weeping in her parents' arms. Bob and Gloria were livid by her betrayal and raged at her until her father threw them out of his house. Other friends, good friends, were afraid to tell Bob and Gloria just how deep into drugs Matthew had fallen. He'd told his friends that his life was over, that he'd have to marry Madeline because there was no way he would let her get an abortion.

For Bob, the more time passed, the fuzzier the memories became, both the joy and effervescence of the good and the paralyzing and debilitating pain of the bad memories. Remembering fun times as a family on vacation helped Bob get to sleep at night. Well, that and a shot of scotch—sometimes two shots.

Bob now wished that he and Gloria had tried harder, that they'd turned to each other instead of sinking into silence. Bob wouldn't agree to counseling back then unless it was with their church's priest. Gloria refused to go at all. He'd give a lot to be able to really talk to her. She'd understand how he felt: how defenseless, powerless, and empty.

* * * * *

In the time of day between sleeping and waking, there was the time of half-formed thoughts when Bob's brain was slowly purring back into gear. His eyes were closed, but he became aware of a weak light filtering in between the bedroom shutters. A sound that wasn't really pure sound but was part sound and part feeling woke him up.

Matthew was seated at the end of his bed. His image waivered in the early morning light.

"Hey, Dad. It's me, Matthew," he said.

Bob closed his eyes again so he could relive the dream of his son sitting on his bed.

"Dad, it's me, really."

Bob lifted his head from his pillow and asked, "Matthew?"

"Yeah?"

"Am I in heaven, Matthew?"

His son laughed. "No, Dad. You're just waking up. Look, I don't have much time. I wanted to tell you how much I love you and Mom. And, I'm sorry for screwing your lives up. I didn't kill myself. I wouldn't commit suicide. I promise."

Tears streaming down his face, Bob whispered, "I know you wouldn't, son. I know how much your faith meant to you."

"I knew you'd listen," Matthew smiled.

"Mom just screamed when she saw me and started lighting candles. Eventually, she calmed down, but she got the broom out and started waving it at me. She misses you, you know."

"Oh. No, I don't know," Bob said.

"Anyway, I've come back to do something. I haven't been told what or how long I'll have. But, I'd like to hang out with you if I'm allowed."

"You're allowed anytime. I wish you could stay. I really miss you, son. And I love you."

"I love you, too, Dad," Matthew said. The air shimmered, and he was gone.

Bob wept.

CHAPTER FOUR

I n a piss-poor mood, Bob slurped his black coffee from the chipped plastic cup and burned his tongue.

"Goddamnit," he said. He glanced around to make sure none of the hospital staff had heard him and craned his neck looking for Tony. It was 8:10 a.m. and they'd agreed to meet at 8:00 a.m.

Where is that asshole? I'm not waiting much longer for the prima donna.

As if summoned from the air, Tony plunked down his warped beige tray across from Bob and greeted him. "Good morning," Tony said.

"What's so damn good about it? We've got to go tell some decent folks that not only is their daughter dead, but she's cut up in pieces, and we have no idea who did it. Or, where the rest of her might be." Bob growled, plunking down his cup, then snatching it back up to go get more coffee.

Tony's plate teetered. It was piled high with scrambled eggs, bacon, sausage, fruit, biscuits, and muffins. The smell of the fatty bacon hung in the air.

"Damn," Bob said. "I wish I were young again and could eat like that without having to fast for two days and run ten miles afterward."

Smiling, Tony bent over his plate and enjoyed every bite. When he was almost finished, he updated Bob on yesterday's developments. There were none. The officers had turned in the various store recordings and the grocery store's recordings, but that was it. No tips on the Crime Stoppers tip line. No anonymous phone calls to the nurse's station on the fifth floor.

They discussed the order of staff interviews to check out Dr. Graham's alibi for the night before. They first had an appointment with a hospital administrator that Bob would lead, and then they'd go to the nurses' station on the fifth floor.

Tony stared into his coffee cup for a minute. "Want some more coffee, rookie?" Bob asked.

"Nah, I'm good. I just want a minute to say something to you—in all seriousness." Tony cleared his throat and went on, "You've been a great partner and helped me to feel at home."

Bob started to say something, but Tony held up his hand. "Please," he said. "Let me say this. Not everyone would have wanted me as their partner, and I appreciate you toughing it out. I don't like to fuel rumors or to listen to crap that is third and fourth hand. So, I want to be straight with you. Bob, you've been down in the dumps for a few weeks. Is there anything that I should know, or is there a way I can help?"

Bob sat in silence. He hadn't kept his promise to spend more time with Tony and cursed himself. He let the hospital sounds ebb and flow around him. Slowly, he shook his head.

"Okay," Tony said, "but what I'm hearing is that you've been so depressed that you want to die. That you've had a lot of tough shit happen to you. I get it. Sometimes all life hands you is a bunch of crap. I know we gotta go in a minute, but I want to tell you a story."

Bob nodded for him to go on.

"Oh boy. I haven't really put this into words. My granddad, who half-raised me, called me back to Oxford because my Dad was back to drinking and drugging. My granddad was tired of putting up with it: bailing him out of jail, literally pulling him out of the gutter, and making excuses for him. Granddad didn't tell me the worst of it until I'd already rented a place and got this job. My Dad has liver cancer and has only a few months, if that, to live. So, I moved back to look after the only two men in my life who ever meant anything to me. Now, that's sad, but we're all going to die someday, and my granddad's eighty-nine and my dad's seventy-three. They've pretty much lived like they wanted."

"That's terrible. Having to watch your dad die and your grandfather get old. Do you have any siblings—brothers or sisters—who can help out or support you?" Bob asked.

"Bob, I know what siblings are," Tony smiled. "The answer is both yes and no. I'm going to tell you something I hope you'll keep in confidence, or at least only talk about with people as stand-up as you are. I'm only telling you this now because I want to clear the air between us and be totally straight up." Tony paused for so long that Bob thought he'd changed his mind.

"I decided to live my life on my terms, which means I identify with the LGBTQ community. My birth brothers and sisters don't speak to me. Haven't spoken to me in years. I saw them in the distance at my grandmother's funeral, but that's it. My fellow police officers in New Orleans were either cool with it or ignored it. I don't expect you to understand or 'deal with it,' but I wanted to put it out there so you know I'll always be honest with you even if I am hot-headed, arrogant, and a fine-looking specimen of humanity."

Bob sat back in his uncomfortable cafeteria chair. "I appreciate the honesty," Bob said. "I'm really glad you felt you could be open and honest with me instead of letting me hear it around the station. It takes an old codger like me a while to process things. I'm slow in that way, but I've got your back no matter what, even if you decide to show up one day for work in stilettos and glitter. You're dedicated, and you're doing a good job for a rookie. Now, come on, let's go see if we can rattle the good doctor's alibi."

* * * * *

The hospital administrator looked down her nose at the detectives and looked back at her computer screen. "Why are you here?" she asked again. She looked like the head nun at Bob's elementary school in Boston: straight back, gray hair in a high bun, and half-glasses perched on her nose.

Bob sat up straighter. "We're here because we need to check the work assignments for Dr. Graham, Dr. Mark Graham, from the other night. We'll need to talk to the nurses and other doctors who worked with him. Just a formality, really."

She cleared her throat and shot him another look. "Well, I guess there can't be any harm in letting you do that."

Bob hesitated. "I get the feeling the doctor has been in or is in some kinda trouble. Can you confirm that?"

She busied herself straightening the already straight blotter and squaring the letter opener at a right angle. "I'm calling Legal," she said. "Now, if you'll excuse me, please go back to the waiting area. Thank you." Her frosty demeanor turned positively glacial as indicated by her pursed mouth and rigid back.

Bob and Tony glanced at each other but went back to the waiting area as directed. Tony went into the hall to check in with the department on his cell phone. Bob picked up a magazine that had a three-year-old Christmas feature.

The young receptionist kept glancing at them with open curiosity. The brass wall clock ticked and ticked. Finally, the door to the administrator's office opened. She poked out her head and said, "Sandy, call me when Legal gets here. They can come back in with them."

Sandy kept sneaking glances at Tony when she thought he was not looking at her. Each time he looked up, she'd giggle and start shuffling the papers on her desk.

The hospital's legal team arrived a few minutes later. A short, heavily built man, followed by a young, slender redhead dressed in a black suit with a white blouse, didn't bother knocking on the door but strode in and shut it firmly. Neither of them acknowledged Bob or Tony. After several minutes, the door opened, and the redheaded female beckoned to the two detectives.

"Detectives," she said. "I'm Michelle Clarkson. Seated next to me is Mitch Sternberg. You've already met Cordelia Thompson, our hospital administrator. Please come in and have a seat."

Mr. Sternberg carefully reviewed their credentials. He glanced down at a Redweld folder on the small conference room table in front of him. The veneer had pulled off the edges, and coffee mug rings were branded into the medium-toned wood. "You've been asking about Dr. Mark Graham," he said. "Can you help me understand what your questions have to do with his fiancée's death?"

Bob leaned in, arms on his knees. A fresh toothpick from the cafeteria slewed around in his mouth. "We're checking on a couple of things. One, we're checking on his alibi, and two, we're checking on what motive he'd have to kill his fiancée. We'd like to exclude him as a suspect. Seems to me, you'd like the answers to those questions yourself, him being a doctor employed by your hospital and all."

Tony braced himself. Bob's cadence slowed, and his accent became more pronounced, which meant he was really mad.

Mr. Sternberg coughed. "Er, yes, that's right. Well, you asked about complaints. We've had one or two in which the staff said he got a little too *handsy.*"

"Handsy? What is that when it's at home?" Bob asked, deliberately playing obtuse.

"Well, let's just say that the staff thought Dr. Graham took unwarranted advantage of their persons," Sternberg said.

"Tony, what is the *unwarranted advantage of one's person?*" Bob asked.

"Ya got me. Look, Sternberg, my partner wants to know: What did the doc grab? Boobs, ass, what? And who complained and when?"

"No need to get crass, detective," he said. Sternberg looked offended. To his left, Ms. Clarkson was stifling some emotion by faking a cough.

Bob narrowed his eyes at her. "Look, we ain't got all day. We're trying to solve a murder here. If you don't give us what we want, then we'll get an order or a search warrant for the records. C'mon, Tony, we need to get going."

Tony stood up and followed Bob to the door.

"Wait," Sternberg said. "Let's just wait a minute here. This is a respected surgeon who has a sterling reputation. No need to get angry."

Bob turned and shoved his hands into his pockets. "I'm not angry. I'm going to call Judge Jones and ask him for a court order. After I get it, I'm going to ask the sheriff to serve it to you. Then, I'll get what I need this afternoon from you after you appear in court with the documents. You'll get to deal directly with Judge Jones."

As they passed through the door to reception, Tony said loudly, "Not Hanging Judge Jones? Oh my God. He has a terrible temper. The last guy who messed around and wasted his time is still in jail."

In the administrator's office, Sternberg blanched and rose heavily to his feet. "Detectives, detectives! Ms. Clarkson will get you a copy of the files before you leave," he huffed.

The hospital administrator rolled her eyes at Clarkson, who just sighed. Tony poked his head back into the room. "Thanks, man. See you in a bit, Ms. Clarkson."

Ms. Clarkson glared at Tony.

Bob and Tony laughed themselves almost sick in the elevator on the way to the fifth floor.

"Did you see his face?" Tony screamed.

"I know. I thought he was going to have a coronary. 'Hanging Judge Jones' did it for him," Bob snorted.

Settling down, Bob mused, "What the hell can be in all of those files? Whatever it is, we may have to do a more detailed background on the Doc."

The elevator opened, and they stepped out into a moderately well-lit hallway that smelled of disinfectant, urine, and cabbage. Locating the nurse's station directional sign, they headed down several hallways before getting to it.

When they arrived, Tony asked the nearest nurse for the head nurse. The nurse at the small station gave him a once-over and stared at his gold badge hanging from a chain around his neck. "She's on break," the nurse said, mimicking someone smoking a cigarette.

"She knows those things can kill you, right?" he asked.

The nurse shrugged her shoulders and went back to looking at a chart.

Bob gave it a shot. "We're here to talk to the person who has this week's schedule for the staff for this floor."

Without looking up, she said, "You're looking at her. What do you need?"

"We need to check the schedule to see when Dr. Graham was here and who he was with," Tony said.

"Give me a minute," she said, turning around to a plastic divider on the wall. She pulled out a folder and handed it to Tony.

"Here's this week's rotation. The head nurse notates on the right side of the schedule whether the employee showed up and when."

"Thank you," Bob said. "Is there somewhere we can sit down with this. We'll bring it back to you."

"Sure. Go back down the hall, and at the end on the right is the family waiting room. There should be a couple of seats in there."

The family waiting room was dim. The only window had a dusty plastic blind pulled down over it. A toddler was playing with the cord while his parents were slumped on opposite ends of a musty couch, glued to their cell phones. An elderly man sat stiffly in his chair with his arms crossed. No one looked up when the detectives came in and sat in the corner in two chairs with a small sofa table in between. Tony took out half of the papers and handed them to Bob. He found the handwritten roster for the last two days and saw notes indicating that Dr. Graham had been in on Sunday night, even though he was not scheduled. There were eight others scheduled for the shift, and seven had shown up. Wordlessly, he handed it over to Bob.

"Let's go find these seven folks and hear what they have to say," Bob said. "It'd be nice to have an interview room."

The toddler walked jerkily over, put her hand on the file, and threw it on the floor. She giggled. Her mom looked up. "Constance, doll, pick those up," she said lethargically. Constance laughed and helped the detectives pick up the papers, crumpling a few in the process.

"Thanks, angel," Tony said. Constance beamed up at him and reached for him.

"No, Constance. The nice man doesn't want to pick you up. Come over here," she said and smiled apologetically. "Constance is bored sitting here every day. Waiting on her big brother to get better."

"I certainly hope he gets better soon, ma'am," Tony said.

Tears began slowly rolling down her cheeks. "I'm not sure he will. He had a stroke after snorting too much cocaine. He's in a coma," she said. "They operated a couple of days ago to relieve the pressure on his brain." The man on the other end of the sofa leaned over and awkwardly patted her arm. Constance went over and stood between her mother's knees.

"You've been too lenient with that boy, Martha," the man in the chair added. If you'd kept him home, none of this would have happened. Back in my day, children went to school, to their job, and then home," he sniffed.

Bob started to leave the room but turned back at the old man's words. "She loves the boy and needs support, not criticism. You need to give it to her or head on home," Bob said.

The old man looked affronted but said nothing more. He turned his head toward the window.

"That's a terrible tragedy," Tony said.

Bob remained silent until they reached the nurses' station. "We need to interview these folks on the roster," he said. The same nurse, Janie Abbott, on her name tag, shrugged. "None of those folks are here on day shift except Allison. Let me go and check. The best thing you can do is head to the cafeteria. I'll send her down. It'll be more comfortable, and she could probably do with another cup of coffee."

"Fine. When can we talk to the rest?"

"Let me see the list again," she said. After a few minutes, she said, "You can talk to the rest tonight after seven."

"Thanks. I appreciate it," Bob said.

"Dr. Graham is a great surgeon. He'd never do anything to hurt Cassie."

"I appreciate your input. Have you known him long?"

"I guess a couple of years now. He really is wonderful with the patients," she said.

"How about with the staff?" Bob asked.

Janie looked down the hall and then back at Bob. "I don't care what you've heard, the man is a gift to this hospital." She put the file back into its slot on the wall and picked up another chart.

Bob and Tony stopped by Sandy's desk and told her they'd be in the cafeteria if Ms. Clarkson stopped by with the file. Sandy batted her eyelashes at Tony and giggled before she agreed to deliver the message.

Once in the hall, Bob turned to Tony.

"That girl's got it bad for you," Bob said.

"Yeah, apparently. Not going to happen. Too young, too female…" Tony trailed off, seeing Ms. Clarkson striding toward them.

She handed Bob a large folder and had him sign the receipt for the hospital.

"Look," she said, hesitantly. "I knew Cassie a little bit. We were in the same law school class. There's no way Dr. Graham could do this. Those two had a whirlwind romance, and it was true love. I'm sorry, but I think you're barking up the wrong tree."

Bob looked down at his phone. "Excuse me a minute," he said and stepped away. A few minutes later, he said to Tony, "We gotta go."

"Okay. Ms. Clarkson, can you tell Nurse Allison we were called away, but we'll be back to talk to her?"

"Sure. Everything okay?" she asked.

"Keep this confidential. They found another female body part. Let's go, Tony. You drive," Bob said tersely.

Ms. Clarkson gasped and put her hands over her mouth.

CHAPTER FIVE

"This shit must be bad," Tony said. "You never let me drive." They got into the illegally parked car and nodded to the security guard out in front of the hospital.

Bob glanced up from his phone, then back down. "Yeah. It's another body part, but they think it's from another body."

"God damn. That is bad," Tony said.

"Patterson's sending an assistant because he's in the middle of the postmortem on Cassie. Plus, her parents are coming over. What a nightmare," Bob said.

"Same parking lot as Cassie?" Tony asked.

"No, this one's over in the library parking lot," Bob said. "Some poor dog-walker found it partly in the bushes separating the library property from the armory lot."

"Blue lights and siren?"

"Yeah, better. We don't want a crowd gathering around our crime scene," Bod said, then added, "Hopefully, any curious bystanders will hear us and scatter."

Unfortunately, the blue lights and siren did little to shift the crowd that had already gathered. The patrol officers tried to move everyone toward the white Victorian gazebo at the front of the property, but people kept pushing in to get a view.

The burly patrolman in the front, working on crowd control, nodded to Bob and lifted the crime scene tape for him and Tony to enter. People called out to Bob, "Hey, what's happening? Is there a body over there? What's going on? Is that a cadaver dog over there?" they shouted.

At the last question, Bob looked to his right and saw a young patrolman leaning against his car bumper. His patrol car blocked a good bit of the crowd's view. "Hey, Junior," he said. "How's it going?"

Junior smiled and pulled on his Belgian Malinois' lead. "Hey, boy, there's your friend, Bob," Junior said. The normally saturnine dog wagged his tail so hard that he shook all over. Bob leaned down and scratched the dog's silky ears.

"Hey there, Blue. What's happening?" Bob asked.

His tongue lolling out, Blue gave Bob a doggy smile. His ears perked up when he spotted Tony, and he sat back on his haunches on alert.

Bob looked over at Tony, who was standing about fifteen feet away. Tony was frozen in place.

"Don't tell me you're afraid of dogs," he said.

"Not the ones that know me. That one, he don't know me. I want to make sure he likes me," Tony said.

Fortunately, Tony had been friendly to Junior early on, so Junior issued a command for Blue to lie down and waved Tony over. Tony hesitantly patted the dog's head and told him he was a nice dog. Blue thumped his tail.

"Wasting time, Tony, c'mon," Bob said. He glared at the crowd behind him to no effect.

The crime scene techs were already on site. The assistant medical examiner came toward them first.

"Hey, Bob," she said, stripping off her latex gloves. "Looks like the same MO, but it's not the same victim." She nodded to Tony.

"Tony, this is Dr. Heidi Mitchell. She works with Dr. Patterson and is the best thing about that office," Bob said.

Heidi laughed and turned to Tony. "He only says that when he wants something. The rest of the time, it's whine, beg, insult, and threaten. Okay, Bob. You'll get the report pretty quickly since it looks like the same professional job as last time."

"How do you know it's not from the same victim?" Tony asked.

Dr. Mitchell moved aside to let the detectives see the crime scene. A woman's leg, from the foot to the thigh, rested in the pine straw and partly under the bushes. Tony went in closer for a better look.

"Oh," Tony said.

The leg was cut with precision right below the groin. The skin color was clearly that of a Black woman. Bruising covered the ankle.

"Well, damn," Bob said. "Tony, we got any missing person reports recently that fit this?"

Tony hit an app on his phone. "No," he said. "Not if this thing has been updated. I'll check in with Sarge when we get back to the station."

After Bob instructed the crime scene techs on some photo angles that he particularly wanted, the two left for the police department.

When they walked through the front door of the station, Sarge called over to them. He'd worked the front of the police department for about twenty years and brooked no nonsense from anyone.

"Hey. Got a misper report in from another county on the community alerts this morning. A young gal from over in Henderson didn't come home last night. Chief wants you to look at the report and get on over to Henderson," he said while swatting at a patrolman who was trying to lunge around his girth to take Sarge's stapler.

"I done told you a hundred times, Dunleavy, leave my shit alone. Go steal someone else's," he barked at the hapless officer. Dunleavy skulked off, making a face at Sarge's back. "And you better quit making faces at me or you'll be looking out the back of your head," he bellowed and gave Bob the report. Sarge nodded to Tony, who politely nodded back.

"Okay, Tony, get us to the Henderson Police Department," Bob said.

"Damn. I'm getting to drive twice in one day," Tony said.

"Put a lid on it," Bob said.

* * * * *

Bob read the report while Tony zoomed down I-85 north to Vance County, where Henderson was located, bordering Virginia, and was on the way to Richmond. A former mill town like Oxford, Henderson was filled with unskilled labor and a few artisans, but no factories to hire them or their children. Unemployment, teen pregnancies, STDs, and high school dropout rates were high.

Tony pulled into the Henderson Police Department at the Sally port. Several uniformed officers were outside smoking or talking. They gave Tony and Bob the once-over, then one of them hollered, "Look who's here, look who's slumming, the big dicks from Oxford," amidst catcalls. Bob laughed and headed into the nearest elevator. Tony gave them the finger.

"Ooo, we've made the kid mad. Oh, no. Don't arrest us, officer!" the same guy jeered.

Tony turned around and thrust both middle fingers into the air.

"Quit playing around and come on!" Bob barked at him.

The Chief of Police, David Franklin, was seated in a glass-walled conference room on the second floor. He had the missing persons' report in his hand. "Hey, Bob, hey, Tony," he said without rising. His face was like a Shar Pei's—wrinkled, sad, and sagging. "This is some shit," he continued, holding out the report. "This girl, this child, is one of our own."

"What do you mean, Chief?" Tony asked.

"The gal in this photo is the niece of my first lieutenant, Johnson Taylor. She's a third-year law student over at NC Central Coast—a straight arrow. The family's been looking for her all night. I've got guys working double shifts so the others can keep looking. Now, what is it you guys have over in Oxford?" the Chief asked.

Bob looked at him steadily, then took the toothpick out of his mouth. "I'll tell you, I think we'd better wait until we can get some kind of DNA before we share this with your folks."

"Is it that bad?" the Chief asked.

"It's worse. All we have located is a leg and not the rest of the poor woman, if it's her. The assistant medical examiner can confirm it's a young Black female, but that's all they can confirm right now. You have anything you've collected here I can take back for them to compare to the leg's DNA?"

The Chief, lost in thought, sat for a few minutes. "Yeah. I think I have something or can get something without raising the family's hopes unnecessarily. Sit here a minute, and I'll be right back."

Several of the Henderson officers stopped in to say "hello" to Bob and to be introduced to Tony. A couple of the patrol guys remembered Tony from his high school days over in Oxford. They stood quietly talking with him in the back corner of the room, but straightened up when the Chief came back in.

"Alright, guys. Better get on the road. The shift started ten minutes ago," he said. When they'd gone, he turned to Bob. "Here's her hairbrush. The parents found her purse in her room and brought it in. Get back to me as soon as you can, okay?"

"As soon as I hear from the medical examiner, I'll call you," Bob said. "We may need your help on this one, Chief. We may have a serial killer out there. I'll keep you posted."

The Chief thanked both detectives for meeting with him, then sat down heavily at the conference room table. He pulled the department's old telephone toward him, taking longer than necessary to pick up the receiver. His hands shook as he dialed.

CHAPTER SIX

Bob drove back to the Oxford Police Department and headed for the small conference room. He directed Tony to close the flimsy plywood door. The black-and-white linoleum tiles on the floor had turned gray with years of use. The long tables were battered, and the chairs were dented gray metal.

Bob put the phone in the center of the nearest table on speaker and dialed the medical examiner's office in Chapel Hill. He asked for Dr. Patterson and then Dr. Mitchell when Patterson was unavailable.

"Dr. Mitchell speaking," she said.

"Hey, Doc. You got the leg from over here in Oxford earlier today?"

"Just a minute," she said. "Yes, they brought it in a few minutes ago, but I haven't had time to get to it. We had a three-car collision over here on the highway, or a two-car and tractor-trailer collision, and I was called out to the scene. Hopefully, I can start on your case this evening. What do you need?"

"Got a report of a missing girl in Henderson now, and I've got her hairbrush," Bob said. "Can I send someone over with it? We'll bag it up as evidence and put all the right labels on the bag. We'll use our case number on it, but the description location will be Henderson, if that makes sense. That's where her home is."

"Yeah, do that. Will your courier be here before five?" she asked.

"I'm sending Tony over. He's not been there since he came back to work in Oxford. Anything else you need, you let him know," Bob said.

"Got it. Will do. Tell him to ask for me when he gets here."

"Thanks. He'll see you in a few."

Tony had picked up a plastic evidence bag from the box in the metal file cabinet and was filling out the label. "Is there SATNAV in the antique car you've been driving, or do I need one of the new patrol cars?"

"Better get a patrol car," Bob said absentmindedly.

"What are you thinking?" Tony asked.

"I don't know. I just can't see a clear motive if these two cases are connected. Plus, we still haven't found Cassie's car. And, it'd be hard to think that there were two knife-happy people running around out there. This is going to be tough going. I'll brief our Chief while you're gone. He may want to call a press conference or keep a lid on it. I have no idea. I'll let him decide. Call me on your way back and update me, okay?"

Bob got to his feet and lumbered down the tiny, dim hall to the Chief's office. Tony scooped up the bag and headed to the front to wheedle Sarge for the keys to one of the new cruisers.

* * * * *

The Oxford Police Chief sat quietly in his office while Bob went through the case and the evidence they'd collected so far. A prior military man, the Chief liked discipline and order, neither of which appeared in a murder investigation. Bob told him they'd picked up Dr. Graham's file from the hospital, but he'd not had time to read it. He planned to do that tonight. The Chief spun his pen around on top of his new legal pad. When Bob had finished summarizing the case, he leaned over toward Bob.

"Just what the hell are we supposed to do with all this? We don't have a clear lead. We don't have any damn answers. If we tell the public that women's body parts are showing up all over Oxford, there's going to be mass pandemonium. The farmers and rednecks are going to buy more shotguns and rifles. Every drug dealer on or near Granville Street is going to ride dirty. All the rest: every man, woman, and child who can get their hands on a gun will. This is a nightmare."

"It's a nightmare," Bob agreed. "But, what about telling the public about the threat so everyone can be vigilant. Also, advise them to report anything, no matter how trivial, to the police. Not a damn thing has come through the tip line. None of the usual snitches are talking."

"This is a shit storm. We're damned if we do and if we don't. If there's another killing, they're going to burn the department down. I've been here thirty years and never seen anything like this. Robberies, shoplifting, shootings, some DWIs, domestic violence, I've seen all that, but cutting up people and throwing away body parts? That I've never seen. Maybe it's time to retire." He pulled a drawer out from his battered fake wood desk and reached down into it. He set a bottle of scotch on the old desk blotter that featured a calendar from five years ago. Drink?" he asked.

"I'd like to, but I'm going home to read the doctor's files and wait for Tony to call me. I'll update you later. Chief, you'll make the right decision. You always do. If you want my two cents, you can't keep anything in either of the two counties a secret. The grapevine works fast—half the folks in Oxford are related to half the folks in Henderson. I think you need to get ahead of this and schedule a press conference at the courthouse tomorrow morning."

The Chief sighed heavily and knocked back his drink. He shuddered as it burned down his throat. "I expect you're right," he said. "I'll talk to you later tonight, but wear your good suit tomorrow for the dang press conference."

"Right. I'll even get a clean shirt out of the closet," Bob said, hefting up the heavy file. He headed for his car in the small gravel lot.

* * * * *

Bob pulled into the driveway of a small brick house sitting on the corner of Royal and Hunters, a modest home built in the 1970s. It had a small porch on the front with spindly white posts, but everyone entered the house from the side door facing the driveway. The grass was brown, dead through years of neglect and the never-ending heat. A basketball goal with a rotting net sat on a small concrete pad near the drive. Out back, there was a slate patio Bob put in for Gloria on her fortieth birthday and a wrought iron fence she'd been begging for. He'd surprised her with it one weekend. Delicate scrolls framed the gate. They talked about getting a dog, but then their son died, and Gloria left.

Bob never has anyone over, and he doesn't talk about his house at work. He's ashamed of how badly he's let the place go. It was never a showplace, but now, the neighbors give him side-long glances. They have gone from subtle and gentle questions to flatout asking him when he's going to cut the grass and trim the shrubs in the front yard. Most days, the house looks abandoned.

Bob hates the hot summers in North Carolina. He cranked his car's struggling air conditioner up as high as it would go. Moving down here from Boston and taking the job at the Oxford Police Department had all been to make Gloria happy. She'd hated the cold Boston winters, the violence of the combat zone, and didn't want to raise their infant son in the huge, dirty city. She'd wanted to live close to her relatives.

He smiled as he thought back to his first weekend in Oxford. The roasting humid heat, even at Easter, had his shirt stuck to his skin in five minutes flat. Neighbors came over to talk and asked a hundred questions, mostly about his thick South Boston accent. Still, each one brought something with them: watermelon pickles, casseroles, a cake, or a pie. Gloria's relatives had shown up in droves. Aunt Myrtle—who was once married to Uncle Fred but now they're divorced but Aunt Myrtle is still part of the family—Grandma Minter, not really their grandma but a nice old lady from next door, Pastor Cleveland Royster, their family's prior church's pastor, now retired, who was a second cousin, and the list went on and on and on. Gloria's mom and dad had passed when she was in college, so she'd clung to every family member that turned up like a life raft. By Sunday afternoon, his head was spinning from the heat, the incessant talk, gallons of iced tea, and the names and nicknames of all of the relatives. All of it and more was worth it to see Gloria so happy.

With a sigh, Bob cut off the car engine and picked up the file. Looking at the backyard, he thought again about getting a dog. He had the space, and he definitely could use the exercise of walking one. His next-door neighbors' Heinz 57 dog was forever having puppies, but that bitch was about the ugliest dog he'd ever seen with mean golden eyes and short fur to match. The puppies always looked just like her. He shivered. No way he'd let Mike talk him into taking one of those monsters. He'd head out to the Granville County or Vance County rescue shelters and find one to suit him. He'd have to conduct his search under the cover of darkness because if Mike caught on to him looking for a dog, he'd bring over the whole litter or drop off some lean hound or hunting dog his nephew raised. Thinking about finding a nice little mannerly dog gave him something to look forward to, and he opened the door to the house with more enthusiasm than he normally did.

After he'd fixed and eaten dinner, baked beans and hot dogs, he settled down at the scarred kitchen table to read the hospital's file.

No wonder the hospital fought us on these documents, Bob thought. File after file revealed a pattern of harassment and systematic bullying. The files dated back three years and stopped in the last three months. Nurses and staff filed complaints that Dr. Graham kept asking them out on dates, despite repeated negatives from the staff; touched them inappropriately; or made sexual references or jokes throughout shift hours. Two members of the staff had transferred to other hospitals and had given Dr. Graham's conduct as the reason for their move. Bob looked but couldn't find any disciplinary letters or any communication at all from the hospital to Dr. Graham. Odder still, none of the complaint files had been closed out.

His cell phone rang. Tony's number came up. "Hey, Bob," Tony said. "Got an update from Dr. Mitchell."

"What'd she say?" Bob asked.

"The cuts on the leg look very similar to the ones on the parts we retrieved from the dumpster. She thinks they were made by the same instrument. She's put a rush on the DNA analysis of the hair in the hairbrush and a sample from the leg found at the library. I took the samples over to the state lab to make sure they got them right away. After looking at the leg, she thinks it's that of a young woman or older girl."

"So, we have a serial killer, is what she's saying," Bob said.

"She can't say that yet. She's running tests to see if they can determine the cause of death. They probably can't without the rest of the body."

"Can she at least say if the women were alive when they were being hacked to pieces?"

"I don't think so," Tony replied. "She's pulled in several experts from UNC's pathology and surgery departments to help her with the analysis. She's even found a certified butcher to examine the cuts on the body parts. That's a little unorthodox, but they're trying."

"Okay. Hey, I've been looking at Dr. Graham's file. The staff complained about him pretty regularly until about three months ago," Bob said.

"Sexual harassment?" Tony asked.

"Yeah. From verbal to physical abuse, and it was constant."

"Does that behavior make it more likely for him to chop up his fiancée?" Tony wondered aloud.

"I wouldn't have thought so," Bob answered, "but here's what bothers me: The hospital didn't discipline him at all. At least there's no record of it in any of the files. Seems like this is the sort of thing they'd be covering their asses on."

"It doesn't make sense. Why don't we talk to one of the attorneys at the hospital when we go over to talk to the hospital staff tomorrow?" Tony asked.

"Good idea," Bob said. "Oh, and there's a press conference at nine at the courthouse. I'll meet you there."

"People are going to freak," Tony said.

"Yeah, but how long can this kind of thing be kept under wraps? It's better to get it out there and see if we can shake out someone who saw anything at all to help us."

"People are still going to freak," Tony said and hung up.

CHAPTER SEVEN

In the hour between when the night fled and dawn stretched her fingertips across the sky, he waited. Admiring the knife he'd sharpened a few hours ago, he crouched, listening for footfalls. The short holly bushes provided all the cover he needed in the gloom. He felt a faint reverberation and then heard the whoosh, whoosh of nylon rubbing together as the runner neared his hiding place. It only took a moment to reach out and slash her Achilles tendon. With a cry, the runner fell, and he was on her. He shoved a towel into her mouth and quickly bound her hands with the duct tape he'd brought. She kicked out at him with her uninjured leg. He hit her hard in the jaw. Dazed from the blow and the drug-soaked towel, she was more compliant as he dragged her over to a car. He'd busted out the window and managed to unlock the trunk. He lifted her up and gently placed her inside. "We're going to have fun today," he whispered to her.

CHAPTER EIGHT

The Granville County courthouse sat majestically at the corner of Main and Williamsboro Streets. One of the oldest courthouses in the state, it featured dark red brick and white trim with a large cupola. Despite its massive girth, it only boasted two courtrooms. On district criminal court days, these burst at the seams with persons charged with crimes, their families, their rides, their girlfriends or boyfriends, and their victims.

Standing on the front steps, in front of the higher-ranking officers and several detectives from both Oxford and Henderson Police Departments, including Bob and Tony, the Oxford police Chief motioned for quiet. The television vans took up most of the nearby parking and recorded from their locations. Press from all over Eastern North Carolina shouldered their way up to the first step.

"Thank you all for coming here this morning," the Chief began. "I'm coming to you for help. We need the public's assistance with the disappearance of two young women from our communities. One was a young woman from here in Oxford, and the other one was a young woman from over in Henderson. At the end of the conference, officers will hand out cards with our number and a special email for tips related to this case. Each contact will also be posted on our Facebook page."

The press interrupted him. "Where'd you find the women? What manner of death? Do you have a suspect?"

The Chief put his hand up for quiet. "I'll get to a few questions in a minute," he said. "Now, one was found in the Food Mart parking lot over at Hill Top, and the other near the Richard Thorndale library parking lot. That's about three miles from one another. And, well, these ladies were dismembered."

Shouts rang out. "Who could have done this? Do you have any leads? What are you doing about it? What did you find?" The press surged forward with microphones held out like swords, but were stopped by uniformed officers and sheriff's deputies.

The Chief shook his head and waited for some order. He held up both arms in a placating gesture. "Please. Have some respect for the grieving families. We are devoting almost everyone in our department to finding out who did this and have enlisted the additional help of the Granville Sheriff's Office, the Henderson Police Department, and the State Bureau of Investigation. Thank you for attending the press conference."

The press pushed forward, with microphones extended and cameramen trying to reach Bob and Tony, but they turned and went into the courthouse. Normally, the two huge wooden doors were kept locked for security purposes, but they'd been unlocked for the department's press conference.

"We going to the hospital for interviews?" Tony asked.

"Yeah. I need to let Detective Branch from the Henderson PD know since he said he'll meet us. He's sitting with the SBI agent, Flannigan, until he gets our call. Hard to know who has jurisdiction at this point. The library victim could have been killed over in the next county and then dropped off here. If it's looking like we have a possible serial killer, then the SBI or the FBI may take over." Bob's cell phone rang, but as Bob turned away to answer, Tony could only hear Bob's part of the call—Bob's tone worried him.

"I'll be goddamned. Yeah, okay. I'll tell him. No, the Chief is stuck outside with the reporters. We'll go get him. Thanks," Bob said.

Bob snapped his old flip phone shut and turned back the way they'd come. Tony followed. Bob physically grabbed the Chief's arm in mid-sentence to a reporter and shepherded him through the courthouse doors and over to a quiet corner.

"Chief, the Sarge has been trying to reach you. There's another missing person—a young female from Oxford. She didn't come home from her early morning run. Her elderly neighbor saw her young neighbor head out for her usual thirty-minute run and went over less than an hour later to borrow her newspaper. The young lady's cat was home meowing through the letter box, and the young lady's car was still parked in front," Bob said.

"Maybe the gal has a boyfriend or stopped off for breakfast," the Chief suggested.

"No. The neighbor said you can set your watch by this girl. If she'd gone anywhere for long, she'd ask the neighbor to check on her cat. The neighbor goes over every day at lunch to visit with the cat, Snowball, if she can't make it home from work that day. Plus, she'd told the neighbor last night that she had to get to work early this morning, but there's no sign of her."

"Jesus God. Not another one," he moaned. "Look, Bob. Change of plans. You, Detective Branch, and Agent Flannigan go talk to the neighbor. Tony, you grab another detective from Henderson and interview the hospital staff. I'm going back to the office to call the Bureau. A serial killer is their bailiwick. I just hope we get a local agent and nobody from DC, Boston, or New York. Sorry, Bob, no disrespect, but you know what I mean."

"I get it, Chief. I'll call you after we talk to the neighbor. Tony, call me?"

"Got it," Tony said, pulling out his cell phone. After a minute of listening, he hung up. "C'mon, Chief, I'll give you a ride back. The Henderson PD detective is picking me up at the department."

Bob, Tony, and the Chief exited the courthouse's side door to avoid the press.

"If the goddamned hotels weren't so damn full of drug dealers and bed bugs, the press wouldn't be hunkered down here all night. Where's the bureau going to stay? If they stay over in Henderson, the thieves will strip their cars clean down to the frame. Better check and see if Mamie's still renting out," the Chief muttered to himself. "Or, maybe that Royster B and B is back open."

Tony looked worriedly over at Bob and then said, "Chief, you closed them down—the Royster B and B—for prostitution last month."

"Damn. You're right. I did. Okay, any other ideas?" he growled.

"Nope. Mamie's is nice and clean. Get Sarge to give her a call. She loves Sarge. Brings him baked goods once a week," Bob suggested. He climbed into his old 4Runner and headed over to meet law enforcement at the possible missing person's townhouse.

Tony took the Chief to the Oxford Police Department, which was only a few blocks north of the courthouse.

"What kind of car is this?" the Chief asked Tony.

"It's a Lexus. You like it?" Tony asked.

"Well, it sure is nice inside. Nothing like that tin can Bob drives. We must be paying you too much."

Tony laughed. "I like working with Bob. He's solid. No taste in clothes or cars, but he's sharp," he said.

"You've been good for him, too," the Chief said. "He's either frustrated, angry, or laughing when he's around you. Never depressed. That's a good thing."

The Chief looked at Tony mournfully when they got out of the car. "Gotta call the Bureau," he said. "I'd rather have all of my teeth extracted. I'll get some snotty kid answering the phone who'll keep me on hold half the damn day. Y'all keep me posted." He brightened. "Hey, I think Sergeant Johnson with the Granville County Sheriff's Office has an in there. I'll call him first."

Henderson Police Detective Johnny Mills pulled up beside Tony in a white Cadillac Escalade. It idled loudly while Tony finished talking to the Chief.

"Damn, detective," Tony said, opening the passenger's side door. "Who'd you take this ride off of?"

"This is one of those cars we seized that'd been passed around from drug dealer to drug dealer. Somebody took care of the motor. Sweet, isn't it?" Mills laughed.

"Man, it sure is. Y'all roll right over there in Henderson, but we got the Cookout restaurant here."

"Yeah? But we got the Starbucks," Mills shot back.

"We got Popeye's and Bojangles," Tony added.

"Damn, ya got me there. We have a Bo and are building a Popeye's."

The detectives one-upped each other about their respective towns, back and forth, until they parked at the hospital. The outdoor security guard came running over when the Escalade pulled up and parked on the curb. Each flashed their badge and nodded to the guard. Deflated, the guard moved back to his post.

"You got the doc's file?" Mills asked.

"Yeah, here," Tony said, handing it over to the other detective. "You can take a look at it. We're supposed to meet the staff, one every twenty minutes, in the cafeteria. I'll get coffee. How do you take yours?" Tony asked.

"Nothing in it. Trying to keep the weight off," Mills said.

"I hear you. I'll meet you at the far table against the wall on the right."

After interviewing the nurses who were assigned to work with Dr. Graham, the detectives were no closer to confirming or breaking Dr. Graham's alibi. One of the nurses, Allison, remembered him coming into the hospital Sunday night but couldn't recall the time. She'd been in one patient's room most of the night because he'd coded and she'd pushed an emergency button that alerted a team of health care workers to resuscitate him. Some of the staff did not stay the full shift because all seven weren't needed for the half-filled floor. The short-timers did not recall seeing or talking to Dr. Graham.

"We're not getting anywhere," Mills said, stretching his arms over his head and exhaling in frustration.

"Just got to slog through it," Tony agreed. "At least we got some first-hand insight into the Doc's roving hands."

When pressed, Allison tearfully told the detectives that Dr. Graham was constantly criticizing her in front of the other nurses after she'd turned down his offer of sex in an empty patient room. A few months ago, he'd backed her into the supply closet and rubbed himself up against her. She'd complained to the head nurse and then to the administrator. Nothing had been done. Now, she tried hard to schedule herself for shifts or for days when he wasn't scheduled to work.

"What a damn jackass," Tony said to Mills later.

"He's got it all," Tony said, shaking his head, "looks, position, money, a fiancée, you name it, and he has to get his thrills harassing women who work for him? I don't get it."

"Yeah, some men with power are like that—they want more and don't care who gets in their way. Narcissistic assholes," Mills said. "But, you know, it'd take someone with a lot of confidence to kill and maim those girls. Just cutting them up and leaving their body parts out like an Easter egg hunt. You've got to be one cold-blooded bastard to do that."

"True," Tony said. "Hopefully, the FBI can help out with that psychological stuff." He looked down at his phone. "Bob says to meet him and the Chief at the police department. They're done talking to the neighbor. Let's roll."

CHAPTER NINE

Bob and the other members of law enforcement arrived at the same time at the townhouse over by the former Thistledown Tennis and Golf Club to meet with the concerned neighbor, Mrs. Flossie Mae Currin, a retired schoolteacher. The townhouses had been built about fifteen years ago to provide a sorely needed housing option for singles and retirees. Thistledown's nine-hole golf course had closed primarily because its dining room wanted to elevate prices from $5.00 for a sandwich combination to $6.50, and because the manager-cum-chef frequently appeared during the well-attended Friday night buffet in the dining room with copious amounts of animal blood on her pants. Most of the patrons speculated it was deer blood, but no one got close enough to take a good look.

Mrs. Currin peeked out through her lacy curtains on the lookout for them. She walked out once the officers pulled up outside her neighbor's small townhouse. "Oh, thank God. You've got to find Michelle. That poor dear girl. What do you think's happened?" she asked in a tremulous voice.

Bob steered her toward the tiny porch of the brick townhouse, gently asking her in a low voice, "Can you help us get into the apartment, Ms. Currin? We'd like to see inside."

"Oh, yes, of course." She patted her fluffy periwinkle angora cardigan pockets. "Here's the key. I'd better let you in, though. Snowball doesn't like strangers."

The men, suited up in tactical gear, chuckled as they lined up single file behind Mrs. Currin to enter the townhouse. Fluffy kittens didn't faze them; they were used to pit bulls and trained attack dogs.

Bob was first behind her. When she moved to the right, calling to Snowball, he saw the big cat.

"Goddamn it," he exploded. "That's not a cat, that's a cougar!"

"No, dear," Mrs. Currin patiently explained. "He's part snow leopard. Michelle adopted him from an animal rescue, but he's a sweetheart, aren't you, Snowball? And I don't countenance cursing, Detective." She frowned at him until Bob mumbled an apology.

The enormous cat rubbed against her twig-like legs. It glared at Bob and the other men, keeping them locked in its blue-green-eyed gaze.

"My apologies, ma'am, but could you put Snowball up somewhere, so we don't, uh, disturb him?"

"Well, sure. I'll just let him out in the back for a minute. He likes the fenced-in backyard," she said.

Detective Branch and Agent Flannigan entered the room cautiously. Each man kept his hand on his service weapon.

"Mrs. Currin, do you know which bedroom belonged to Michelle?"

"Sure, I do. Go down to your right, and it's on the right. If you don't mind, I'll just sit in here on the sofa." She pulled out a well-worn crossword puzzle book and pencil stub from her skirt pocket and sat down in the corner of the blue and white flowered love seat.

"No problem. Thank you," said Bob. The others followed him into the medium-sized bedroom. It had a queen-size bed, neatly made up with a pink duvet, a bedside table, and a padded stool at the foot of the bed. A few silver-framed photographs stood on the walnut bureau.

Bob picked up one of the photos and looked at it. He then took it to the window for a better view. "Oh dear God. I know this girl, er, woman. This is Michelle Clarkson, a young attorney who works at the hospital. I really hope the Chief got up with the FBI. We're gonna need the extra help right away."

"Damn. We gotta get the crime scene techs in," Flannigan said.

"I'll call the Oxford techs over," Bob said, taking out his flip phone.

"No way," said Flannigan. "They've got to be our guys from the State crime lab, not your locals," he said and punched in some numbers into his iPhone. He looked over at Bob. "Shouldn't that phone be in an antique store or museum?" he asked.

Bob looked at his phone. "No, this is a great phone. Why? What's wrong with it?"

Detective Branch distracted Bob by offering to help clear the house now. They should have done it on entry, but had been over-whelmed by the mountain lion. No one other than Mrs. Currin was in the townhouse. She was patiently waiting on the couch with a quilt over her knees, and Snowball curled up beside her. She saw the officers looking at the cat. Snowball growled low in his throat.

"Snowball wanted to come back in, poor dear. He loves Mi-chelle," she said. "Did you find out where she went or when she'll be back?"

"No, ma'am," Bob shook his head. "We're still working on it. Do you want to go back to your house? One of us needs to formally interview you, and you may be more comfortable over there."

"I'm fine, detective. I eat lunch over here with Snowball all of the time. I'll just fix him a snack, and then we can talk."

Waiting for her to bring out half a haunch of venison or some big steaks, he was surprised to see her go to the freezer. "Snowball loves vanilla ice cream. He can have a small bowl now," she said.

Snowball sat up and eyed Bob with suspicion. "Easy, Snowball. I'm not going to eat your ice cream. Promise," Bob said, easing away from the puma. "Uh, Mrs. Currin, what're you going to do with Snowball until Michelle comes back?"

"Oh, it's no problem to feed him until she gets here. "Now," she said, seating herself at the small ice cream parlor table, "What did you want to talk about?"

Detective Branch and Agent Flannigan took this as their opportunity to exit the townhouse and gladly grabbed it. *Cowards*, Bob thought. "What's Michelle's full name? What was her usual morning routine?" Bob asked Mrs. Currin.

Mrs. Currin confirmed that Michelle was Michelle Clarkson and worked as an attorney at the hospital. She'd taught Michelle AP English when Michelle attended C.G. Webb High School. According to her old teacher, Michelle was a delightful student and a delightful young woman. Mrs. Currin was overjoyed when Michelle bought the unit next to hers last year.

"Do you have her parents' phone number?" Bob asked.

Mrs. Currin's thin lips trembled, and she made small, bird-like sounds of distress. Snowball growled menacingly. "You think she's dead, don't you?" she asked querulously.

Bob moved his feet further away from the big cat. "No, no, Mrs. Currin. I just wanted to, uh, talk to them. You know, ask them some of the same questions I've asked you."

She dabbed her eyes with a crumpled tissue she took from her cardigan sleeve. "Okay. I have it at home on my fridge. Or maybe in my address book. Or, you know, it may be on a Christmas card they sent last year. If you want to, you can wait with Snowball while I go look for it."

Bob stood up at the same time she did. "Oh, er, no. That is, it's such a nice day out. I'll wait in the sun until you have a chance to look for it."

"Okay. Come on, Snowball. I'll get your lunch meat out and see you in a little while," she cooed to the snow leopard.

Bob fled before she opened the refrigerator door.

CHAPTER TEN

The Chief wiped his eyes, which were streaming with tears because he'd laughed so hard at the retelling of Bob's adventures with Snowball. Bob looked ruefully around. "I'm telling you, that was one big cat. We don't have enough money in the budget to feed that cat for more than a day or two."

The Chief sobered. "The FBI is sending an agent who should be here in a few minutes. I explained our situation and asked for an experienced agent or at least one who'd worked on a case involving a serial killer. A professional profiler is coming too or will be patched in on speaker phone, depending on who's available," he said.

Bob sighed. "We took a quick look at the route that Mrs. Currin says Michelle normally runs and didn't see anything out of place. I called her parents, and they're heading over. That was one tough call."

Agent Flannigan nodded. "At some point, we're going to need to get the families together and see if the girls-ladies-had anything in common. It doesn't sound like it, but they may come up with something. I've seen it happen before," he said. "I guess I need to let the FBI tell us how we can help. I don't want to step on any toes at the Bureau."

There was a knock on the conference room door. Lt Katie O'Connor and Sgt Johnson strode into the room and greeted everyone.

"Sorry, guys," Katie said. "We meant to get here earlier but had a dust-up at the jail that we had to sort out. Some fools arguing over the TV remote managed to shiv each other. The paramedics came in and stitched them up." Katie's dark hair escaped her high ponytail in the back, but her lean frame gracefully sank into the wooden chair in front of the Chief. Sgt Johnson stood in the doorway.

"Bunch of fools," Johnson said. Sergeant Walter Johnson was big, well over six feet, and muscled. He'd played football at C.G. Webb High School and then on scholarship at the State University. Only his mama called him Walter. Everyone else called him Johnson, Sarge, or sir.

Young, smart, and more than competent, Katie had recently been promoted to Lieutenant by the Sheriff. Her father had worked in local law enforcement until a drunk driver ended his career.

"You tell the Sheriff that I'm grateful he's let you two go over there to work on this case. The FBI is sending one of its agents. Katie, are you still a task force officer for the FBI?" the Chief asked.

"Yeah, but it's really on more of a case-by-case basis instead of me going over to Raleigh all the time. I know a lot of the guys in the Cary office. Johnson has a lot of friends there, too. Do you know who's coming over?" Katie asked.

"Not a clue. Hey, anybody need coffee, water, a soft drink?" the Chief asked.

Katie favored her dad: tall and slender with long brown hair, blue eyes, and a laid-back disposition. Even the local criminals found her easy to talk to and would ask for her by name if they got picked up on a charge. She'd been in law enforcement for about fifteen years, proudly following in her father's footsteps. As an FBI task force officer, she'd gained the respect of her state law enforcement colleagues and the Bureau. The Oxford Police Chief had tried to woo her away from the Sheriff a time or two, but she was loyal to him and her team. She and Johnson had been working together for a long time and usually caught assignments on the toughest county cases.

The conference room phone buzzed, and the Chief told Sarge to send the FBI agent on back to the conference room.

Sarge himself escorted the petite, curvy, mahogany-colored woman into the room.

"Afternoon," she said.

All chairs scraped back as the men stood. Katie stayed seated but smiled at her.

The agent smiled back. "Hey, Katie. I'm glad you're on this one. Good to see you again," she said going around the office to shake hands with everyone.

"I'm glad it's you, too, Gus. I was dreading the sight of Agent David."

Gus snorted. "Not a chance. I don't think he's allowed back in the state. I think he's on the TSA watch list in Raleigh."

Katie and Augusta got to know each other right after the murder of the federal judge, Patrick O'Shea, in Raleigh last year, and had become close. Agent Bullock's out-of-town colleague, FBI Agent David, had pissed off everyone involved in the murder investigation and everyone who'd worked at the federal courthouse.

Katie made the introductions around the room. Gus explained how her dad desperately wanted a son after the birth of three daughters, but was stunned that another daughter appeared in the delivery room. He'd stubbornly refused to call her anything but Gus. Her mom won the second round of the name debate with "Augusta" on her birth certificate.

"Hey, Gus, heard you're bringing in a profiler on this one. Are they heading over, or are we calling them?"

"Yeah, about that…" Gus grimaced.

Sarge interrupted, came back into the room, and yelled, "Chief, FBI for you on line two!"

The department's office phone only had two lines because the city's tight budget only stretched so far. It had taken a lot to get a couple of new patrol cars. Years of carting around felons and drunks ruined the patrol cars' backseat upholstery awfully fast.

"Chief Evans, here. Yeah? Let me put you on speaker phone, Doctor. I've got a group in here that needs to hear you," he said.

"As I was saying, I'm Dr. Felix Fulcher, assigned provisionally to the FBI. I'm going to help you with the case you have there. I understand Agent Bullock has arrived?"

"Hi, Doctor," Gus said. "Glad you had time for us today. I'm going to let one of the detectives summarize what they have so far."

Bob took the lead and, over the phone, introduced everyone and their respective agencies. "Okay, Doc, here's what we've got. Three missing persons and body parts from two of the three. All are young women. For the first victim, we have a head, one arm, and one leg. For the second, just one leg. The cuts on these two look professional, according to the ME. The third gal we're still looking for. There hasn't been much to go on between the two separate scenes of the amputations or whatever you'd call it. The ME said the cuts are precise and surgical."

After a few minutes of silence, the profiler said, "I need to see the bodies or body parts. Agent Bullock, can you square it with the Bureau? Or do you want me to call over there?"

"Better you make the call for travel so you can explain the reason and get the approval," she said. "Oh, speaking of travel. Katie, you want to explain the accommodation problems?"

"Yeah," Katie said. "So, there's really nowhere to stay in the two cities or counties except Mamie's off College Street here. She rents rooms but cooks supper and sometimes breakfast. It's nice and clean at her house, but it's not a hotel, so to speak. No bar, no breakfast buffet, but plenty of local gossip," Katie said to both the agent and the profiler. "Oh, and afternoon sherry if you care for it," she added.

"I'll book a room for me and a room for Dr. Fulcher," Gus said. "After I check in, can we go over to the ME's and see what evidence is in and let me read the ME's draft report?"

"I'll be glad to take you over," Tony said. "Anytime you're ready to head out, let me know."

It took several minutes for everyone to exchange cell phone numbers and for the profiler to call back and confirm his flight for the early morning. Katie and Johnson offered to pick him up in Raleigh.

"That won't be necessary. I've already rented a car for the trip. Sometimes I like to drive around and get a feel for a place. See it for myself. Assimilate the aura. I'll meet you in the morning," he said and hung up.

Everyone looked at Agent Bullock in silence.

"Okay, I get it," she said. "Yeah, he's a little odd, but pretty good at what he does, I think."

"What do you mean, you think?" Bob asked.

"I haven't worked with him before, but I've heard stories. I think he fancies himself part scientist, part medium."

"Unbelievable," the Chief said. "That's all we need now. Some paranormal psycho."

"Don't you mean psychologist?" Katie asked.

"No. The way I heard it, that guy is more along the psycho spectrum," the Chief said.

* * * * *

While Katie left to brief the county's deputies to be on the lookout for Michelle Clarkson, Gus and Johnson headed to the Medical Examiner's office in Chapel Hill. Bob and Tony drove over to Henderson, following the Henderson detectives.

After a short conference with the FBI agent before Agent Bullock left Oxford, Agent Flannigan worked out with Agent Bullock that the SBI crime scene techs would process Michelle Clarkson's house. He headed there to oversee their ongoing efforts. A sack of ribs from the Sunny Side filled the floorboard of his car. He was taking no chances with Snowball.

Bob and Tony drove by the two-story brick house in Henderson where the law student Mia's family lived. They slowed while navigating the residential street, which was filled with people walking and crossing to get to the house. Flyers for Mia adorned the street-side mailboxes and telephone poles. Mia's heart-shaped face on a petite frame shone from the black and white photo. They pulled over at the end of the crowded street but hesitated before going into the house. Due to the family's close ties to the local police department, they'd been asked to re-interview the family. Detective Branch called ahead and made the arrangements with Mia's father, Joe.

Unexpectantly, it was Mia's mother, Doris, who opened the solid front door. Grimly, she stood aside as Bob and Tony slid past her.

"Come into the dining room," she said, without looking at them. She was of medium height, slightly overweight, and dressed in a black knit suit. "Anything to drink?" she asked, looking at each in turn. "May I get you some iced tea or coffee?"

Another heavier-set lady walked into the room. "Doris, do you need anything?" she asked, keeping her eyes on Bob and Tony.

"Louise, these are the two officers we're supposed to talk to. Can you get them something to drink, please?"

Bob asked for coffee, and Tony asked for sweet iced tea. Louise patted Doris's shoulder as she passed by her. Behind her back, Louise directed a hard stare at the two officers.

"Mrs. Hargrove, is your husband available to talk to us?" Bob asked.

"He's in the back resting. I made him lie down because he's been up all night, and he has hypertension. Can you talk to me first?" she asked.

"Yes, absolutely," Tony said. "Where do you want us to sit?"

The dining room had an inlaid dining table big enough to serve twelve. The crystal chandelier's soft light picked up the persimmon-flocked wallpaper. Cut glass vases filled with stargazer lilies sat on either end of a handsome buffet.

Louise brought in drinks on a silver tray for everyone, including herself and Doris. Unapologetically, she took up sentinel on Doris's right side. "Let me just clear the air," Louise said. "I ain't going anywhere. So y'all can just go on and talk. I'm here to support Doris while her husband gets his rest. Y'all just go ahead and pretend like I'm not here."

Tony smiled at her and thanked her for the iced tea, which he carefully placed on a crystal coaster on the table. It would be hard to ignore Louise, who was a vision in a deep purple pantsuit, pearls, and white and pink high-top sneakers. Her neck featured an impressive number of rolls, and her gold bracelets clanked every time she moved.

Bob cleared his throat and took a sip of coffee. He dreaded further upsetting this gentle woman. "Mrs. Hargrove, please tell me what you remember about the day your daughter didn't come home. Take your time and let's go through everything you can recall." Tony unobtrusively took a small notepad out of his jacket and took notes while she talked.

Mrs. Hargrove described her daughter Mia getting up early, making coffee for her and her husband, and getting into her small blue Corolla to head to class at NC Central in Durham. Her daughter wore her usual uniform of jeans, a brightly colored top, and a jean jacket. Her backpack was black with a Nike swoosh and slung over her shoulder. It was packed full of books, notebooks, pens, and her laptop. About noon, her daughter sent her a text message saying she would not be home for dinner but would be going out with friends and would be home before nine. She'd sent a silly selfie to her mom from Jimmy's Pizzeria in Durham. Posing by the giant pizza character inside the small restaurant, she grinned into the phone's camera.

"And that was the last I heard from her. When it got to be ten, then ten-thirty, her dad and I started to worry. I'm Lieutenant Taylor's sister, and I called him and woke him up when it got to be eleven. He told me she'd probably gotten caught up with friends and didn't notice the time. But it wasn't like her not to let us know. She's our youngest and is so considerate of us. She would never just *not* come home." Doris started to quietly cry, and Louise put her beefy arm around Doris's shoulders.

"That's right," Louise said. "That child never gave them a bit of worry. She was a straight-A student in high school and got a scholarship to college and law school. She'd never ever upset her mama like this."

A shuffle of feet preceded Mr. Hargrove's entrance into the dining room. His face was ashen, and his shoulders were slumped. He sat down heavily on the other side of his wife. "Any word?" he asked quietly.

No one said anything for a minute. Doris stroked her hand down his arm and said, "Joe, shouldn't you be resting? You haven't had any sleep. These detectives are here to go back over Mia's day."

"I'll be glad to try to help y'all in any way I can," Joe said. "I've reported the car stolen to the Durham PD, hoping somebody would spot it. I told them why—I didn't lie to them. But, they've been all over that restaurant and neighborhood. Nothing. Some off-duty guys with the highway patrol have driven up and down I-85 looking for that car and Mia. We've called all of her friends that we've met from school and her high school friends. No one heard from her after six o'clock last night. We've called the Apple store to help with the phone, and the Chief here got a subpoena out for the phone records even though we gave permission and they got 'em. Her brothers, uncles, and I rode around all night, all over town, looking down every road, going to every club and hangout we could think of. Just in case." He dropped his head down, looking at his feet. "Ain't nobody seen her or will admit to seeing her after dinner. I've even hit up old boyfriends, screaming at them to tell me where she is. I'm lucky none of them have filed assault or threat charges."

When he looked back up, tears filled his large brown eyes. "This doesn't make a bit of sense. That girl was, *is*, as good as gold."

Louise, dabbing at her eyes, stood up and went into the kitchen. Neighbors who'd come to lend support were talking quietly in groups of twos and threes in adjoining rooms.

The Henderson Chief had warned Bob and Tony explicitly not to divulge any part of the investigation. He personally was going to call in his lieutenant and give him the option of being the one to meet with the family.

Bob felt terrible for playing a part in Mia's parents' suffering. How well he knew what it felt like to have your whole world disintegrate and plunge into a dark hell. His own Chief had come over to break the news of Matthew's death to him and Gloria. Bob still sort of hated him for tearing his and Gloria's life apart, even though he knew rationally that the Chief would've rather been anywhere else than holding onto his sobbing, screaming detective.

Bob and Tony rose from the table and thanked the Hargroves for their time. Halfway down the brick sidewalk, Louise rushed out to catch up to them. Breathing heavily, she looked each man in the eye. "I want you to tell me the unvarnished truth. You think our girl is dead, don't you?" she asked. Neither answered her. She looked from one to the other. "I can see it in your faces. These good people's lives are about to be destroyed." She held up her hand, turned, and slowly walked back into the house.

CHAPTER ELEVEN

Johnson drove Gus over to the medical examiner's office in Chapel Hill. He'd cleared out the passenger seat for her after she'd raised her eyebrows at the state of his deputy's car and refused to get in it.

"You're mighty particular," Johnson said, scooping up Bo wrappers and sheriff reports and tossing them in the back. A lone Coke bottle rolled around in the foot well while he continued his efforts. Satisfied there was no longer any hiding places for vermin, Gus lowered herself into the bucket seat and fastened her seatbelt. A few coffee cups rolled around on the floorboard in the back. She'd had to pick errant strands of pine straw off her jacket.

While Johnson drove, Gus read reports generated by the Oxford Police Department, Henderson Police Department, and the State Bureau of Investigation. After the last page, she exhaled.

"So, now there are three women? Have they found anything on Michelle Clarkson? Anything to rule her in or out as a victim related to the first two?"

"Not a thing. We can give Agent Flannigan a call to see what, if anything, his techs turned up at Michelle's townhouse." Johnson dialed the SBI agent and put him on speaker phone. He handed the cell phone to Gus for her to hold while he drove. "What'd you turn up, Flan?" Johnson asked. "I've got Gus with me."

"Hey, Johnson, Gus. Not a damn thing. We're looking outside around the townhouses now and canvassing the neighbors. No one's seen Michelle since last night. Mrs. Currin saw her car pull in and park, and it's still here. Katie is organizing search teams along the route she normally ran in the mornings. I called her boss, Sternberg, but he was no help. He doesn't know anything about her. Mrs. Currin gave us the parents' phone numbers, so Katie said she'd call them for me. Goddamn it! I've got to go. That damn Snowball bit one of my officers. Hey, hey!" he yelled, then cut off.

"Snowball?" Gus asked.

"Michelle's got a big ass cat. She swears it's half snow leopard," Johnson said.

"So, you knew her?" Gus asked.

"Yeah, a little bit," Johnson said. "I usually coordinated with her on serving court orders for medical records for things like driving while impaired charges, wrecks, hit-and-runs, and felony assaults. She was very nice, unlike her boss, Sternberg. He's a colossal jerk."

"You know what these women, if Michelle winds up a victim, all have in common?" Gus asked.

"No, what?"

"Cassie and Michelle were attorneys, and Mia was a third-year law student," Gus said.

"Well, that's a damn big list of suspects—people who hate attorneys," Johnson said. "Joking aside, who'd want to kill these women? Cassie was a transactional attorney and rarely went to court. Same for Michelle. She worked for the hospital. And Mia was set to graduate and had interned for the same Raleigh business and for Buck's firm both summers. None of them did any high-profile work as far as I know. Now, I can see someone hating the courtroom barracudas with their snarling and their slashing claws enough to take them out, but these women? No way."

"How well did you know the law student, Mia?" Gus asked. "She seems to be the only one who was with a group of people before she disappeared."

"Not very well. I know some of her family, the Hargroves, and her uncle over at the Henderson PD. Her uncle was so damn proud of her. He'd update me on her law school progress every time he saw me. This is going to kill them, if it's her over at the ME."

Johnson and Gus were silent for the rest of the trip until Johnson stopped at a fast-food restaurant on 15-501. "Want anything?" he asked.

"What're you getting? Oh, hell. Yes. I want a ham biscuit combo with Bo rounds," Gus said.

He used the drive-thru to place the order. After paying and getting the food, he parked in the "pickup only" parking space, rationalizing that he'd "picked up" his food. He rustled around in his bag before pulling out his bacon and egg biscuit and taking a healthy bite.

"This busts my diet wide open," Gus said, frowning at her ham biscuit.

"Hell, a skinny girl like you don't need to diet," Johnson said.

"I gotta keep in shape to keep chasing the bad guys. Besides, there's enough cholesterol in this good country ham biscuit to clog up all of my arteries," Gus said.

"Yeah," Johnson said, reaching for his fries. "But what a way to go."

* * * * *

Chapel Hill was a lovely southern town with the University and its hospital system sprawling through its middle. Charming houses and lavish gardens dotted the wide main street, which abutted the university. Like an amoeba, the medical and government buildings associated with the hospital system took over everything in their path. Glittering steel and windows did little to soften the structures or provide aesthetic appeal.

The nondescript building that housed the state medical examiner's office looked like a federal prison. Its boxy shape wasn't adorned in an attractive manner or relieved by window placement—its dumpsters were the first thing visitors saw.

Johnson pulled up almost to the door and parked in the spot labeled: "Visiting Medical Examiner Only." Gus looked at him, and he shrugged.

"You see anywhere else to park other than by those dumpsters? You got no idea what's in those things, and I don't either. This is safer," he said.

A glass partition separated the visitors from the receptionist. On the other side of the glass, an attractive woman looked up from her desk.

"Hey," Johnson said. "We need to meet with Dr. Patterson. I'm Sergeant Johnson, and this is Agent Bullock. We should be on your list." He pointed to the paper in front of the lady.

"If you're on this list, you're in trouble," she drawled. "This is the list of cadavers we currently have in the morgue."

Gus started laughing. Johnson quickly recovered. "Oh, well. Another list, then?" he asked.

"Let me just call up and see if they're ready for you. Go ahead and sign the visitors' log. And, if that's your Dodge out there, you can go ahead and move it out of the medical examiner's space." She dialed the phone in front of her and spoke to someone about their visit.

"Busted," Gus said.

"Ain't that a damn shame," Johnson said, pulling his car keys out of his pants pocket. "That woman's got eagle eyes."

When he came back in, the two were buzzed through the locked door and directed to the examiner's main office floor. Dr. Patterson's assistant, Jim, dressed in a white lab coat and sporting a minuscule goatee, met them at the elevator and walked them over to the room where Dr. Patterson was standing over a body on a metal gurney. He looked up when they entered the small, concrete-walled room.

"Johnson, good to see you again," Patterson said.

"Good to see you, Doc. This is Agent Augusta—Gus—Bullock. She's been sent in by the FBI to assist and wants to see the evidence in the cases we're working," Johnson said.

"Nice to meet you. Can you take a few minutes to show us what you have in here that's associated with the cases?" Gus asked.

Dr. Patterson pulled the sheet up on the man on the steel gurney. He stripped his gloves off his hands, opened a trash can by putting his foot on the pedal, then led them down the hall.

Johnson avoided looking at the poor man on the table. The sheet had shifted when they first went into the room to reveal massive head trauma. His skull caved in, and a dangling eye flopped on the gurney.

"Doc, I don't know how you do it," Johnson said. "Dealing with the dead day in and day out. That guy in there? Well, I don't know how you cope."

"You get used to it, like anything else," Patterson smiled. "Plus, I couldn't do what you all do: looking for missing people, talking to their grieving families, searching for clues, and hunting for suspects." His cowboy boots clicked rhythmically on the ancient linoleum. "I don't have to run after my folks," Patterson chuckled.

His assistant, Jim, helped the doctor locate the body parts that law enforcement recently collected from Oxford. Dr. Patterson asked him to double-check the computer and find out if the DNA report on the leg collected outside of the library had been uploaded by the SBI crime lab.

No one uttered a sound as the parts were retrieved and placed on a white cloth-covered gurney. Gus looked over each one and then reviewed them a second time. She pulled out her cell phone and asked the doctor, "May I?"

Dr. Patterson handed her a manila file filled with eight-by-ten-inch color photographs. "Will these do?" he asked. "If not, you may go ahead and take your own. Those are your copies. Johnson, I've got a folder for you to take back to give to the PD."

"What do you think was used on the victims to make these cuts?" Gus asked.

"I've thought about it. Maybe a circular saw, a sharp machete, or a large sharp knife could have cut or made marks like these. Obviously, if you all collect something along those lines, I can compare it next to the lacerations."

Seated at the computer, Jim interrupted. "They've uploaded the DNA report comparing the material in the hairbrush to the leg collected outside of the library. I'm printing four copies." He handed out the copies. Each scanned the SBI report in silence.

"Motherfucker," Johnson whispered under his breath.

"You're damn right," Gus agreed.

"The leg is a match to the girl missing from Henderson," Dr. Patterson said. "Officers, you've got a serial killer on the loose—these girls almost certainly are dead—and you've got to stop the killer before he kills again."

* * * * *

Tony dropped the groceries on the stained laminated kitchen counter with a thump. Dust motes danced in the fading afternoon light. The smell of old cooking grease was overwhelming. He opened a window that still had its screen to air out the kitchen. He'd forgotten to go shopping for his family earlier because he'd been totally distracted by investigating the murders.

Tony's dad, Albert, shuffled into the room. "Hey, boy. Good to see you. What's up?" Albert asked in a low, gravelly voice.

Tony stood still, trying to figure out if it was one of his father's good days or bad days. On good days, his dad liked conversation and would share a meal. On bad days, his dad stayed hunched down in his worn-out chair, trying to hide the white powder he normally kept on the coffee table down in the sofa's seat cushions.

When his dad smiled at Tony and asked him to sit down, Tony relaxed and released the stress in his shoulders. He put a few groceries away before pouring iced tea for both of them and taking a seat at the small kitchen table.

"Hey, Dad. Grandpa here?" Tony asked.

"Nah. He's courting the Widow Douglas, who stays over in the next street. He's been at it about three or four days now. Today, he took her some pepper jelly he got at the store uptown."

"How's he doing?" Tony asked.

"Pretty good. They're going to the Elks hut to a dance this weekend. It's an afternoon dance. Neither one of them would make it past seven o'clock. He's been polishing his shoes all week."

"You going?" Tony asked.

"Nah. I'm good right here."

His dad was anything but good: overweight and diabetic, with a drug and drinking problem. Tony played along. "You might find the perfect match. Fall in love," Tony said.

"I'm good," his dad repeated.

His dad pointed to the empty grocery bags. "What'd you bring?"

"I brought dinner. Thought I'd make some for you and grand-dad, and some for a friend that's coming over after a while."

"Hmmm," Albert said. "Suit yourself. I'm sure it'll be good whatever it is. Your mom sure enough taught you to cook."

"It'll be ready in about forty minutes. Go sit on the porch and keep an eye on the interlopers next door." His dad's feud with the neighbors was long-standing. No one could recall what started it.

"I just might," he said. "Them neighbors planted two tomato plants on the property line and put out a damn gnome. It's ugly as sin. I hate that thing grinning at me every day. Who'd want that in their yard?" he shook his head.

"I get you. If you see a big ol' Lincoln and a bigger guy com-ing in the driveway, that's my friend coming over for dinner. And, Dad, be nice."

His dad stopped walking through the front door of the old shotgun house and turned back to Tony. "Fair enough. What's this one's name?"

"Patterson. He's a doctor. Over at Chapel Hill. In the medical examiner's office."

"A doctor, you say. Well, well. We could use a doctor around here. Your granddad's about to fall apart at the seams with his asth-ma and goings on, and my ticker isn't acting right. I might even go put on a clean shirt for this guy," his dad said while slowly walking back down the dark hall to his cramped bedroom.

Tony rolled his eyes at Albert's hunched back. He just hoped his dad's good mood lasted through dessert.

* * * * *

A few hours later, Dr. Patterson pushed back from the wooden table and sighed. He'd had a tough time easing his long legs under the gate-leg table and almost tipped the whole thing over when he sat down.

"Tony, that was pure heaven. That cornbread and that peach cobbler. I'm going to need bigger pants," Patterson said.

"Your pants get any bigger and you can put a family of four in 'em," Tony's dad muttered.

"How's that?" Dr. Patterson asked.

Tony jumped in before his dad could repeat the comment.

"Who wants more cobbler? There's plenty of it. Here, Dad, give me your plate. I'll put it in the sink."

His dad snatched the plate away from Tony's hands. "Whoa, boy. I'm not done with the collards or the fish. I'm just enjoying it. Who'd a thought baked fish could taste that good? I'll clean up. You guys go sit on the porch or on the patio."

Tony poured white Burgundy for himself and Patterson and took the solo cups out to the patio. It was almost dark, and a few fireflies appeared. The streetlamp backlit the gnome. "Sorry about the glassware," Tony said, handing the red plastic cup to Patterson.

"I can do solo cups," Patterson said. "I used to drink out of jelly jars and four different colored aluminum glasses my granny had. Some of them were even clean."

Tony laughed. "How was it growing up in Texas?"

"It was great and terrible," Patterson said. "Great when you're a football star. Terrible when you're the 'fairy football star.' My older brother fought a lot of fights for me, but he didn't talk to me about it much. "How about you?"

"Oxford wasn't bad until my folks got to yelling and screaming terrible insults every day. Lots of things breaking and them shouting. The neighbors called the cops almost every weekend. My mom and I moved out when I was in middle school. My siblings—really my half-siblings—had already left home. New Orleans was just… different. A lot more going to church with my mom and her cousins, and a lot more of the live music. I missed my dad and granddad, though. The police force was cool about my 'orientation' as the guys called it, but I didn't advertise the fact. I was lucky. I had a lot of friends down in N'Oleans, both gay and straight."

"How are you liking it here and with Bob? He's a good ol' guy."

Tony took another swig from his cup, then set it on the black wrought iron table after pushing aside leaves and his dad's scrawny one-eyed gray cat, Toot. The affronted cat stared at him, walked back to the same spot on the table, and sat down with his back to Tony. Toot got his name from drinking the dregs of alcohol out of random glasses and cups, then puking it up in bedroom shoes or on the bathroom floor.

The late honeysuckle and small gardenia bushes perfumed the humid air. The temperature slowly dropped into the eighties.

"Bob treats me right," Tony said. "He works hard, and he expects me to work hard. He treats me just like everybody else. He told me to take off tonight when I kept falling asleep over boxes of hospital documents we'd been trying to get through. He pulled in another detective to help me."

"Bob's a good cop and a nice guy. Don't see that combination all the time," Patterson said. "A shame about his boy."

"Yeah. I can't imagine the pain of losing a child. That'd be horrible," Tony said. "Bob's the sort that'd be a great dad, too… well, as long as his son liked the Sox."

Patterson laughed. "And didn't mind his dad talking about them nonstop. Is he working tonight?"

"He is. Said he'd call if something develops. He ordered me to take off since I haven't been to bed in over twenty-four hours. I've been living on coffee, tea, and soft drinks today, but I'm going in early tomorrow. Bob's not a morning person, so he's okay with it."

"I'll let you get some sleep then. Sorry to keep you up. You must be wrecked." Patterson stood up.

Tony faced him. He gently took Patterson's cup and put it down far from Toot. Tony put his arms around Patterson, who smelled faintly of tobacco and mint. "I enjoyed spending time with you tonight," Tony said, muffled against Patterson's shoulder.

"I did too," Patterson said, drawing Tony gently away. "And you can cook," he added with a smile. He closed his eyes and kissed Tony softly.

* * * * *

Tony's bed in his old room wasn't the most comfortable spot in the house. He woke up disoriented. Realizing he was at his dad's and not his own place, he looked over at the dark head on the pillow next to him, smiled, then closed his eyes for a few more minutes of sleep. A faint humming noise started toward the end of the bed. He opened his eyes. Toot came walking his way up to Tony's head, licking Tony's hair. A warm, rumpled Patterson started laughing.

Tony's dad and grandad were up in the kitchen, coaxing the old percolator to give it one more go. Tony introduced Patterson to his granddad, and both heard about granddad's courtship, in great detail, of the widow Douglas over breakfast.

Patterson made his excuses, and Tony saw him to his car.

"Later?" Tony asked.

"I'll call for a dinner reservation over in Chapel Hill one night in the next week. Let me know what night you're free," Patterson said. The big old Lincoln ambled off down the street.

Back inside, Tony's dad smiled at Tony. "We got ourselves a doctor in the house," Albert said with a big grin.

"Hallelujah," Grandad said, pumping his fist in the air. "I need him to see about my sugar before me and the widow get serious.

"He's not that kind of—" Tony began over the hoots and the laughter. *Oh, what the hell. At least they like him.*

CHAPTER TWELVE

ob hadn't seen Matthew since he'd last seen his son sitting on his bed. Today, he awoke eagerly, looking for him, keeping his eyes partially closed before checking the room. Sometimes, in the car, he felt Matthew's presence and looked around in the back seat for him. The investigation had gone from bad to worse and then worse to worse with another woman missing. Bob gave up looking for his son.

He picked up his flip phone to answer Johnson's call. "Hey, Johnson. You and Gus made out okay over at the medical examiner's late yesterday?" Bob asked.

"Yeah, we got in and out and picked up the latest report. Listen, I've got some bad news."

"Okay, let's have it."

"The hair in the hairbrush and the leg are a positive DNA match for Mia."

"The missing law student from over in Henderson?"

"Yeah."

"That's awful. Her folks are going to be destroyed."

Johnson continued, "I called Katie, and I'm notifying law enforcement over in Durham now. You want me to call Chief Mills over in Henderson, or do you want to?"

"You do it," Bob said. He thought for a minute and changed his mind. "No, no, I'll do it. God, this sucks. I'll let my Chief know about the match and see if there's any other agency we can call in to help us. Our guys aren't trained to look for some sicko like this guy… or girl. We're gonna need more officers."

"I hear ya," Johnson said. "I took Agent Bullock over to Mamie's last night. She said she'd get up with you and Katie early this morning."

"Okay. Is that Fulcher guy over there, or do you know?" Bob said.

"I have no idea where the profiler ended up. Maybe in a séance somewhere?"

"Okay. If you talk to Gus before I do, tell her there's still no word on Michelle, the young lady who didn't make it back from her run."

Several hours later, Bob made another pot of coffee in the department's microscopic kitchen even though it was well into the afternoon. While he waited for it to percolate—no money in the budget for a fancy coffeemaker—he looked at the days-old newspaper someone had left strewn on the square table amidst takeout salt and pepper packets.

"Dad?" Matthew whispered.

Bob looked up. "Matthew? Oh, son. I've missed you."

Matthew smiled. "I've missed you, too. I've been hanging out with Mom some. As in, I've been trying to convince her it's me, but she keeps calling me Uncle Waldo." He rolled his eyes.

"As if that guy would ever talk to her. He barely acknowledged her while he was living," Bob said.

"Right? Anyway, I'm not allowed, I can't say much, but that girl, Mia, she's around here somewhere with me. I mean, I haven't seen her, but I get this feeling."

"Mia's leg, the way it was cut, we thought she was gone. What about Michelle, are you allowed to say?"

Matthew frowned. "I think so, but I don't know anything about her. Maybe that's a good thing? Anyway, Dad, once I do whatever I have to do—and I still don't know what it is—I've got to go, like permanently. Okay?"

"Yeah, son, okay. I just... I could just stay here all day talking to you."

"I know," Matthew said and smiled. "But that didn't happen in real life, did it?" He laughed.

Bob smiled. "No, it didn't. I'm glad I got a sliver of time with you now."

Sarge poked his burly head into the kitchen and looked around. Matthew faded. "Who you talkin' to, Bob?"

"Just talking to whoever will talk to me," Bob said.

"You're getting weird, Bob," Sarge said.

"Tell me about it." He poured his brew into the only non-cracked clean coffee mug in the cabinet labeled "Officers Get All The Calls" with disgust and followed Sarge to the Chief's office. Katie was seated in the other client chair. Her hair was partially out of the usual ponytail she favored, and her pants were stained with dirt and debris. She looked as exhausted as Bob felt.

"We gotta get more manpower and step up the search for Michelle," the Chief said.

"I had about twenty deputies and volunteers to scour her usual running route, and we came up empty. We even had a couple of

K-9 officers join us. Nothing. We've been to every park, culvert, field…" Katie said.

"The leg is a DNA match for Mia. We need some more help," Bob said. "We need some trackers and that profiler to do his damn job and tell us who we're looking for out there. We can't lose another one."

The Chief reached into his bottom drawer and brought out the seriously depleted bottle of Scotch. He unscrewed the lid and offered it to Bob and Katie. When they said no, he put it to his lips and tilted it back. "Let me see what favors I can call in and try to sweet talk the FBI into providing us with more agents," the Chief said. "This is a complete nightmare. We don't have the officers for this kind of case. Everyone has been working overtime. The city's going to have my head on a plate if I put in for all the overtime and no results."

"Yep. I gotta go call Chief Mills and tell him about the match. I've been putting it off," Bob said.

"No, no, you don't. I'll do it," the Chief said. "Y'all go on home, and we'll meet here early in the morning to get briefed by the teams out searching for Michelle tonight before we start over again. I'll get Sarge to drive me over to Henderson and call the FBI on the way," he said, ruefully looking at the amber liquid in his bottle.

The Chief shared the news about Mia and the DNA match with Sarge and the few officers who were left in the conference room.

Sarge took the news about Mia hard. He was good friends with the Hargrove family and doted on little Mia. "I'm gonna kill the son of a bitch that did this," he said, cracking his big knuckles. "Mother-fucking asshole," he sniffed, wiping away tears. "Goddamnit."

For a few minutes, the officers were quiet, each lost in his or her own thoughts. A few radio beeps and the soft voice of the 911 operator from down the hall disturbed the silence. Sarge pushed through the double glass doors and into the small, paved lot. The Chief followed him and put on his suit jacket.

"Come on, Sarge, let's go on over to Henderson," the Chief said, patting Sarge's wide back. "I'm with you, but you know you gotta be strong so you can be there for the Hargroves when we have to break it to them."

Sarge spat beside the cruiser. "Mother fucking coward asshole," he said. "Dirt bag, peanut pecker, donkey balls…" He slammed the cruiser's door shut and spun gravel out of the parking lot while the Chief held onto the interior door handle with a look of resignation on his face.

When the others left, Katie turned to Bob. "Where in the hell is the rest of Mia? We can't stop searching for her, and now for Michelle. Chief's right, this is a goddamn nightmare. I'm going over to meet with the Sheriff now to beg for more men, but I get it, the Sheriff has to cover the whole county with his staff, so I just don't know what he'll say."

"Do what you can. We appreciate you and Johnson coming over to help," Bob said.

Looking more closely at her, he said, "Hey, is that a ring on your finger? Let me look at that. That's a big honkin' diamond! You and Buck getting married?"

Katie blushed and held her hand still for his scrutiny. "Yes. You and Gus are the only ones who've noticed. Johnson knows because Buck had to ask his permission to marry me since my dad's gone. Buck said that Johnson grilled him for hours, cross-examining him all about Buck's plans, his finances, everything he could think of. Buck said it would've been easier to just elope and endure Johnson's anger afterwards."

"You tell Buck he's a lucky man," Bob said. "If I were a couple of years younger, I would have stolen you right out from under his nose." He laughed.

"Bob, you're one of the good ones. I'll be sure to tell him," she said.

"Is the big day soon?"

"I think his mom is torn between speeding us down the aisle and taking her time buying out the florist, hiring the caterer, and drawing up elaborate plans for doing up the venue. That woman is a force," Katie said.

Bob had met Mrs. Davis, and he agreed. Once she was on a mission, it was best just to get out of her way.

"We're planning for next month," Katie said. "It's a good compromise, I think."

They promised to meet up at Sunny Up Biscuits when it opened at 6:00 a.m. unless they got called out that night.

* * * * *

Sarge and Chief Mills solemnly walked up to the Hargrove residence. Lights were on, but few cars remained in the drive or out front. Sarge had expended his anger on the ten-mile drive from Oxford to Henderson. A Henderson PD officer stood by to take the Oxford Chief home after he had told the assembled group of Henderson officers and the Henderson Chief the devastating news that the leg found near the library in Oxford belonged to Mia.

The front door of the Hargrove house opened. Louise studied them for a minute, then sagged. She clutched the door for support and said, "Dear God, no...."

Sarge gently removed her grip on the door, put his arm around her shoulders, and ushered her inside with a few murmured words. The Hargroves were seated at either end of the table in the dining room, moving food around their plates. Mia's four brothers were in the adjoining living room, quietly watching television. Louise hovered in the doorway between the dining room and kitchen. Joe Hargrove spotted the men first and started to rise. The Chief waved him back into his seat.

"Joe, Doris, there's no easy way to say this: The leg found in Oxford is Mia's."

Joe banged his hand hard onto the table, and Doris wailed, "Nooooooooo!" Louise staggered over to a chair.

Hearing their mother's cry, the boys jumped up and poured into the dining room. "Mia's dead?" the oldest asked. The youngest sat next to his mother and held her hands.

"Where is she? Why haven't you found her?" Joe demanded.

"I'm so sorry, Mr. Hargrove, but we've been looking. Each shift is assigned a team to look for her. We're out looking for her around the clock. There's another young lady missing over our way and we're looking for her too," the Chief said. "Oxford has called in the FBI to help, and they've agreed to work on Mia's case as well."

"What the fuck can the FBI do? My baby is missing and probably dead is what you're telling me," Joe howled.

"Let me call someone for you," the Chief started. Doris let out a moan and fainted. Her son chafed at her hands and looked at his father in alarm.

Sarge came back into the room. "Joe, I've called the pastor and Doris's brother. They're on their way." When Joe didn't respond, he pulled up Joe from his chair, hugged him to his big chest, and rocked him like he was a child. The sons stood by helplessly with tears rolling down their tired faces.

Louise swayed in her chair, wringing her hands. "My poor baby," she kept repeating.

CHAPTER THIRTEEN

Early the next morning, before sunrise, the team met back in the Oxford Police Department's conference room. Each had a warm bag of biscuits or a Styrofoam plate of eggs and grits wrapped with silver foil from Sunny Up Biscuits, and the room quickly filled with the smells of country ham and sausage.

Dr. Felix Fulcher arrived while the last bites were being taken. Although he was dressed in a blue button-down and gray suit, he looked disheveled. His tie was crammed into his suit pocket. Fulcher was a petite man with slicked-back hair and a clipped way of talking. His shoes sported lifts or what looked like heels. Around forty years old, wrinkles fanned from his dark eyes and up to his salt-and-pepper eyebrows. He walked to the front of the room and asked for silence.

"My apologies, everyone. I can't tell you the night I've had—or the morning rather. It's been terrible. I checked into a hotel in Henderson late last night. I had to wait thirty minutes before I could rouse the receptionist. She was dead asleep in her office. Then, all of the restaurants were closed, so I had to go to the Sheetz out by the highway for some food. That place was packed, but most of the customers were loaded down with beer and wine. Some woman propositioned me, right there in front of everyone. I finally got my food and ate it in my room. Someone in the hall played music all night long," he said. "No one answered the front desk when I called down to complain. The phone just rang and rang. After three hours of sleep, I'm late getting here because someone broke into my rental car and stole everything not bolted down: the floor mats, the cup holders, my change, my sweatshirt, my cokes, and my spare socks." Forlornly, he looked at his sockless ankles.

He paused to take a breath, then sank tiredly into the room's spare chair. "You were right. Big Mistake. I'm going over to stay at Mamie's tonight."

"Tried to tell you," Bob muttered.

Gus stood up. She put her fingers in her mouth, and her whistle pierced the air. When everyone quieted, she spoke.

"Everyone, meet Dr. Felix Fulcher, FBI profiler. He's been with the Bureau for about five years and has assisted on numerous cases, primarily kidnapping cases.

"Listen up, guys. Before we meet with today's search teams, here's what we've got: two dismembered females and one missing female. The dismembered body parts recovered are one leg, one arm, and one head from one victim and one leg from another. We don't know if the missing female, Michelle Clarkson, is connected to the first two, but we're treating each case as a homicide."

Gus turned to the profiler and said, "Dr. Fulcher, we've got copies of the ME photos, crime scene reports, and interviews in these folders. I'm teaming up with Katie and Johnson to lead the Sheriff's team. He's generously allowed ten more deputies to join us today. Bob and Tony are coordinating with both the Oxford and Henderson police departments, and Agent Flannigan will lead the officers of both of those departments and the SBI teams. The SBI processes any crime scene we discover. The FBI interviews any suspects. All clear?" she asked. Today, she was dressed in dark pants and a jacket with "FBI" emblazoned in white across the back and chest.

Somberly, the officers nodded their heads. They were getting ground down by the long hours, double shifts, and lack of sleep. They'd never complain and wanted to catch the monster preying on their young women.

While they were finishing up, a church group brought in more canisters of coffee and breakfast foods. The Area Congregations United in Service, or ACUS, coordinated with the Chief to bring lunch in for the patrol officers and sheriff's deputies later in the day. One of the volunteers led those assembled in prayer for the safe recovery of the young women, succor for their families, and strength for law enforcement as each continued to search for the women.

The group left Dr. Fulcher happily munching on a huge wedge of coffee cake and slurping his coffee while he immersed himself in the files. All agreed to meet back there around lunch, absent any new discoveries or leads. An old office phone sat on the scarred table within Dr. Fulcher's reach. His laptop was open, and he scrolled down every few seconds. Abruptly, he patted his pants pocket and cursed. His work cell phone had also been stolen while he was over in Henderson. Upon consultation with the FBI local office near Raleigh, he'd get one via overnight mail.

Bob's phone rang twenty minutes into their morning. He and Tony drove over to College Street, which featured some of the largest and oldest Victorian homes in Oxford, which was once a thriving tobacco town. Prestigious farmers and tobacco buyers had built big sprawling homes for their expanding broods. Now, some large homes were divided up into apartments for the single teachers coming in from out of town to teach. Other houses were slowly falling into disrepair, with peeling white or yellow paint and rotting columns or gingerbread.

Bob told Tony to alert the members of the SBI and FBI teams to meet them at the Orphanage. Tony pressed his foot on the accelerator and turned on the blue lights and siren to move past slow traffic clogging College Street in front of Crescent Elementary School. The crosswalk guard glared at them and hugged tiny children to her side.

The orphanage sprawled down a good bit of the main city street and up to its neighbor, the Granville Medical and Dental Center. Visitors mistook the grouped buildings and cottages and their Georgian architecture for a college campus, often driving past it before turning around.

The security guard met Bob and Tony at the graveled entrance on the side near the photography and thrift shop. They walked over to the back of the soccer field. A morose young man dressed in jeans sat on an upturned wheelbarrow smoking.

"Okay, Billy, you can go over there a few feet, but wait for these detectives," he said. Bill fairly sprinted away.

"It's bad," said the guard who sported a name patch on his navy-blue uniform that read *Jimmy*. "I'll let you see for yourself," he said. He moved aside where they'd stopped walking near uncut brush and small shrubs. What first appeared to be an old soccer ball was, in fact, a head. Blood oozed down the cheeks and onto the ground.

Bob crouched down, careful not to disturb the earth. He could see one pink shell-like ear and a small gold earring glinting in the sun.

"Let's back out of here carefully, Tony," Bob said. "Call Dr. Patterson, will you? I'd like him to assist on this one, too." Tony walked over closer to Billy and pulled out his cell phone.

A few minutes later, as they trudged back over to the drive, the SBI forensic team pulled up. Bob pointed to the location, and six white-suited members hustled over the soccer field. He turned to Billy, who was chain-smoking and shaking.

"Billy, you the one who found her?" Bob asked.

"Yes, sir. I found her. Oh my God," Billy began to cry. Smoke, snot, and tears mixed, and he coughed uncontrollably. Bob motioned Jimmy over.

"Got anything you can give him to drink? He's a mess, which I don't blame him for being," Bob said in low tones.

Jimmy grimaced. "He's new in the twelve-step program and gets a little shaky in the mornings anyway. This just…"

He brightened and said, "He loves Diet Mountain Dew. Let me go across the street and get him a big cup—a fountain drink—and some little chocolate cakes or something. Billy's got a real sweet tooth."

While Joe headed over at a swift trot to the convenience store catty-corner from the orphanage, Gus, Johnson, and Katie rolled up and were briefed by Tony and Bob.

Katie walked over to Billy. "Hey, Billy. Man, tough break coming in and seeing what you saw first thing this morning." She spoke quietly and put her hand gently on his arm. She crouched down to where he was now sitting on the ground. "Look, Billy, it'd really help us if we could talk to you about it. You okay to do that?"

Billy nodded and wiped his streaming eyes with a grubby bandana he'd pulled out of his back pocket. "Yeah, okay," he said. Eying Johnson, "I'll talk to you but not him," he said, pointing to the Sergeant. "He's arrested me before. I don't like him," he said with a pout.

"No problem, Billy. I'm gonna see what the SBI has found," Johnson said and walked off.

"Billy, this is Agent Gus Bullock. Is it okay if she stays while we talk? I thought we'd sit in Bob's car. It's more comfortable," Katie said.

Bob unlocked the car, and the four of them sat in it. Tony leaned in the open window on Bob's side of the car. The back seat was as big as a sofa, and Billy and Katie sank into it. Jimmy thrust the Diet Mountain Dew and the box of cookies through a window for Billy. Billy smiled, revealing a few holes in his stubbly smile.

"What time did you get here this morning?" Katie asked.

"It was a little after six. I always gets here early so I can open up the shop and check phone messages to see if anything broke during the night. Plus, it's nice and quiet early on," he said.

"When did you find your, uh, your discovery? How long had you been at work?"

Billy gulped down his drink. "I went down to check the shrubs, to see if they needed weed-eating. I have a schedule where I mix up what I do outside. When I went to check on 'em it was about seven, and I… and I…."

Katie said quietly. "It's okay. Just take your time."

"I found that, I found her, I found her about seven," Billy said. He opened the box he'd been holding against his chest and extracted a large chocolate chip cookie. Offering one to the others, who declined the treat, he peeled off the plastic and began to chew. With it half-chewed, he continued, "I radioed Jimmy to come over 'cause he'd know what to do."

"You did exactly right, Billy. Now, Joe told us you can go on home if you want to. Can you write down what you just told us and sign it before you go?" Katie asked.

"I don't write too good," Billy said.

"Here's some paper," Bob said, peeling some sheets off his pad. He rustled around in the console and located a pen.

The group stayed in the car until Billy had the statement written to his satisfaction. A lot of words were scratched out, but he signed his name with a flourish. He gave his boots to Katie so the SBI could exclude his shoe prints from any they collected. Billy grinned when Jimmy told him that the orphanage would buy him some new ones. He let one of the sheriff's deputies drive him home.

Bob looked up just as Dr. Patterson's big Lincoln pulled up. The tall man got out slowly and stretched his back. Without him noticing, a long, dark dog eased out behind the driver's seat before Dr. Patterson shut the car door. The dog took off across the field.

"Franz, damnit, Franz, get back here! Franz!" he yelled while running after it. His polished cowboy boots forced him into an awkward lope.

The crime scene techs looked up in horror as the dog barreled toward them. A few valiantly tried to shoo the dog away. Tony bolted after the dog at the first yell and was catching up to it. He dove for the dog's collar, but not before it had teased something out of the undergrowth and clenched it in its teeth.

Dr. Patterson finally caught up to Tony and the dog and leaned over his knees, winded. "Franz," he yelled. "What have you got, you bad dog?"

Franz did not give up his treasure until Dr. Patterson grabbed him by the scruff. Out fell a bloody piece of cloth—a pair of running shorts. "Franz, so help me God, if you've botched up the DNA, I will…" he said, but stopped when Franz looked at him with mournful eyes and slinked over to his feet.

Tony tried to scrape the mud and leaves off his pants with a stick. Leaving damp patches on the fabric, he blotted away the worst of it with an old Sunny Up Biscuits napkin. Diving for Franz had ruined his shirt, but the suit pants could be salvaged.

A member of the crime scene tech group came over and bagged the shorts using an official evidence bag. Short and square, her face was almost totally obscured by the white covering.

"If it makes you feel better, Dr. Patterson, none of us had seen the shorts, so your dog did us a favor. We've been searching the same area and coming up with zilch." The tech bent down to scratch behind Franz's ears.

Dr. Patterson sighed. "Okay, thanks, Wilma," he said. "I guess you'd better swab Franz for DNA exclusion." He clipped the leash on Franz and headed first back to the Lincoln to put up the subdued dog, then back over to the gruesome discovery to see it before it was gently laid in a cloth-lined box.

"Wilma, do y'all have an ID for the victim?" Tony asked, striking a tone between conciliatory and businesslike. His Louisiana accent crept in as it usually did when he was nervous.

Wilma wordlessly considered him for a minute. "Not yet, but one of the techs pulled up Michelle's graduation photo from the university, and it looks an awful lot like her," she said. "I just called Agent Flannigan, who's headed over to the townhouse to get a recent photo of her from Mrs. Currin."

"Thanks," Tony said. "I appreciate it."

Wilma then said, "You know, a few of us usually get together for dinner over at the Oak Room on Friday nights, just law enforcement types—crime techs, law admin, a few officers, dispatch, lawyers, court reporters, and sometimes their wives or girlfriends," she said. Defiantly, she raised her chin and added, "I bring my wife too."

Tony smiled and said, "It sounds like a good time and beats the heck out of cooking for myself or my dad and granddad."

"Come join us sometime if you like," she said. "We're going there this Friday. Just a warning, it's named after the famous Oak Room in New York, but that's all it has in common with the one at the Plaza."

"I would like to come, and thanks," Tony said. He smiled brief-ly, then turned and headed back to where Bob was parked.

Before he'd made it to within twelve feet of the car, Bob hol-lered at him. "You're a mess! You're crazy if you think you're getting into my car."

"For God's sake, Bob. What am I supposed to do? I gotta get home and get changed."

"You're damn right you do. Jesus," Bob sputtered.

After consulting with Jimmy, the orphanage loaned Tony a golf cart to drive over to his dad's house to clean up. Tony had to promise to pay for the gas and hose off the cart before he returned it later.

Tony ran the cart at about fifteen miles an hour on the far side of the right lane. That didn't stop folks from blaring their horns at him, yelling at him, or throwing a couple of apples at him. His dad's mouth dropped open when Tony swung into the driveway of the white shotgun house.

"Whew, boy. What're you doing driving that thing in your suit?" Albert asked. As Tony pulled closer, the older man stepped back. "Ooo-wee! Man, you are filthy. Go 'round back and take them clothes off. I'll burn 'em for ya."

"No, Dad, that's alright," Tony sighed. "It'll come out okay. I'm going to head in and shower. I'll put my clothes in a garbage bag and put them out back to wash later. Bob's picking me up here in half an hour."

"You gonna be home for supper?" his dad asked.

"Probably not. You and granddad go ahead and eat without me."

"Okay, son. You be careful out there."

Tony stared at him hard. His dad's pupils looked normal, and the cadence of his speech was normal. His dad's shoulders slumped as he turned away. There were a lot more white strands mixed in the grizzled black hair on top of his head.

"You don't need to keep staring, boy. I'm not on the powder. Been off it several days, really weeks now."

"I'm glad, Dad. You look good. I'll cook you and granddad something special this weekend. I miss you guys." Tony said as he disappeared from the covered porch into the house.

CHAPTER FOURTEEN

He snickered to himself and watched the cops clamber over the soccer field like ants. He took care that no one saw him looking or heard him laugh. His soft-soled shoes made no sound. His clothes were purposefully plain and utilitarian.

He'd elected himself the president of Seniors Who Walk Seniors at the local animal shelter. He was far from a senior, but his dog of the day wasn't—a slobbering arthritic Pitbull, named Sweetie. Sweetie jerked on the leash, pulling him out of his reverie. The other volunteers kept walking, or shuffling on, while he savored the scene.

The cops would only find what he wanted them to find and nothing more. He'd been meticulous and scrutinized the field first with a flashlight and then in the natural early morning light before he'd left his "gifts."

He had big plans, and these yokels weren't about to stop him. He'd already selected his next victim and relished the upcoming hunt. The only thing he worried about was the ever-growing amount of "trophies." They were well hidden now, but he liked to take them out and look at them, fondle them. He couldn't help himself. He felt they'd speak to him if he could just be patient and still. Each piece had a story to tell.

CHAPTER FIFTEEN

Promising to meet Dr. Patterson at the ME's office later that day, Bob and Tony headed back to the Oxford Police Department. They'd radioed the rest of the team about the gruesome discovery on the soccer field. Bob was the first to walk into the precinct.

Sarge growled out, "You seen the conference room?"

"No, we're just getting back. Why?" Bob asked.

"You're not gonna believe it is all. Not gonna believe it." Sarge shook his head but would say no more about it.

With trepidation, Bob and Tony walked to the back and into the conference room. Bob eased the door open. It was like Disney, The Wizard of Oz, and Law and Order all rolled into one. Victims' photos and crime scene photos were put on different colored poster paper, and colored string led from one to the other. Arrows pointed around the room to various photos and Xeroxed interview notes. A final red poster board featured large block writing and was labeled *suspect*. All the room lacked was balloons. Bob pulled up a chair in front of the suspect poster. Tony sat on a table nearby. Dr. Fulcher stood by like a proud parent while the two scrutinized his work.

Bob finally asked, "Dr. Fulcher, you mind going over this here on the wall?"

Dr. Fulcher smiled modestly and said, "Let's wait for the others, shall we? I'd hate to go over it twice."

"You buy out all of the birthday decorations at the Family Dollar?" Tony asked.

"What do you mean?" Dr. Fulcher asked, affronted.

"Well, this is a lot of, er, color and drawing and all. I thought there'd at least be some glitter, a birthday cake, or maybe even a picture of the suspect?"

Dr. Fulcher stalked out of the room. They could hear the taps on his shoes click-clacking down the hallway, and his distinctive smell of mint combined with moss or dying logs went with him.

"You pissed off the hired help—the very expensive hired help, Tony," Bob said. "Go get him and be nice. Apologize to him for acting like a donkey's ass."

Tony sighed. "Yeah, okay, but what the hell has he been doing? I don't see his crystal ball or whatever he uses to commune with the spirits."

"Tony, I'm too damn old to go chasing after prima donnas. Get up and go fetch him back before the others get here."

"I liked chasing after Franz a whole lot better," Tony muttered, getting up from the table.

"And apologize!" Bob barked at his retreating back.

It took Tony several minutes to soothe Dr. Fulcher and several more to convince him to come back into the conference room. Members of the team were gathered around the lunch spread from the ACUS, and a few hunkered down over full plates. Tony asked Dr. Fulcher if he could get him a plate, and he looked slightly mollified by his offer. Tony used two paper plates to support the potato salad, ham biscuits, pimento cheese sandwiches, and Jello mold with unrecognizable bits that he loaded onto the doctor's plate. Dr. Fulcher ate slightly apart from the group.

In a few minutes, most of the team was seated in front of an enormous display of food. Helpful but somber volunteers poured sweet and unsweetened tea. Once they'd left, Dr. Fulcher cleared his throat and stood. He motioned for Tony to close the conference room door.

"I've been analyzing the method of murder—or murders—and the locations of the evidence," Fulcher started. "Now, this person has to have some skills or training to wield a knife like this."

"Come again?" said one of the deputies. "What's a wield?"

Dr. Fulcher smiled a tight little smile. "The perp needs to know how to *use* a knife. He or she needs to be able to cut things up quickly but with finesse," he said. Looking at some blank faces, he added, "Skill, like I said. You're looking for someone trained in using knives and someone very careful and controlled. Probably a male, probably white, probably older than thirty years old and younger than fifty."

Johnson snorted. When he finished chewing, he said, "How the hell did you conclude all that?"

"One, the knife skills demonstrated with the evidence that's been collected are fairly unique. Two, it's mostly white men who deer hunt or hunt large animals in this area. Three, a person has to be fairly strong to subdue these healthy and fit young women," Fulcher ticked his points off on his fingers.

Johnson raised his hand. "So, we have two victims who are white and one who's black. Are you saying we can forget about the brothers and focus only on the whites?" he asked. "That seems a bit presumptuous. You're assuming a hell of a lot about this sicko."

The officers snickered but ducked their heads as Dr. Fulcher glared around the room. "Look, officer—" he began.

"Johnson," Johnson said.

"Yes, okay, look, Officer Johnson," he began again.

"Sergeant," Johnson helpfully added.

"Sergeant Johnson," Dr. Fulcher bellowed. In a quieter voice, he added, "These are deductions I've made based on the evidence you collected, previous case studies, and psychology."

"Alls I'm saying is that we don't know what ties these victims together. It could be a black boyfriend or a girl's grudge," Johnson said patiently.

"You're absolutely right," Dr. Fulcher acknowledged. Johnson smiled around the room. "But probably not."

Johnson glowered at him.

* * * * *

Katie and Gus sat down at the table across from Mr. Sternberg at the hospital. Their serious faces had the attorney sweating before they started talking.

"Mr. Sternberg, we're sorry to inform you that we found Michelle Clarkson a few minutes ago," Katie began.

"So, she's okay? She'll be back soon?" Sternberg said, clutching at straws.

Katie shook her head and looked down at the table for a minute. "No, Mr. Sternberg, she's not okay. She's dead, and we have reason to believe she was murdered," Katie said.

Sternberg blanched and continued to sweat. He dabbed a limp handkerchief across his heavy jowls. "This is terrible," he moaned.

"Yes. Yes, it is," Katie said. "I need to get her personal information. Her next of kin? Her neighbor couldn't find it."

Sternberg sat in a daze. Visibly, he shook himself. "Yes, quite right. I will have someone bring it in here." He continued to sit there.

"Mr. Sternberg? May I get you a glass of water?" Katie asked, concerned.

"I'm sorry," he said. Heavily, he got to his feet and pushed a few buttons on the telephone. A few minutes later, Cordelia Thompson bustled in with a sheet of paper she handed to Mr. Sternberg. He asked her to take a seat.

"Cordelia, something terrible has happened. Michelle, Ms. Clarkson, has been killed."

Gasping, her face turned ashen. Ms. Thompson looked to Katie and Gus for confirmation. They nodded silently.

"Oh, dear God. That poor, lovely girl. How did it happen? Car wreck?" Ms. Thompson said.

"No," Gus said. "It's confidential at this point, but she died in, uh, mysterious circumstances."

"Are you going to tell her family, or do we need to?" Cordelia asked, looking from Gus to Mr. Sternberg and back again. "I've met her parents just once, but if you need me to contact them, I will."

"No," Gus said. "That's one of the reasons why we're here. To get her parents' information or her next of kin. Her neighbor misplaced their contact details and couldn't help us out."

Sniffing, Ms. Thompson blindly reached for the box of tissues in the middle of the table. I'll need to let the staff know. They'll be devastated. Everyone loved Michelle. May I let them know today?"

"I'd rather you didn't, not just yet," Gus said. "Maybe after five this afternoon or even tomorrow morning. Let me try her parents first. I'll let you know if we reach them. We'll need to interview those she was closest to here. Today, if they're onsite, and no later than tomorrow."

"Yes, certainly. I'll arrange it," Ms. Thompson seemed to recover herself after being given a task to do.

"Mr. Sternberg," Gus began. "Can you think of anyone who'd wish to harm Ms. Clarkson? An ex-boyfriend, a litigant with a grudge against her or the hospital, anyone?"

"No one," he said. "You can take a look at the files on her desk upstairs, and I can give you a list of those in storage that she worked on this year. I can't imagine someone whom the hospital sued to collect on their past due account hating her or killing her. You can ask Sandy if Michelle ever got threatening calls or letters. Sandy, out front, took most of our messages if we weren't in our offices and kept a log of some sort. Again, I can't think of anyone. Michelle was exactly the same to everyone: sweet, personable, efficient, and smart. Who could do such a thing?"

Allowing them to use his office, Sternberg left in bewildered silence. The call to Michelle's parents was every bit as awful as Katie and Gus anticipated. In advance, they'd contacted the Franklin County sheriff and asked him to send some deputies over to sit with her family until they or other law enforcement could get there. Hearing that reporters had called into the precinct with a lot of the crime scene information already in their possession, the two felt it was best to make the call now.

Gus and Katie hunkered down over boxes of files from the records room and Michelle's office. They sipped coffee from delicate pink and oyster-colored bone china cups that Ms. Thompson had brought.

A red-eyed Sandy had been in and denied taking any threatening or angry calls for Ms. Clarkson. She'd gone upstairs to empty the rest of the young attorney's desk into boxes so the officers could sift through it.

Five or six nurses and doctors came by, one at a time, to be interviewed. Each had seen Ms. Clarkson at least two days before. Three had met with her to discuss issues and had been gently referred back to human resources. The doctors discussed threats of malpractice suits that they'd had from overwrought patients. Under their contracts, the doctors were obligated to report every threat of legal action to the hospital's Legal Department. Most of the younger set at the hospital talked to Michelle because she was quiet, unassuming, and did not talk down to them like her boss did. Unanimously, the employees described her in glowing terms and denied that the attorney had seemed stressed or anxious.

Surprisingly, the last employee who came in was Dr. Mark Graham. Reluctantly, he took a seat at the conference table and introduced himself.

"So, did you see Ms. Clarkson recently, Dr. Graham?" Gus asked.

"Yeah. I needed to ask her about some pending complaints with the hospital. It'd been a while since I'd talked to her. I got a message up on the floor that she needed to speak to me, too," he said. "We usually met every other month to discuss the employees on my floor, including the doctors, since I'm the doctor in charge of the surgical floor."

"Was this your regular meeting or a special one?" Gus asked.

"I wouldn't call it special, but I hadn't gotten an update in a while, so I went by to see her."

"How did she seem to you?"

"Same as always. Tried to spare my feelings from the worst complaints about me. Updated me on a malpractice suit that got filed a few weeks ago. Nothing out of the ordinary," he said.

"Did she take any notes or provide you with any paperwork?" Gus asked.

"No. Look, it took about five minutes. She was fine when I left," he said.

Katie stopped taking notes and interjected, "This must be really hard for you. Having to answer questions about another missing young lady."

"Doing what I do, I'm supposed to be hardened to injury, illness, and death. I've seen enough of death. You don't get used to it," he said.

He shrugged but put his shaking hands in his surgical pants' pockets. Dark circles under his eyes and a web of fine wrinkles belied his assertion.

"Thank you for coming in, doctor," Gus said.

He got up and slowly walked to the door. Turning around before he left the room, he said softly, "I hope you catch the bastard soon."

CHAPTER SIXTEEN

Bob looked at himself in the mirror. He looked pretty good for a guy who was getting really close to fifty. Shoes shined, hair in place, he didn't look too shabby. He sucked in his small gut. *Can't do that all night.*

He didn't have time for this and should never have let his neighbor, Mike, talk him into it. Mike had been on him to sign up for internet dating. Mike texted him site after site on the weekends. Truth be told, Mike enjoyed scrolling down the various dating sites and seeing photos of beautiful young women. He'd be here in two minutes, with his wife Martha, to go with him to the Oak Room and meet his dinner date.

When he finally agreed to go on a date, he hadn't been in the middle of a murder investigation. The email he'd been using for his "date" did not acknowledge his last-minute appeal to reschedule. He couldn't just stand her up, so here he was in his best suit and tie, getting ready to head to a place he didn't want to go with people he didn't want to be with.

Mike honked the horn outside. Bob grabbed his house keys and wallet. When he got to the car, he saw only Mike.

"Where's Martha?" he asked.

Mike wouldn't meet his eye.

"She decided to stay home," he said.

"What? Why? She was gonna help the conversation get going," Bob said. "This whole thing is a bad idea."

"Let's just go. You don't want to be late."

Bob grumbled but put his seat belt on. He almost fell asleep during the two miles it took to get to the Oak Room.

Mike looked over at him in sympathy. "You've been working really hard, haven't you?"

Bob rubbed his eyes. "Yeah. It's been brutal lately."

"Here we are," Mike said, easing his car into a space up front.

Bob got out and waited for Mike. Mike rolled down his window. "I'll pick you up in two hours. Call if you're ready beforehand."

Dumbfounded, Bob stood where he was for a minute. *What the hell? Fuck it, I'm hungry. I can at least eat. If the lady is a no-show, I'll just get rid of this tie.*

The restaurant was dim, not dim for ambiance, just dim due to ill-fated lighting decisions. He saw the hostess coming toward him. "Hey, Wanda. I'm meeting a lady."

"Yeah. I put y'all at the best table in the house," she said and waggled her eyebrows at him.

"Well, that's mighty nice, but I'm not sure how long we'll be here," Bob said.

"Follow me."

Bob almost tripped over Charles, attorney Buck Davis's big Lab, on the way to his table. He stopped to speak to Buck and his brother, Jeb, who were in the middle of a heated discussion about basketball's best teams, power forwards, players, icons, etc.

"Hey, Bob," Buck said. "Maybe you can help settle this. Who was the best forward? Surely, being a Celtics fan, you know a little about basketball?"

Jeb sneered. "Naw. Celtics never had nothin' after Kevin Garnett. Bob wouldn't know."

Bob almost sat down with them. This was a hell of a lot more interesting than where he was headed, he'd bet. "Sorry, guys. I'd like to argue with you, but I'm on my way to meet someone."

"A date? Bob, it's about damn time. Good luck," Buck said.

"Hey, I saw Katie's ring. Congrats," Bob said, patting him on the back. "You got a great one there. Katie's first class. The folks she arrests and charges, and even the criminals' families, love her. Jeb, it's your turn now. Turn on the charm, cut that mountaineer beard, and find somebody that will put up with you."

Charles thumped his tail, and Buck and Jeb laughed while Bob continued to follow Wanda to the back of the restaurant.

He'd already decided. He'd get a couple of appetizers and make excuses about needing to get back to the investigation. Mike be damned. He'd call the town's one-car taxi service and go home.

Wanda waited patiently by the two-top table covered in a burgundy tablecloth adorned with fake flowers and flickering candles. It even appeared to be made of actual cloth instead of the usual plastic. Seated at the table was a strikingly good-looking woman. Wanda handed him his menu and backed away.

Bob started to apologize for being late. His voice died in his throat as he took in his companion.

"Hi, Bob," said Gloria. "Long time no see."

"Gloria," he whispered.

"I can see you've still got your detecting skills. No, I don't mean that. It's good to see you, Bob. You look great," she smiled up at him. She hesitantly rose from her seat and gave him a slight hug.

Bob grabbed her wineglass, took a sip, then spit out the fruity drink into his water glass.

"Not alcohol. Just a virgin daiquiri," she laughed.

He started laughing along with her. "You look fantastic. How have you been?" he asked.

"Pretty good. Don't be too hard on Mike and Martha. I asked them to help me set this up. I've wanted to see you for a long time and just didn't know how to go about it. I was afraid you wouldn't show up if you knew it was me."

Wanda came back, and they ordered dinner. Bob stared at Gloria. She'd put up her blond hair and had a trace of lipstick on. Her earrings sparkled in the candlelight. One stubby candle lit up her smile. She had a few more wrinkles around her eyes than the last time he'd seen her, but she looked tan and healthy.

"Bob," she said. "You're making me uncomfortable."

"I'm sorry. I just can't believe you're here. It's really great to see you."

"I'm really glad to see you, too." She laughed, then turned serious. "I need to make amends. You know I've been following the twelve steps?"

He nodded.

"I need to apologize to you for deserting you at a time when we both needed the most support. I didn't act like the person I want to be by just taking off. I ran away from my grief, our grief, and I'm not proud of it. You're a good person, and I let you down in the worst way."

Bob began to speak.

"No, please. Let me finish. I think about you often and hope you are well. Martha said she didn't think you'd met anyone. I don't know if we can start over, but I wanted to tell you how I feel about you, just in case. I think you are the strongest, kindest, and most loving man that I've ever met."

Bob teared up. His eyes glistened, and he cleared his throat to speak. "Gloria. I've missed you every single day. I hate prowling around the house on my own. There's a big hole in my heart. Should we take things slow and get to be friends again?" he asked.

"I think that's the smart thing to do. I'm so glad you're not mad about this deception. Martha thought it would be okay."

"No. I'm not, but what about your life in Myrtle Beach? I thought you had a lot going on there with a new real estate job."

"I've loved the job I have. I've met a lot of great people, but none of them have felt like home."

Their steaks, salads, and baked potatoes arrived all at once. There were no steak knives or salad dressing, but eventually, those materialized, one at a time, as Wanda tried to overhear their conversation.

"Where are you staying?" Bob asked, putting down his fork. He tried to hide the pieces of grizzle under the lettuce leaf garnish.

"Next door, at Mike and Martha's," she said.

"Are you staying over long?" he asked. "I don't want to ruin the night, but I have to tell you, we're in the middle of investigating a series of murders. I just didn't want you to think I'm abandoning you or that I am not making this a priority."

She smiled at him. "That's very thoughtful of you to tell me. Martha and I had planned a day trip for shopping tomorrow, so you're off the hook. I just hope, well, I just hope that one day you'll forgive me."

"I do. I do forgive you. It was a terrible time for us. No one should have to live through losing a child." He stopped for a minute. "I didn't know how to reach out, to say what I wanted to say when it all happened. I'm just glad I got to see you again." He looked at his watch. "Mike's probably outside. Are you ready?"

"Yes, and thank you for dinner. I was prepared to pay," she said, scooping up her clutch and putting on her wrap.

"No, this is my treat."

Wanda's eyes were shining as she needlessly escorted them to the front door.

CHAPTER SEVENTEEN

Bob woke to the earthy smell of coffee beans. Disoriented, he looked over at the cheap plug-in clock. He bolted upright. He had twenty minutes to shower, shave, and get to the meeting at the precinct on time.

Gloria stood at the bedroom door dressed in one of his old t-shirts. "If that's what you call taking it slow," she said, "I'd like to know what you call taking it fast." She smiled at him and handed him a cup of coffee while he started throwing clothes around the room with his free hand.

"Here, let me," she said. "You go shower and I'll pick out your clothes."

He walked over and kissed her hard on the lips. "That was the best date I've had," he said and smiled when he held her in front of him. "I'll miss you when you leave tomorrow."

"I'll be back soon," she said, "or you can visit me when your case is over. You take care of yourself. Be safe." She hugged him to her fiercely, then shooed him into the shower.

She left out a suit, shirt, and tie for him, even socks and shoes. Dressed, he found her downstairs sitting in front of the mantel. She was looking at the family photographs. Instead of tears, there was a gentle smile on her face.

"You know, Bob, it's almost like Matthew's been talking to me lately. I just can't explain it. That sounds so weird, I know. It's just a feeling I have, but I think he'd be happy that we're friends again."

Bob hugged her to him and kissed the top of her head. "I think you're right. I think he'd be happy. I'll call you tonight," he said and headed out the door.

* * * * *

The mood at the police station was grim. No one was talking. The Henderson officers trickled in and sank into the cheap plastic chairs at a table in the corner away from other law enforcement. The church volunteers silently brought in the filled coffee canisters and some ham biscuits, sweet rolls, and coffee cake. Officers wordlessly hunched over their plates or slurped their coffee. Part of Dr. Fulcher's photo display hung off the wall in limp strips.

All of the officers and deputies looked tired and despondent. The only one looking the least bit upbeat was Dr. Fulcher, probably because no one had proved his theories wrong or right.

Dr. Fulcher positively chirped when he saw Bob. "You were so right," he said. "That Mamie's B and B is an absolute wonder. I had the best sleep, and she's such a dear. We stayed up talking after dinner. She's so very knowledgeable about Steiff, Murano glass, Limoges, and Royal Doulton."

When Bob looked at him blankly, Dr. Fulcher impatiently said, "The teddy bear, glass, and china companies?"

Bob couldn't believe he was having this conversation. He looked around for Johnson or Katie. Johnson caught his distressed look and walked over to the two men.

"Hey, doc. How's it going? Got any paranormal feelings today about our guy? Hair color or height? List of favorite songs?" Johnson asked..

Dr. Fulcher drew himself up to his full height of five feet six inches and said in a plummy voice, "That's not funny, Sergeant."

Bob steered Johnson away as an excuse to get him out of whatever was about to happen and be blamed for it. "Er, Johnson, come on over here. I want to show you something," Bob said loudly to distract the officer.

"Okay, Bob. I get it. Don't rile up the professional help, but that guy gets on my nerves. We're out here wading through creeks, pushing through shrubs and trees, and talking to every snitch we've ever signed up and what we have is a big fat nothing. And *that* guy is not helping us."

"I agree, but the Chief will blame me if the Bureau pulls out," Bob said.

"Gus is alright. She gets her hands dirty and is trying to interview people," Johnson said. "What are we going to do today? I feel like we've been over every square foot near where the victims lived or worked."

Teams of officers and volunteers spent hours the day before combing the neighboring forests, backyards, and residential streets near where each victim had lived or where she was recently seen.

"Oh, Bob," Johnson said with a smile. "Heard you had a hot date last night. Yeah," he said in response to Bob's startled expression. "Wanda sometimes babysits my kids. She told me all about it this morning."

Bob sighed. "Is nothing sacred in this town?"

Johnson laughed. "Not much. Maybe we should call in Wanda on this case. She's got good powers of observation."

The two were interrupted by Gus and Katie coming in together.

"Y'all are mighty late. What's up?" Johnson asked.

Gus's jacket was rumpled, and she looked exhausted. She poured herself a generous cup of coffee from the fresh carafe.

"We've got another missing lady," Gus said.

"Her name is Letitia Royster. She's a nineteen-year-old. Everyone, suit up. Johnson, you, Bob, and Tony head over to the house. It's on Granville Street. Katie and I are headed over to the girl's grandmother's house, where she normally stays."

Tony walked up at the tail end of the conversation. "Bob, we headed out?" he asked.

"Yeah. Pick about six guys over there and give them the address here," Bob said, handing off a piece of scrap paper to Tony. "Tell them to meet us there in five," Bob said.

Johnson went over to the tables with Tony and instructed the remaining officers to follow Katie and Gus over to the grandmother's address. Most poured a "to go" cup of coffee for the ride and headed out for the patrol cars and deputy vehicles.

Katie turned on blue lights as she left the precinct. There wasn't a lot of traffic, and what there was pulled over to the shoulder when the officers' cruisers streamed down the street.

She pulled up to the curb in front of the small wooden structure on Maple Street. Two people were fighting in the dirt. A muscular black-and-tan dog strained at the end of a heavy chain and barked. An elderly man sat on a sagging sofa on the front porch. Next to him, a woman in a purple-print housecoat, curlers, and fluffy violet bedroom shoes screamed at the two on the ground.

The blue lights and sirens didn't penetrate the shouting combatants. Katie pulled a whistle out and its screech at least silenced the dog. Gus grabbed one's arm, and Katie took the other's arm, and they pried the fighters apart.

Katie's fighter was a small, wiry woman who was spitting and still cursing at the other one. "You mother fucker! You're a goddamn liar and a thief!"

The small man Gus held lunged forward. She kept a tight grip on both of his arms so that he only got a step closer. "Calm down! Neither one of you is going anywhere except the patrol car if you don't settle down. I'll cuff you in a heartbeat."

The man glared at the young woman being held by Katie and said, "Ho," which started another round of cursing and of the officers tightening their holds on them. The other cars pulled up, and sheriff's deputies jumped out. Johnson got to them first.

"Buster, I told you last week that if I caught you fighting again, you were going in, didn't I?" Johnson said to the short man.

"Yeah, but this goddamn ho has made me mad as hell. She done stole my liquor and slept with my brother," he said, gesturing to the older fellow sleeping on the porch.

"That's a damn lie," Letitia said. "I didn't steal your nasty liquor."

Buster lunged toward her, but Johnson grabbed him in a full Nelson. "Nope. You're going in this time, Buster," Johnson said, frog marching him to the car. Shoving him inside, he slammed the door closed, told the deputy to book him, and came back over. "Letitia, we thought you were missing, and here you are screaming down the neighborhood and fighting. Your Grandmama is ashamed of you—she taught you better," Johnson said.

The lady with the curlers moved closer.

"Walter, you tell her. My granddaughter won't listen to a thing I have to say. She's gonna get herself shot if she keeps messing with these two sorry men," she said with a contemptuous sneer toward their house.

"How you been, Ms. Jackson? I'm sorry these two fools disturbed your peace today, but we're glad she's safe. We thought we had another missing girl."

"Oh Lord. Thank mercy, no. She's been in and out, but thank goodness she's back. I called the dispatcher earlier when she wasn't here this morning. It's been over a day since she's been gone, and it's not like her to not call," she said, glaring at the young woman.

"Granma, I'm sorry. I just lost track of time. And Buster took my phone and broke it. I didn't mean to worry you," Letitia said, reaching for her grandmother. She enfolded the older woman in a hug.

"Okay, then. Guess we'll head out and back to the hospital for a few more interviews," Katie said.

"C'mon, Letitia, you've got to go with me," Johnson said. "Don't look at your grandmother for help. I hope she leaves you in jail for a while. Then she'll know where you are."

Ms. Jackson waved forlornly as Johnson buckled himself into his car. Johnson waved back and took off toward the county magistrate.

Katie's phone rang. She looked at it and then at Gus, "Sorry, I've got to take this, but we can go and get in the car."

Katie climbed in the driver's seat and said, "Um hmm, um hum. Yeah, well, um hum, um hmm." She sighed and said, "You're right. Okay, see you tomorrow night."

Gus gave her a few minutes before she asked her what that was all about.

"Pink! It was all about pink, as in frosted pink, dark pink, peach pink, mauve, blush pink, and fuchsia. That was Buck's mama, Mrs. Davis. I forgot to call her yesterday, so that was her going on and on about the pink I was supposed to pick. My poor mom would rather garden all day than have to pick out wedding froo-frahs, as she calls them. So, Mrs. Davis is taking charge. She loves it because she has two sons—Buck and Jeb—and this way she can do the girly stuff. But, she is driving me bonkers. I thought saying 'I do' was the sum total of what Buck and I would plan. But, oh no, no way, huh uh. This is a Cecile B. DeMille production, kinda like Ben Hur," she said as she ran out of steam.

"So," Gus said. "Which pink?"

"Aaahhhggg! I have to decide that by tomorrow night. Mrs. Davis has given me a deadline. Look at me. I wear a uniform every day, which is the worst possible brown biscuit color. It has no style—zero, zip. It washes me out—I look paler than normal—and it adds twenty pounds. Any color of pink is a positive."

"Is pink the color of your dress?" Gus asked.

"No, it's the color of the flowers on the altar and the bouquets. We haven't even started on the wedding dress. I tried to lobby for the thrift store, but I thought Mrs. Davis was gonna pass out on me. No, dress shopping is this weekend. Thankfully, my mom's coming too. She can distract her while I pick out what I like. My mom's picking out her mother-of-the-bride dress too, and made the mistake of asking Mrs. Davis's opinion. Mrs. Davis will have her hands full because Mama likes some glitter and tends to pick things inappropriate for her age. Plus, I don't think she's worn a dress since 2010 when my cousin Junior electrocuted himself on the tractor engine and had a massive funeral. Well, I guess it would be since Junior weighed about 350 pounds."

"Sounds like a blast. I'd hide a bottle of something strong in your purse in case of emergencies."

"I should make Buck and Jeb go, too," Katie smiled.

"That'd fix Buck's cavalier attitude toward the 101 things I have to do. Buck just tunes it all out and says, 'whatever you think' while he watches television. Jeb's my man of honor, so he ought to go."

"Is Jeb going to style you barefoot with flowers in your hair and wearing a filmy floaty white dress?" Gus snorted.

"Actually, he has pretty good taste. He's picked out some Vera Wang and Panina Torne from the Modern Bride magazines. He won't admit it, but I think he helped find my engagement ring. Buck was going to give me Aunt Tilley's Art Deco monstrosity of sapphires, garnets, and European cut diamonds set in a huge, heavy setting. Fortunately, he showed the ring to Jeb before he showed it to me. Jeb told him he was going to get a big fat 'no' if he pulled that ring out and proposed. So, he and Buck headed over to Bailey's in Raleigh and picked this one out," Katie said. She held up her hand and admired the two-carat, emerald-cut diamond set in platinum with diamond baguettes.

"That's one beautiful ring," Gus acknowledged. "I wish my husband had gotten a little help," she said ruefully, looking down at her plain round diamond set in a gold setting with a matching wedding band. "I get the feeling that he picked one in the first cabinet he came to in the jewelry store and the one he could make payments on."

"Listen to you. Your husband showers you with little presents and gifts all the time. He bought you that diamond tennis bracelet for Valentine's. He cooks dinner for you and checks the kids' homework," Katie said, smiling and starting up the car.

"Yeah, I guess he's a keeper," Gus said. Gus and her husband remained besotted with one another even after fifteen years of marriage.

"I've decided. I'm definitely going to call Jeb to go dress shopping with me. He can keep my mom out of the pageant dresses, and he won't badger me like his mom," Katie muttered as they headed back to the precinct.

CHAPTER EIGHTEEN

He was pissed off. His face turned a dangerous shade of red as he started perspiring profusely. His thoughts rushed, and his knees trembled. Consciously, he slowed his breathing and practiced some breathing techniques that his old therapist had taught him. Back when he was made to go to therapy because his bitch of a mother and sister belittled him, laughed at him. So, he'd had to set fire to field mice, then to old Mrs. Thompson's cat next door. All hell had broken loose.

But that was a really long time ago—back when he was a child.

What the hell were the cops doing? He saw blue lights buzzing all over town. Most were headed to the south side. He hadn't left anything there. No, it must be another crime that had caught their attention. Why weren't they looking for those missing girls instead of wasting time on something else?

He tugged on Louie, a disgruntled, ill-tempered Pomeranian who was today's senior dog.

He started laughing. Forget him? When he was finished, no one would forget him.

CHAPTER NINETEEN

ob watched the sweat trickle down Buck's forehead and disappear into his shirt collar. Bob liked Buck. Bob thought he was good for Katie, but this was his job: to ask questions, and Buck knew it. Buck Davis had been at the small Oxford law firm of Hobgood and Davis since finishing his federal clerkship in Raleigh, North Carolina.

"Bob, dammit, I didn't kill those girls. I gotta find my calendar and give you details on where I was? This is insulting and a waste of time!" Buck's voice ended an octave higher than when he'd started.

Bob continued to stare at him. "Yep. That's right. C'mon, Buck, work with me here," Bob said. Tony silently watched the interplay.

"I'm giving you the courtesy of interviewing you in your office instead of down at the precinct. Here, I have a fifty percent chance of getting burnt or electrocuted by your sweet but clumsy legal secretary, Emma Jean. Now, Mia interned with you for a few weeks last summer. Michelle was hired as a summer intern by your partner, Cal Hobgood, her first year out of law school. Sternberg said you recommended her for the job opening that came up at the hospital."

Tony looked from one man to the other like he was watching a ping pong tournament. He rubbed his shin where he'd bumped it trying to avoid a collision with Emma Jean and her idea of a tea tray—an old bamboo affair that leaked. His pants' knees were wet from the weak tea that dripped from his saucer. Tony hated tea.

The lawyers' office faced Main Street and the courthouse. Paper files erupted across the large mahogany desk and spilled from stacks on the floor. Emma Jean, Buck's legal assistant and sometime dog sitter for Buck's Lab, Charles, sent one stack skittering when she hit it with her foot. The top file slid to a stop on top of Tony's shoe.

"I told you I've been tied up in a trial in Raleigh. I haven't been here all week. You can check the Marriott's records. I've been staying in that big new one downtown."

Bob moved his toothpick from side to side. Finally taking it out, he pointed it at Buck. "Don't screw with me, Buck. I'm not taking your word for it. I don't care if you are Katie's fiancé. That's the only thing keeping me from dragging you down to the precinct. When you get out of court today, you head straight back to the department, and we're gonna talk again."

"Whoa. I can't believe Lt O'Connor...." Tony started.

Buck glared him into silence.

"Look, Bob. I'll get you timelines, receipts, whatever, but I don't have time to go through this again right now."

Buck stood up and started shoving files into his briefcase.

"I've got to get to Raleigh. Oh shit," he said, looking at his watch. "I'm going to be late. The judge will kill me."

Bob and Tony stood up and gingerly balanced their teacups on the partially functional tray. Outside the two-story brick building, they watched people hustling over to Donna's Donuts for a ham sandwich, cup of coffee, or biscuit. Donuts featured on the menu only occasionally,

Bob yelled to Buck as Buck opened his car door. "Get Trooper Graham to run the blue light and bird dog him over to Raleigh."

"I'm avoiding Graham. He lost his last DWI trial to me, and the judge chewed out his trainee for sloppy work," Buck hollered back.

"Get Emma Jean to get your hotel receipts over to me this afternoon," Bob said as Buck's door slammed.

After Buck sped away, Tony turned to Bob. "What's his story? Why's he so uncooperative?"

"He's a good guy," Bob said. "His wedding is coming up in a few weeks, and he's stuck in Raleigh in that jury trial. Plus, he's got old Judge Williamson, who is cantankerous as hell on his best days. He shoulda brought Emma Jean over to Raleigh with him for the trial. The old judge loves Emma Jean..." Bob trailed off for a minute. "Plus, like most lawyers, he needs to feel like he's in charge. This time he's not. I think he's hiding the fact that he's upset by these women's deaths. Look, you follow up with Emma Jean in a few hours if she doesn't email those receipts and timelines to you. Speaking of lunch, let's head over to Donna's and get a sandwich."

Tony winced. Donna's place was an old-fashioned part diner, part store. It featured a couple of low lunch counters dotted with Texas Pete, dusty red and yellow condiment bottles, all underpinned with spinning stools. Nothing was electronic—no cash register, no WIFI, no charging station. A pad, a pencil, and an old cash register, fashionable during World War I, got the job done. Donna didn't take any credit cards, no exceptions. The food was okay. Donna now had wheat bread in addition to the usual white, and fried bologna wasn't the featured special every day. It didn't compare to the menu of shrimp po' boys or gumbo from New Orleans that Tony was used to, but it wasn't terrible.

The old Christmas bell tied on the inside handle tinkled when they pushed open the glass door.

* * * * *

At the courthouse, Assistant District Attorney Grady Capps looked over his shoulder at the packed courtroom and then down at the dregs of coffee in his lopsided ceramic mug. He smiled at the memory of his daughter throwing her first pottery piece, but quickly looked up when he heard Judge Jones clear his throat.

The judge scowled at him from the minute the judge took the bench. His black robes settled around the chair like a bird of prey folding its wings. Grady's shucks, once in alphabetical order, according to the defendant's last name, spilled all over his table. The defense attorneys picked them up and waved them in his face. The attorneys talked all over each other, trying to get a deal done and get out. No one wanted to face Judge Jones in his foul mood.

A few officers and deputies sat in the jury box waiting for their cases to be called for trial. Each immaculate uniform boasted the insignia of its department: highway patrol, sheriff, police department, ALE, and wildlife. The grays, blues, and browns were sharply creased.

Around the courtroom's wooden bar, lined with curved white wooden pickets, inside its rails, the defense attorneys gathered on club chairs. Most women attorneys were dressed in dark colored suits or pantsuits. The men wore suits or blazers and khaki pants. Every so often, an out-of-town attorney would show up for court without a blazer. Those attorneys sporting less than sartorial splendor were turned around at the door by the bailiffs. Judge Jones was old-school conservative. Far better for the attorney to correct the wardrobe problem than get blasted by the judge in front of their clients. It was bad enough when their DWI clients wore graphic t-shirts advertising beer or bourbon.

Grady scanned the jury box, looking for an officer so he could try the next case. Judge Jones drummed his fingers on his bench and fixed Grady with a frosty stare.

"Got anything else for hearing, counselor?" the judge growled. "Are we done here?"

"Your honor," Grady began, an octave too high. He cleared his throat and started again. "Uh, your honor, the State calls for trial the case of State versus Turner Sullivan."

From the wooden pews outside of the bar, where defendants and victims both sat, a silver-headed, stately man rose and began his progress down to the defense table.

Novice attorney Jordan McNamara stood up inside the bar. He was unclear what Dr. Sullivan had decided about his legal representation, but he'd brought his new leather briefcase with a copy of the relevant statutes in it just in case he got the nod to be counsel. He glanced hopefully at Sullivan.

Judge Jones squinted at him.

"You got an attorney?" Jones asked Sullivan.

"No, sir, I'm going to represent myself," Sullivan said.

McNamara sat down, deflated. He opened his briefcase, trying to look busy and evade Judge Jones's sharp eyes.

"Is that a good idea? It's a pretty serious charge," Jones added.

"I'm aware of that," Sullivan said, straightening his club tie. He wore a dark blue pin-striped suit and white button-down shirt.

"Suit yourself," Jones said. "Arraign the defendant."

"Mr. Sullivan," Grady began.

"That's Doctor," Sullivan interrupted.

"Okay. Dr. Sullivan, how do you plead to the charge of carrying a concealed weapon?"

"I plead not guilty," Sullivan said. Sullivan pulled out the defense table's chair and settled into it gracefully. McNamara sank awkwardly into a chair along the rails of the bar where other defense counsel waited. The attorney beside him whispered, "Tough luck."

"Call your first witness," Jones said. He pulled out a fresh, yellow-lined legal pad and a blue pen.

"The State calls Lieutenant Kathleen O'Connor to the stand," Grady said.

Lt Katie O'Connor was sworn and took the witness stand. Her brown sheriff's uniform consisted of a light brown long-sleeved shirt and dark brown pants. Her hair was pinned back in a low bun.

"Lt O'Connor, tell us about your background, starting with your education and then law enforcement experience," Grady asked.

She turned slightly to face Judge Jones and the defendant. "I attended high school here and community college in Henderson. I transferred to a four-year college after two years and pursued a degree in criminal justice. After graduation, I attended law school. I decided against practicing law and joined the Sheriff's Office about fifteen years ago," she said.

"Why didn't you want to practice law?"

"My father had worked his whole career as a police officer. I admired him and wanted to follow in his footsteps." Katie said.

The judge muttered under his breath, "Smart girl." This earned him icy frowns from the older lady clerks. "Er, woman," he amended.

"Now, Lieutenant, can you tell us if you were working on January 2nd of this year?"

"Yes, I was."

"Did you come into contact with this Defendant?"

"Yes, I did."

She detailed a late-night traffic stop she'd assisted a colleague with and her discovery of a firearm on Dr. Sullivan that he'd failed to declare at the outset of the stop under the then-current carry conceal permit regulations. Her pat-down of the doctor's waistband revealed the expensive weapon. The Walther PPK 9mm was loaded. She also testified that he'd smelled of alcohol but that he'd passed a battery of field sobriety tests well enough that he wasn't charged with driving while impaired.

On cross-examination, Dr. Sullivan began with questions as to her qualifications.

His first question targeted her vocational choice.

"You expect me to believe that you chose law enforcement over being an attorney? You probably couldn't pass the bar," he sneered.

"I could and I did," she answered. "It was an informed choice. I decided that I wanted to follow my father's career path. His career was cut short by a drunk driver."

Dr. Sullivan tried another line. "It's not a crime to have a gun is it? Or do you believe only lawmen should have them?"

"No, sir, I believe in upholding the Second Amendment and the laws of North Carolina and applying them equally to all persons. You didn't declare your weapon. The law requires that you do so."

After thirty minutes of Dr. Sullivan's minimally relevant questions, the judge scowled at Grady. Grady took this as a time to make an objection. The objection was sustained.

The State rested.

"Any evidence for the Defendant?" Judge Jones inquired.

"I would take the stand, but I can see how this is going," the doctor started.

"Say again? What are you talking about?" Jones barked.

"This backwoods town isn't interested in my side," Dr. Sullivan said.

"That's not the way I see it, but it's up to you, doctor. Your case. What do you want to do?" Jones asked.

"I just want to be heard," Sullivan said.

"No evidence for the Defendant?"

"No."

The judge listened to closing arguments from both sides. He took a break before entering his decision.

During the break, the attorneys swarmed the ADA, and he worked to continue cases and listened to law enforcement tell him about all of the other places they needed to be, other than the courtroom.

After the break, Judge Jones asked Dr. Sullivan to stand.

"The State has a heavy burden, and that burden is beyond a reasonable doubt. I find the State has met its burden in this case."

Sullivan's face turned red, and he started toward the bench, arguing with the judge. The bailiffs stopped him and backed him up to the defense table.

Judge Jones looked at him for a moment and entered a sentence suspended on the condition that the doctor complete a carry conceal class and pay a fine and court costs.

Sullivan gathered himself and said, "I give notice of appeal."

"That's your right, doctor. Bail stays the same."

Grady called his next case for trial, and the doctor left the courtroom, mumbling under his breath.

Dr. Sullivan passed Katie in the courthouse lobby on his way to get a copy of the judgment and court file. He paused for a moment, then stepped in front of her. She could feel his breath on her face.

She refused to back up one step despite the venom in his eyes. Sullivan's eyes were red and bloodshot. He smelled faintly of tobacco, stale alcohol, and something less salubrious.

"Bitch, this isn't over," he whispered to her.

* * * * *

A short time later, Bob and Tony were the first ones back in the precinct's parking lot. They'd been called to assist in clearing traffic behind a turned-over truck hauling tobacco. All of the patrol guys were tied up with the investigation or other traffic investigations on the various highways in and out of town.

The Chief met them in the parking lot and handed them a piece of paper. The Chief had bags under his eyes, and his coloring did not look healthy. His suit jacket was wrinkled and smelled faintly of mothballs. "What do you make of this?" he asked.

"It's either some nut job or it's our guy," Bob finally said. The faxed-in paper read: "You're a bunch of assholes. You need a road map to find your asses. I'm still out here, and you'll be sorry."

Bob and Tony studied it further in silence. "It sounds like the emotional rant of an eighth-grader. If it is him, our killer, it means he's gearing up to kill again," Bob said. "Have you asked the FBI expert his thoughts?"

"No, it just came in this morning's mail. This is a copy. They're bagging the original and placing it into evidence inside. They've already dusted it for prints. There are a couple of partial latent prints on it. They're running the partials through the system, ours and the feds, to see if they can get a match."

"Can we get the FBI to locate the post office used to mail the letter, and maybe, in the interim, the profiler will have some insight?" Tony asked.

They all headed into the precinct to find Dr. Fulcher in the conference room. He'd spent the morning tacking up the peeling display and was now on his computer, staring intently at the screen.

"Doctor," the Chief said, starting to hand him the paper.

"Not now. Give me a minute," Fulcher said. His hands moved swiftly over the computer keyboard. His shirt sleeves were rolled up, and his suit jacket was hung over the back of his chair. Every time Fulcher slowed down and the Chief moved to give him the paper, Fulcher waved the Chief away.

After a few minutes of this, Tony rolled his eyes at Bob. He eased the paper from the Chief's hand and pushed it in front of Fulcher. "We think this is from our guy," Tony said. "Can you give us a minute here?"

Fulcher pushed up his glasses with one hand and took the paper with the other. "Hmm," he said. "There's an address at the top. Probably phony. Let me get on that. If I can't find it, I have a guy at the Bureau who's a genius with this type of thing."

Katie and Gus came in, and the Chief brought them up to speed. Gus took a photo of the document with her phone and went over to a corner and made a phone call. Katie, Tony, Bob, and the Chief headed over to the still heavily laden table of lunch meats, sandwich bread, potato salad, and the ever-present Jello mold. The officers, coming in from the field with updates on their searches, ate standing up. All waited on Fulcher to come up with something. The patrolmen and deputies trickled in to wait for orders.

One of the young deputies started studying the graphic photos on the wall. Katie walked over to him. Blond-headed and blue-eyed, TJ was shorter than she was but wiry. There wasn't one perp he couldn't outrun in a foot chase.

"What are you thinking, TJ?" Katie asked.

He didn't say anything for a minute, just stared at the body parts on display. He spent a few minutes going from photo to photo.

"Lieutenant, you know I like to hunt? And I like to eat what I can catch or bring down," he said. "I kept my mom in venison all last winter."

"Yeah, every season you're out there looking for some poor ducks, doves, deer, fish, or something. And, I know not to bother assigning you work on Thanksgiving Day when it's deer season and your whole family is out in the woods," Katie agreed.

TJ grinned. "Well, I'm looking at these here marks and the way the, uh, parts are," he said, pointing to a photo of Mina's leg. "I don't think just anybody could handle it like this. I mean, this took some skill and a super sharp blade. Forget that you'd have to be one mean son of a bitch to do it. I don't see just anybody being able to cut like that. You know, having the strength or the skill."

Katie leaned in closer and looked where he was pointing. "Where do we need to look for this guy? You have some hunting buddies who can give you anything? Anybody they've come across that's odd or, I don't know, too excited about the butchering?"

"I can't think of anybody like that, right off. You know, I hunt mainly with my brothers. I'll ask them, though. One of them belongs to some kinda hunting club. Let me see if I can get any of them on the phone."

TJ's brothers were all in law enforcement. One brother was on the state highway patrol, one with the ALE (Alcohol Law Enforcement), and the third with the Creek Police Department. Their dad was a lifelong Granville County sheriff's deputy who retired and then lost his battle with cancer. TJ stepped out into the hall to make his calls. The cinder blocks lining the narrow hallway were painted a muted green, giving everyone a sickly glow.

Katie walked back over to Dr. Fulcher and the small group gathered around him. His fingers were flying over the keyboard, and sweat gleamed on his forehead. Gus was standing at his shoulder, trying to see what was coming up on the screen. The Chief went outside, ostensibly to wait for the SBI crime scene techs to pick up the original letter, but snuck a cigarette that his wife had forbidden him to have.

Finished with his calls, TJ spoke to Katie. "I talked to my brothers. It's a miracle they're all on day shift this week. Anyway, Patrick, the state trooper, said he knows a guy who isn't quite right, who sometimes hunts with a friend of his. He's heard that the guy talks about perfectly butchering the meat, but he's never seen him do it. I wrote his name down, and Patrick's trying to get the guy's number or where he lives or works. Thought we could at least see if he had a record or something." TJ said, handing over a ragged piece of paper to Katie.

"Thanks, TJ. Let me know once you get a number or address. Good work," Katie said.

TJ's big smile highlighted just how young he was. He had a lot of light-colored freckles but no wrinkles on his smooth face. He went back over to his squad with another helping of chocolate cake.

* * * * *

A group of Granville deputies' cruisers silently floated up to the address in Stem that TJ had gotten from Patrick, not far out of Oxford. On the perpendicular street, a mirror image of Stem and Oxford police cars eased up near the Old Franklin Road address. The house was nondescript and had a deserted feel to it.

Katie approached the door with the leader of the SRT (Special Response Team). Barking "law enforcement" twice, without results, she nodded to the leader, who rammed the battering ram into the front door. The door splintered at the top but swung open. With guns drawn, she and the team entered the front room. A smell of decaying meat and old beer assaulted them.

"Jesus," sputtered Katie, pulling her t-shirt over her nose and mouth. The SRT lieutenant leaned out of the door and called for the crime scene techs who'd been smoking over at the white van discreetly parked across the street. The lieutenant came back in and motioned to Katie.

"Better let the team come in first. This isn't going to be good news," he said. She backed out onto the porch slowly, careful not to touch anything. An old, sagging sofa barred the only downstairs window, which was grimy with dirt and bird droppings.

The crime scene crew hustled in and started working after the lieutenant and one other officer cleared each of the four rooms.

"Damn," the lieutenant, whose name tag read Henry, said and scrubbed the sweat from his face. He drank greedily from the water bottle that Katie offered. "Hot as a bitch in there and not doing those bodies any good. I counted two in the back bedroom and one in the kitchen. Got to have been in there awhile."

"I called the SBI agent for backup. Any idea what happened?"

He shrugged. "Hard to say. They were slumped over, but I didn't see any shell casings or obvious signs of death. Hopefully, the techs will have better luck. You call the ME?"

"Yeah. It's beginning to be a daily thing. Someone should be here in under an hour. Okay to let TJ's brother in to scan for quick ID?"

He thought for a minute. "I don't see a problem with it. Get him suited up first. Should be alright."

The young patrolman put on protective gear and followed one of the techs through the house and back out. He leaned over and put his hands on his knees, trying to catch his breath.

"Hot as hell in there," he gasped. "It's that hunter we know, in the kitchen. I don't know the others, but they've all been in there awhile."

As a courtesy, Katie had called the Stem Police Department before they'd approached the house. Turning the crime scene over to them now, in the cool of her air-conditioned cruiser, she brought Stem's two officers up to speed on who was coming to assist and what was happening inside. She gave them brief details of the murders in Oxford and Henderson so they'd be aware of the neighboring investigation.

Law enforcement dispersed except for the Stem Police, who nervously trod the porch's wooden boards, waiting for the crime scene techs and SBI assistance.

CHAPTER TWENTY

Getting word that the lead in Stem had not panned out and had produced another, but different type of crime scene, Bob and Tony went back to the conference room to grab files and head to the hospital for more interviews.

They spread out at the back of the hospital cafeteria and spoke to the staff who had been working on Sunday. No one remembered anything strange happening that evening. It wasn't unusual for the doctors not to be scheduled to work but to still come by the hospital and check on their patients.

The detectives delicately probed into Dr. Graham's extracurricular activities with nurses or staff that had left the hospital. Each effort was met with a stony silence. Finally, frustrated, Bob asked an older nurse, "Why isn't anyone talking about the good doc and his bad reputation?"

Nurse Undine, a solid-looking short woman of middle years, looked at Bob and Tony for a minute. "Are you crazy? It's not worth my job to talk to you about anything. I have three kids at home and a husband who can't or won't apply for a job. For six months now, he's sat on his ass and watched every damn game show on television. Can't run the damn vacuum or do a load of laundry, but by God, he can lift a can of beer to his mouth." She snorted in disgust, then heaved herself to her feet and walked out of the cafeteria.

Bob slammed the file in frustration. "There you go," he said. "I bet Legal's threatened to fire anyone who talks to us. Guess ol' Sternberg thought he'd get the last laugh."

"Didn't think he had it in him," Tony said. "What now?"

"Now we do what we shoulda done early on. We get a court order or search warrant and turn his office upside down and inside out. Go get the car, and I'll pick up the rest of these files and call Sally at the DA's office. Sternberg is gonna wish he'd cooperated."

Tony jogged to the front of the hospital to retrieve the car from a no-parking zone. He almost ran over Sandy.

"Sorry, didn't see you there," he said.

"Oh, don't worry," she said. "I wasn't really watching where I was going and can barely see over these boxes." She waggled her eyebrows at the two banker's boxes in her arms.

"Let me get that for you," Tony said, grabbing one off the top.

"Oh, thanks," she huffed. "They were heavier than I thought. I'm just parked down here in the fire zone," she jerked her head toward a small Fiat. Tony took the keys from her hand and opened the car for her. "Don't worry. I just moved my car here a minute ago. Have a good evening. And thanks."

Tony smiled. "You too," and watched her drive off, wishing he could have told her how badly her day was going to suck tomorrow once they got the warrant tonight. She seemed like a nice person. He pulled up in the front as Bob came down the stairs, talking on his cell phone.

"Yeah okay. Tony and I will be there in five. Yeah I know it's late but what are you gonna do?" Bob slid the files into the back and got into the front. "Blue lights and siren," he said. "The judge is getting ready to leave for the day."

* * * * *

Judge Jones kept Bob and Tony waiting for an hour. He was conducting an acrimonious pretrial conference in a motor vehicle case when the two slid onto the back bench in the superior courtroom.

The fifth most historic courthouse in North Carolina, the Granville County courthouse sprawled down main street, a four-story brick building with huge double wooden doors, white trim, and a cupola. Unfortunately, it only had two usable courtrooms. The placement of the interior columns in the superior courtroom partly blocked the detectives from the judge's view. The decorative balls on the end of the judge's bench blocked the rest.

The attorney for the insurance company was impeccably dressed. He wore a dark gray suit with a white shirt and a red tie. He had four associates and various boxes and bags at this table.

The plaintiff's attorney wore a rumpled seersucker suit. His brown unpolished shoes were not hidden by the too-short pants. He had a single buff-colored file and no associates at his table. His client, an older bird-like woman, sat hunched in her seat. She coughed pitifully every few seconds and kept shifting her crutches around.

Each side tossed out the words "discovery," "negligence," "last clear chance," and "contributory negligence" about every other sentence. Bob had to nudge Tony awake when the civil attorneys started packing up to leave. Tony had slumped down halfway through.

Trotting toward the judge's chambers in the back, Bob said, "Let me do the talking. You answer questions only if he asks you. It's five o'clock on a Friday. He's not gonna want to chat."

"Got it," Tony said, trying to tuck in his shirt while he followed Bob.

Judge Jones looked up from his too-small veneer desk. Hosting numerous judges from all North Carolina districts over the years, it was pockmarked with rings made from coffee cups, scratches from pens, and dents from dropped staplers.

"What's going on, Detective?" Jones asked Bob.

"Sir, we have an ongoing murder investigation and need a search warrant for the hospital's records. Their legal department is stonewalling us. They're picking and choosing what files we see. We need to get into their offices and get all that might pertain to the staff who could be involved," Bob trailed off as the Judge turned around in his chair. He sat thinking while drinking his coffee. An old percolator hissed in the corner of his chambers.

"Oh, keep going," Judge Jones said. "I just need my afternoon pick-me-up." The smell of bourbon wafted through the small beige room. "Now then, whose records do you need? And why won't the hospital cooperate?"

"We're looking for records of Dr. Mark Graham and any records that may be associated with his work schedule. Their legal department gave us a few things, but we think there's more. Plus, we're having a hard time with hospital staff talking about him or any of the surgeons for fear of retribution."

"Hand me the search warrant and raise your right hand. Do you affirm that you will tell the truth and have told the truth, and that is your solemn affirmation?" Judge Jones looked at Bob over his half glasses.

"Yes, your Honor."

Leaning over and squinting about two inches from the document, the judge signed the search warrant. "Kinda crummy serving it on the hospital this time of day, isn't it, boys?" the judge asked.

"Maybe. But we think we've got a serial killer on our hands and need to follow up on all possible leads. We need to catch him—or her—before they strike again. Thank you for your time, sir."

"You're welcome. Now, it's on to the Oak Room. I think I've finally talked that young court reporter into meeting me for a drink. If not," he shrugged and turned to take his jacket off of the wire hanger, which clung precariously on an old wooden coat rack. He started patting his pockets and then realized his glasses were on top of his head.

Tony raised his eyebrows at Bob behind the judge's back. The "young" court reporter was a solid matron of sixty years and outweighed the judge by at least twenty pounds.

"I'll walk you guys out," he said, turning the key in the lock. "Not that anyone would steal anything in there," the judge grumbled. "A bunch of moldy old appellate reporters and some outdated statute books and a damn phone an MIT grad couldn't figure out how to use."

Tony walked with the old jurist while Bob walked ahead, calling Sternberg to give the lawyer a heads up.

"How long you been a detective?" the judge asked Tony.

"Several years. Most of those years I spent in New Orleans, at the PD. I haven't been back here for long."

"Ahh, New Orleans. I spent one happy week down there during Mardi Gras many years ago. Those people are crazy, but crazy fun, not crazy mental. Everything was purple and green, even the people."

Tony agreed and they started talking about which place had the best remoulade sauce, gumbo, and po'boys. Bob stopped at the exit and told Tony they'd need to head back to the hospital, as Sternberg was waiting for them. "Drop you some place, your honor?" Bob asked.

"No, no. I'm walking to the Oak Room. You fellows have a good night."

* * * * *

When they arrived at the hospital, Sternberg met them at the entrance's sliding doors. He silently reviewed the search warrant, then turned on his heel, gesturing to them to follow him. They and the patrolmen Bob had called for backup silently formed a line. One had a wheeled cart. At the entrance to the administrator's room, Bob gave instructions for what they were supposed to pick up and what they needed to look out for. He and Tony started on the HR files in a separate room. They could hear Sternberg next door screaming at someone on the phone about the police and a search warrant. An hour later, they'd finished the review of the rooms housing the hospital's files and wheeled out several boxes to examine.

Sternberg slammed the doors to the office and faced Bob. "You're a goddamned nuisance. You got all you needed this morning. You want to waste your time, fine. But I sure as hell don't appreciate you wasting mine, and on a Friday night. I'm calling your Chief."

"Okay, Sternberg, whatever. We'll see you later. Call him all you want. Maybe he'll think of something else we need to come back and get," Bob said.

Tony stretched before getting into the full patrol car. He folded his jacket and put it on top of the boxes. "Damn, Bob, that was cold," he said.

Bob stared at him. "What's cold is whining about his precious files and stonewalling us just to protect his golden goose doctor, who might have a motive for these murders."

"Yeah, I get it. Hey, you want to head to the Oak Room for a beer?" Tony asked.

"Nah. I'm beat. I'm going to microwave leftovers and watch the Family Fracas Show. I appreciate the offer, though."

"Bob, you're fifty, not seventy. Come on, go. Just one beer. And you'll get to find out if the judge cozies up to the court reporter. Hard to imagine, but hey, it could happen."

Bob snorted. "Okay. One beer. But that's it," he said.

CHAPTER TWENTY-ONE

Bob's head hurt. The pain pulsed across his forehead, behind his eyes, and in the back of his head. He never drank draft beer, but he'd let goddamned Tony talk him into a pitcher—a pitcher for God's sake—at the Oak Room. At first, it was nice seeing some of the men and women who worked patrol and the crime scene techs. Since Gloria had left, he'd rarely gone out socially in town. The crowd at the Oak Room shared some laughs and stories about the Chief. Then Bob got hungry and ordered wings, which led to more beer, which led to one of the crime scene techs driving his too-old-for-this-ass home sometime after midnight.

Where was the damn aspirin, or better yet, the Tylenol? He put the pillow over his head to block out the low-level light creeping in the window from outside.

The sound of fingernails scrabbling made him sit bolt upright up in bed. He eased his firearm out of the holster sitting on the nightstand beside him. Holding it in both hands at the ready, he eased open the thin bedroom door.

Light spilled through the door at the end of the hall. He listened. A scuffling noise, then the sound of steam expelling. *What the fuck?* He crept down the hall in his threadbare plaid pajama bottoms. His glasses were jammed on top of his head.

Fifty pounds of black fur came hurtling at him, heedless of the flimsy wooden kitchen gate. Bob landed hard on his tail bone. The enormous dog continued licking his face despite his yells of protest. His firearm went flying into the corner. He couldn't shift the big mass. Finally, he grabbed the dog tag dangling in his face and tried to read it. Reaching for his glasses he could make out the letters. "Bella, good dog. That's a good dog. Down now, Bella. Get down."

Bella sat down and looked up at him with soft brown eyes. She had a little tan brown around the muzzle, neck, and ears but otherwise was all black.

Bob rubbed his sore bottom and put the gun up high on the corner bookcase. He picked up the rickety gate and headed over to where his coffee maker was making coffee. *That's strange. Never known it to do that before.*

A note was taped to the cabinet above the coffee maker. It read: "Bob, thanks for offering to take Bella. She's a good dog. I wish I could keep her, but my husband is allergic. I made some coffee for you. Yours, Carol." There was a little "x" after her name.

Bob looked down at Bella and then back at the note. Bella panted in the same spot where she'd sat. Then she started to whine.

What the hell? What does that x mean? What in the hell did I agree to? Why is that dog whining, and why is she pacing?

His head really ached now, and his throat was dry. Bella finally butted her head against the back door. *Oh, she needs to go out.* Bob opened the door, and Bella flew into the fenced-in back yard. She was partly hidden by an azalea.

Mike was just over the four-foot-high fence, putting something into his car's hatchback. He gave Bob a side eye of disgust and then hollered over the fence.

"See you went and got yourself a dog there. Our puppies don't suit you, Bob? You could have just said," Mike said manfully, trying to hide his hurt. His eyes were wet.

"Aw gee, no, it's not like that. It's really hard to explain. I'm, uh, helping out a friend."

"Yeah. Sure. I get it," Mike said, and scooped up the three ugly puppies playing at his feet. Each one was mud brown with large patches of fur missing. They looked rough, just like their mom.

Bella trotted over and sat at Bob's feet. She cocked her head at him. Bob sighed. "Come on, girl. Let's see what I've done and what we can do about it." Bella stood at the door, and Bob let her inside. He found a clean glass and poured some cold water from the tap. He grabbed the Tylenol bottle, making sure it had only expired a couple of years ago before taking two. He found his favorite mug, "Best Dad," and poured in the hot coffee. He took a couple of swigs. After a few minutes, his stiff shoulder muscles started to relax.

He dialed Carol and prayed that she'd pick up.

"Hey, Dad," she said on the third ring.

"Er, hey, yeah, Carol, this is Bob," he said.

"I know. How's it being a new dad?"

"Oh, you mean the dog? She's nice. When are you picking her up?"

"Oh no. Bella's *your* baby now. You begged me to give her to you last night after you saw her and her one littermate. I granted you your fondest wish. Plus, my husband is over the moon. He can put away his nasal spray and quit taking Benadryl. I put some of her dog food on the counter next to the sink."

"Well, yeah. I always wanted a dog. And," he said, looking down at Bella stretched out on the kitchen mat, "she's a really good dog and all, but I don't think I can look after one."

"Guess you'll figure it out then. Y'all seemed pretty cozy when I dropped you off. You were sleeping on her belly in the back seat."

Jesus God. How embarrassing. "Oh, about that. I really appreciate the ride home. Sorry, I was a mess, Carol. Hope it wasn't too bad. Oh, and the coffee. Thanks for making it and putting it on the timer. I really like the coffee. I almost feel human."

She laughed. "Oh, you were fine. A bit more relaxed than usual, but that's a good thing. Bella's about six months old and needs to be spayed soon. She'll end up being close to eighty or ninety pounds when she's done growing. Her mom was seventy-five pounds, and her dad was about 110 pounds."

"No way! You're joking, right? She's pretty big now."

Bella was gnawing on the kitchen mat but looked up with her head cocked. Losing interest in the conversation she could hear, she growled low in her throat at her prey.

"She's eating the kitchen mat. What do you usually feed her?" He listened intently and scribbled down notes on the pad he kept near the fridge. He sighed again. "Thanks again for the ride, the coffee, and the dog. By the way, what is that x on the note?"

She cackled. "Oooo, I bet that had you guessing. Don't worry about it. I didn't get excited over that one little kiss. See you at work."

Bob stared in horror at his phone. *One little kiss?*

* * * * *

An hour later, after running to Food Mart and picking up more dog food and chew toys, Bob walked into the police station to find Tony. He held his drive-thru coffee in a death grip in his left hand. This was his third cup, and his head was still thumping in pain.

Tony was slumped in a chair in the conference room. Dr. Fulcher was typing on his laptop. The room was otherwise deserted. Crime scene photos dotted the wall.

Bob picked up the heavy-duty stapler on the table and slammed it down. Tony jumped, and his eyes flew open. "What the hell, Bob? Boy, you sure look like shit today. You look like I feel," Tony moaned.

"This is your fault, you moron. Just a couple of drinks, just a few minutes, you said. And, wait, the pitcher of draft beer. Who does that? My head is killing me. Oh, and I got a dog."

"You're kidding? A dog, you? What kind? No, let me guess. It's a bulldog, so ya'll can dress in matching sweaters."

"No."

"Okay, okay. Three guesses. It's a Doberman. A squared away military-looking dog."

"Ha. No."

"Final guess. Let me think. It's a poodle. You're getting in touch with your feminine side."

Bob shook his head. "The best I can tell, it's mostly German Shepard and getting bigger by the minute. It's eaten my kitchen mat, a couple of napkins, and a tumbler I dropped on the floor by mistake."

"Never figured you for a dog."

"Well, I've thought about getting one before. I would have started out smaller, but, well, Bella's a good girl. My neighbor's pissed off that I didn't take one of his puppies."

Tony shuddered. He'd seen Mike's puppies and scrubbed his hands for ten minutes after he'd had to pet one.

Bob looked around. "Where is everybody?" he asked.

"They're at one of the schools. A kid brought a gun onto school property, and everyone's in an uproar, understandably. It wasn't loaded, but that doesn't matter. Plus, the kid was in first grade. The school wanted officers around to assure parents and students that all was okay. Parents have been calling here nonstop, and the news stations about as much. The Chief's about to crack open a new bottle of scotch."

Bob nonchalantly put his coffee down and sat down across from Tony. He looked over at Fulcher, but he was immersed in his research and about two inches from his screen.

"What all went on last night? I remember the pitcher, talking to some of the guys, and then it gets a little fuzzy."

"Yeah, it got a little fuzzy for you. You were pounding them back." Tony snorted.

"You left with Carol and looked pretty friendly with her. She'd offered to take you home, and I walked home myself a few minutes after you left. Think you did something you're trying to remember to regret? If you did, you'd better watch yourself. Her husband is a big mother."

"Haha. No, I just can't piece it together. It was kinda nice, though, seeing people outside of work. I saw a couple of friends I hadn't seen in a long time," Bob said.

"It was. I met some good people whom I hadn't met before. Young people. You remember what that was like?" Tony asked.

"Give it a rest. Let's get going." He turned to Fulcher. "What's happening, doc? You got a profile for us yet?"

Fulcher did not look up. After a minute, he pushed back from the computer and scrubbed at his eyes.

"As you can see, I am still working on it. This takes concentration. At least I'm putting in the time, unlike some people who are spending theirs in seedy bars."

Tony grabbed Bob by the arm before he could advance any closer to the hapless doctor. Fulcher jumped up and put the table between them.

Bob jerked his arm away. "I'm tired of you playing around with your pictures and charts and whatever the hell else. You need to get us something, and soon."

CHAPTER TWENTY-TWO

He had a bad feeling. It started at the small gray stone church on College Street. He didn't want to go to the funeral, but he had to, or someone would comment on his absence. Despite the broiling heat, he'd put on his dark gray suit and conservatively striped red tie and headed out with just enough time to lose himself in the crowd. Squeezing into the last wooden pew on the left, he'd felt eyes boring into him. After he rose from the kneeler, a few work acquaintances nodded to him. Cassie's mom motioned for him to join the family in their pew. He couldn't ignore her. The guy beside him in the wooden pew nudged him to get him moving to the front.

He could still feel the eyes on him, an unwavering and malevolent force. Scanning the stuffy chapel lit with diluted reds and blues suffusing the sides of the church, wavering from the stained glass, he tried to find the source. With a start, he found the rector staring straight at him..

He knows, he thought.

CHAPTER TWENTY-THREE

Move over, Tony," Bob huffed, trying to squeeze himself into the already crowded pew.

"Look, Bob. You move any closer to me, you might as well be on my lap," Tony hissed. The elderly couple next to them frowned their disapproval but moved over three inches.

Bob and Tony crossed themselves and rose from the kneeler in tandem. The first hymn swelled up from the big organ, and the wooden doors creaked open to allow in the processional.

Tony had a clear tenor that soared over Bob's raspy baritone. *I should just lip sync this one.* He tried to keep track of the partly visible words in the hymnal without taking out his readers.

The funeral for Cassie was well attended. A sea of mourners, primarily clad in black, settled in quietly for the eulogy. Muffled sniffling came from her family and Dr. Graham, who was seated up front and on the right. The detectives surreptitiously scanned the mourners. No one stood out as not belonging or being unduly nervous.

Bob hated funerals. He focused on the floral arrangements of roses, bells of Ireland, and star gazer lilies, and the massive brass candlesticks to take his mind off of the rector's platitudes and woefully short recitation of young Cassie's life's accomplishments. After a while, he watched Dr. Graham.

Graham's grief seemed genuine. His shoulders were shaking as he tried to gain control. The older woman seated beside the doctor handed him a white handkerchief. She put a thin arm around him.

Neither he nor Tony knew the other people seated in the family's front pew. They swiveled their heads around and scanned the crowd periodically. No one acted out of the ordinary during the service.

They stood for the final hymn and waited until the casket rolled back down and out the double doors. The family followed, and then the mourners, row by row.

"That was tough," Tony said. He'd kept the bulletin and had rolled it up into a thin roll.

Bob agreed. "These things never get easier. You never get used to them."

As they passed through the church and onto the slate porch, they nodded to the rector. The rector had unsettlingly icy blue eyes and a weathered face beneath his full head of white hair. He held onto Bob's hand.

"Good to see you, Bob. It's been a while."

"You too, rector. Yes, it's been a while."

"You know, I'm in my office Monday through Thursday. Or, just call sometime if you want to talk." He paused for a minute, not letting go of Bob's hand.

"I will, and thank you."

The few people behind Bob started pressing closer.

"Look, Bob. I'd like to talk to you about something. Can you call me later tonight?"

"Sure, glad to. I'll give you a ring later."

Tony was waiting for Bob at the foot of the steps and smoking a cigarette.

"What was that all about?" he gestured back up to the rector.

"He wants to know why I quit coming to church."

"Oh. Well, good luck telling him. I don't envy you that conversation. Are you ready to head to the graveside, or are we skipping it?"

"We better skip it if we're going to get to Mia's visitation, too. Her parents decided to go ahead with it tonight and are planning a memorial service for after the visitation. They're holding onto hope but expect the worst based on her only slight chances of living through that type of assault."

"I can't imagine losing a child and what kind of hell you'd go through," Tony said. A second too late, he started, "Bob, look, I'm sorry…"

"No, you can't, and you're right," Bob said. "It's the closest thing to hell on earth. The worst is at night when you're tired and start dreaming about them. You think you hear them, that they're in the next room. You wake up so happy until you realize it's all been a dream, that they're never walking back through the door. That you're alone and you always will be."

"I'm sorry, Bob…"

"You didn't mean anything by it. I know that. I shouldn't have come here. There's no way I can get over to Mia's vigil. Maybe you better grab another detective and head on over to Henderson. I'm not fit to go."

Mr. Lamberti wore a beautifully made Italian suit and greeted the officers at the bottom of the steps to the stone church. Each nodded deferentially to the other.

Bob turned to Tony after Lamberti had passed them to talk to the rector. "That's funny," Bob said.

"What?" Tony asked.

"That's the last guy I'd expect to see at Cassie's funeral."

"Why?"

"I heard Cassie posted a terrible review of the Oak Room and insulted Lamberti personally after she and the lady lawyers had their annual dinner there. I skimmed the posts after someone told me how to get on social media. They were awful."

"That guy looks like he couldn't cut up a grilled cheese sandwich. You don't like him for this, do you?" Tony asked.

"Don't judge a book. He used to be our high school's number one wrestler. I don't really think he's a suspect, but I also heard he was really pissed off about the negative reviews and refuses to serve any of those women who were at the dinner. They have to get takeout or come in at lunch when he's not there."

"Add him to the list of interviews?"

"Yeah. I guess we better."

* * * * *

Tony and Bob drove in silence back to the precinct so Bob could get his car. Bob waved to Tony without a backward glance. Tony picked up the Chief and headed to Mia's life celebration.

A few minutes later, Tony and the Chief pulled up to the church. It was a modest structure set in the country amid mature pecan, oak, and maple trees. The gravel driveway and parking lot were packed full, but they squeezed in next to an old pickup with a dented front panel.

The music swelled inside, then spilled out the front glass door when they pulled it open. Keyboards, organ, bass, and horns joined in a joyful surge. A few folding chairs put around the perimeter were empty, so they sat in those and scanned the crowd.

The family stood up front, swaying with the final notes, and then sat in the polished pew. The preacher praised God's glory and asked for succor and comfort for those waiting for Mia to be found.

Tony sat, lost deep in thought, then shook himself to scan the crowd. No one stood out as a possible suspect, but many people caught his eye and nodded to him.

An hour later, the Chief and Tony met Henderson officers outside, standing a little away from the family, who were accepting well wishes from the congregation.

"Anybody seem off in there?" the Chief asked the Henderson Chief.

"Not that I could tell. We had a few guys out here to scan the people as they left. They didn't see anything suspicious. I don't think someone who's this methodical in his killing or butchering would show up. But you never know," the Henderson Chief said.

They stood in silence while Mia's mother slowly walked over.

"I appreciate you guys being here," she said in a voice shaking with emotion. "Please don't give up looking for my baby. Please find her."

The Henderson Chief pulled her into a tight hug. "We're not giving up. We still have double shifts out there searching. The Vance sheriff's office sent me two deputies this morning to add to our teams. I promise you, we'll bring her home," he said, wiping tears from his eyes as she stepped back to look up at him.

Tony spoke in a low voice to his Chief. "You mind if I head to the car? I want to call Bob and check on him." He'd shared his last conversation with Bob with the Chief on the short drive over.

"Go on. I'll be there in a few," he said, distracted by the approach of Mia's father.

Tony sat with the door to the cruiser open and punched in Bob's number on his cell. Birds dodged in and out of the nearby tree branches, and squirrels rustled in the dead leaves littering the ground left over from the fall.

"Bob? Hey, it's me. Yeah, didn't see anyone that looked out of place or acted funny. You okay, man? I didn't mean to bring up painful memories. Okay. Good. I'm heading with our Chief over to the family's house here. Call me if you need me."

* * * * *

Tony mingled with the other police officers on the periphery of Mia's family's dining room. Mia's brothers, aunt, and parents recognized him from his earlier visit and welcomed him with hugs and handshakes. An aunt brought him a plate loaded down with food after he'd made no move toward the groaning table of casseroles, salads, and heaps of chicken and pork. Tony smiled his thanks and sat in a chair out of the way of the other guests, precariously balancing the plate on his lap.

Bob isn't the only one who hates funerals. Mom's funeral practically killed me. It'd been almost a year, but it was so different from the ones today. His mom's funeral had been joyless and cold. The few people who'd come had said that her passing was a blessing. What kind of blessing is it to have the one person who loved you unconditionally literally rot away in front of you? The shame and the regret he'd felt choked him up. Everyone else thought it was grief. Grief eventually would've been washed away with tears and the care of good people or supportive family. He'd never felt he had that.

The fact that his grandmother was dead and buried in Carville, at the National Leprosarium, under her Carville name ensured

Tony would never find her marker or be able to trace that side of his family. His mom refused to talk about her mother and was tight-lipped about any family she'd had or had lost. She'd kept no birth or death papers with her handwritten will and had no family Bible to provide clues as to who had been before. He suspected his mom used an assumed name most of her life to hide the fact that she'd had a near relative buried at Carville.

Tony didn't know his mom had leprosy or Hansen's disease, as it was more commonly referred to, along with cancer, until her final year. By then, he had been newly made detective with the New Orleans police and had moved out of the small yellow cottage he shared with her, but he still checked on her every Sunday. He found out by accident. He'd been paying her bills for her since she'd been sickly for several weeks, and the treatment letter was in the same stack as the light and water bills.

He'd been stunned and confronted her, a rake-thin and fragile Black woman wrapped up in quilts and reclining on an aged and faded sofa.

"Fuck's this, Momma?" he snarled, waving the letter inches in front of her. Her eyes were dimmed by cataracts, and she swung her head back and forth, trying to see the paper, but he pressed on. "What's this about Hansen's? Isn't that what grandma had?" He was ashamed of himself but couldn't stop the burning rage. "How long have you had this? What are you doing about it?"

His mama had drawn up her small frame and placed her feet on the floor before she replied. She struck a match and lit up one of her Chesterfields, coughing and blowing smoke away from him. "Looka here, boy. They ain't no need to shout at me. Ain't nothing I can do for it but what the doctor says." Her voice softened, recognizing his fear. "A'hm doing what I'm supposed to do. That's all I can do."

He sat on the couch next to her with his head in his hands.

"Look, boy. I know you stayed down here after high school for me. I know you left your friends and your dad, all for me. I know you left North Carolina to come down here and be with me. There ain't ever been a finer son than you," she whispered. "Look at me, Antoine."

He slowly lifted his head. He hoped the gloom and dim light in the little front room hid the tears welling up in his eyes.

She continued in her soft, raspy voice. "But it's time for you to decide what you want for yourself. To choose what you want to do. My path's been written. In fact, you should head on back to North Carolina before, well, before I go home."

He refused to take the easy way out and stayed in New Orleans with her until the end. There was no one he could talk to about her illness except her doctor. His older half-siblings grieved in their own way, closing themselves off and denying the severity of her illness.

He broke up with his casual boyfriend and dared not breathe a word of it at work. People didn't understand Hansen's disease now any more than they did at the turn of the century. His coworkers would ostracize him if they learned of it.

In the beginning, when he first found out she had it, the only thing he knew about Hansen's was that it killed you by inches. People casually talked about it like it was a voodoo curse, and that any reputable witch doctor could cure it, or that you needed a priest and an exorcism to restore the person to health. During the last few weeks, it was a race between the Hansen's, diabetes, and lung cancer as to which would get her first.

* * * * *

Tony went back in the house and talked to the Chief. The Chief assured him he could get another ride back to Oxford, so Tony took the cruiser and headed back. A few miles down the road, he pulled over into a church parking lot and wept.

CHAPTER TWENTY-FOUR

The old rector polished off the silver wine goblet with a faded linen cloth and left it on the altar. Gnarled and bent, his thin hands moved like twin doves in the gloom as he extinguished the candles. The altar itself was draped in white linen, but the railings were burled brown and yellow wood rubbed soft by multitudes of sweaty hands that passed through. The red, blue, and green from the stained-glass windows danced as the setting sun shot light through them.

The gray-headed rector walked slowly and fussed with the silver bowls and spoons on the altar before pulling across the wooden piece that completed the kneeling benches. His worn, dark shoes peeked out from his robe.

He waited in the shadows of the still sanctuary until the old man bowed in front of the altar and moved silently toward the door that took him to the outside stairs leading to the parish hall. The steel of his knife reflected back the light from the few hanging glass lanterns. He hid it in the folds of his clothes and walked softly to where the rector was bending down to retrieve a forgotten bulletin.

CHAPTER TWENTY-FIVE

Bob and Tony studied the photos and mug shots on the wall of the Oxford Police Department's conference room. Dr. Fulcher continued to add photos to the wall. Bob started again, "So, Doc, let me get this straight. You think it's gotta be one of these guys up here on the wall. These are the sex offenders and guys on probation, am I right so far?"

Dr. Fulcher nodded. "Yes, these are the suspects I've selected based on the type of crimes committed. I think you should be looking for a sexual deviant with any kind of prior stabbing crime."

"And all of these guys fit the bill?"

"Yes. Well mostly. I included some that had a lot of prior assaults on women and some that had prior assaults on children."

"What's the science behind all of this?" Bob asked.

"Well, it's not an exact science," Fulcher sighed. "I think that the suspect has significant issues with women, especially women he perceives to be in control, and probably a sexual issue, and also is quite proficient with knives."

Bob and Tony scanned the wall in silence.

"So, do you think we need to interview these, what? About fifty suspects?"

"Well, yes. I think someone needs to talk to each of them and get their alibi if they have one."

"Shouldn't we start with someone who's been picked up for suspicion of stabbing or cutting somebody? I mean, isn't that the most logical place to start?" Bob asked. He winced after sipping the bitter coffee in his paper cup and put it down on the scarred table with other half empty cups. Bob flat refused to drink out of the last clean mug emblazoned with "New York Yankees."

Tony stayed remarkably silent but continued to study each photo. He walked back and forth down the wall. Periodically, he took out his small notebook and jotted something down.

Bob felt his patience ebbing. They were no closer to solving these murders, if that's what they were, and some of their manpower had been diverted when the Sheriff's evidence locker had been broken into. A suspected fifty pounds of confiscated high-grade marijuana had been taken along with stolen firearms. Katie had been apologetic on the phone earlier when she'd called, but she had to go where the Sheriff told her to go.

Tony was standing at his shoulder.

"What?" Bob growled.

"I don't think this is our best suspect pool. Look at the ones over here," he gestured to the far corner. "These guys over here on probation are all, what, maybe sixty and older? And these sex offenders over here? I know for a fact that two of these ten have died."

"Oh, for God's sake." Bob rubbed his face with his hand, trying to eradicate the tiredness from his eyes. Bob turned on Fulcher. "You've got to do better than this. We can't run all over the district trying to corner every sex offender. Most of these guys look like they couldn't lift a knife, much less stab anyone or cut them up. What the fuck kinda program are you running? A Ouija board would help about the same as what you've come up with!"

Bob ended up nose to nose with Fulcher. Gus moved between them. "Whoa, whoa," she said. She grabbed Bob's shoulder and led him to a folding chair across the room.

"I get the frustration. Hell, we're all frustrated and tired. And scared. But we gotta start somewhere," Gus said.

She pointed to the wall. "I'll take a third, you take a third, and these guys over here assigned to the team will take the last third. Now, how do you want to go at them, divide them up? Talk at their homes or here?"

Before Bob could answer, his phone rang. "Yes? What? When? Dear Lord. Yes, we're on the way." Bob motioned to Tony. "Get your coat. The rector's been murdered. Someone cut his eyes out."

"That's terrible about the rector," Gus said. "Be safe. We'll keep working here. I'm going to sit with Dr. Fulcher for a few minutes and try to select some similarities between the ones we have that he can focus on. We'll divide up the list on the wall, at least those under sixty. Catch up to us when you can, and I'll give you an update."

Bob nodded his thanks, not trusting himself to speak, and followed Tony out to the lot.

* * * * *

"Up 'til now, each of these killings all had one thing in common," Tony said.

"What?"

"The victims were female attorneys or female law students. If the rector was killed by the same guy, he's changing the script, or he's running scared."

"I should have gone over to see the rector last night. I should have at least called him," Bob said. His hands shook on the wheel, and he nearly missed bumping up onto the curb when he turned into the street for the rectory.

"Bob, you had no idea that the rector could possibly be in the killer's sights. He is totally outside the victim pool."

"Yeah, but I promised I'd talk to him later, and I didn't. I just decided he'd want to guilt me into going back to church, and I didn't want to hear it."

The car shuddered to a stop on College Street behind a patrol car running blue lights. Neighbors formed tightly knit little groups and blocked the sidewalk. The director from the funeral home across the street stood in the small yard quietly talking to an elderly woman openly weeping into a handkerchief. Tony gently pushed a few of the clusters aside. Not seeing anyone on patrol outside, he and Bob went in the rectory's side door, which stood open.

A patrolman met them in the kitchen.

"Hey, Detective. Let me get you some booties and gloves before you head in there. You too, Tony."

Tony suppressed a quick retort about them both being detectives and just nodded his thanks. He knew he was still the new guy and needed to prove himself, but it sure was irritating.

Bob didn't seem to notice and was gloving up by the kitchen table. The green-patterned linoleum was yellowed and cracked in places. Several windows brightened up the cabinets and tobacco-colored backsplash. The kitchen had missed an upgrade in the 1980s with its white fervor, and the original cherry cabinets gleamed with a warm patina.

Both followed the patrolman into the wood-paneled den. They stopped shy of the dark stain soaking the light brown carpet. The rector was lying on his back as if asleep. A shriveled man seated, unmoving in a chair in the open door nearby, turned his head when Tony and Bob walked quietly into the room. The man's eyes were luminous with tears, and he held a wad of paper towels in his left hand.

The patrolman pulled the detectives over.

"Yeah, I know it's odd, but this is the sexton, and he found him. He's refused to leave the rector alone with us. I've tried to get him to go." He shrugged.

Tony walked over to the old sexton and crouched down to be at eye level with the grieving man. "Hey, Pops. This here is tough. I'm sorry you had to see it. You want me to take you home? I'm glad to do it."

The wizened man shook his head without taking his eyes off the rector.

"How 'bout you and me go into the room off the kitchen, so after the crime scene techs finish processing the kitchen, we can start something hot, maybe some coffee or tea? I bet some of the other folks from the church will be coming over soon. They'll need something to drink."

The sexton wiped his face with the paper towels and slowly stood up. Tony followed him into the mud room, off the kitchen. Bob turned back to look at the rector, who at first appeared asleep.

"Where are the evidence techs?" Bob asked.

"They've come and gone. The techs took photos. They took his glass, which seemed to have a tiny bit of Scotch in it, his plate of food, which was congealed, and put bags on his hands in case there was any material under his fingernails. There wasn't a whole lot to see except, except..." he said, pointing to the rector's mutilated head.

Neither said anything for a minute. Bob could hear Tony softly talking to the sexton and the rattle of cutlery.

Bob bent down closer to inspect the damage. He avoided looking directly at the rector's eye sockets. The right occipital bone was crushed. Bob scanned the room for a potential weapon. Shelves of books lined three of the four walls. A few pipes and an old-fashioned nutcracker sat on one side table. Nothing looked heavy enough. There was a small fireplace but no andirons or poker. He thought back to his last visit here. He remembered that he'd admired a geode on a small mahogany table. The amethyst geode cluster featured dark purple and lavender crystals.

"Get me an evidence bag," Bob said to the patrolman. A minute later one was shoved in his hand. "Naw, better call the techs back. I'll screw this up if I try to lift it." The patrolman stepped back to the kitchen and used his radio to call the techs.

"Lift what?" Tony asked. He'd come silently back into the room once the sexton was busy setting out cream and sugar.

"See the sparkle on the side of his head and on his ear?" Bob shone a small flashlight at the rector's head.

"Yeah, I do."

"There's a geode the Father loved that's missing from the last time I was here. I think these are pieces of it."

"You think that's what killed him? Who'd do that? What kinda bastard… I mean, look at this place. It's obvious the priest had nothing to steal. Even his house belongs to the church," Tony said.

Bob continued looking at the dusting of particles. "I don't know, but the fact that his eyes are just gone…" Bob whispered, then turned to head outdoors.

Tony stood in silence for a few minutes. The ticking of the clock was the only sound in the den. A brass clock with spinning circles of brass at the bottom held a place of pride on the mantle. The smell of old cigars and Old Spice permeated the air. Dust motes danced in the morning sun, coming in through parted linen curtains.

A hand came down hard on his shoulder, and Tony reached for his gun.

The man backed away with his hands out in front of him.

"Hey, sorry, Officer. I just wanted to know if it's okay that I take the body across the street," said the man in a dark gray suit. The man held out a hand that Tony didn't take. "Okay, well, I'm with the Sturgeon Funeral Home, and my guys are here to pick the rector up. Oh, and your police friend is outside, heaving in the bushes."

"No. You just need to hold up," Tony said. "The rector is going to the medical examiner's office. I don't know if y'all take him or he's getting a ride with someone else, but the crime scene techs are headed back here. Don't touch anything."

"No, of course not. I thought something was wrong last night when not one but two doctors were visiting with the old guy, I mean, the rector. Must've been something serious," he said, trying to see around Tony.

Tony pointed a finger toward the kitchen. "Go," he snarled.

"Officer!" Tony yelled over his shoulder.

The patrolman stuck his head in the doorway.

"Did anyone get the funeral guy's statement or canvas the neighborhood?"

Shifting from foot to foot, the officer adjusted his belt. "No. We're waiting on a detective."

"For God's sake," Tony mumbled and headed out to get Bob.

* * * * *

Bob swiped his mouth with the back of his hand. He hadn't lost it like this since he was a young beat patrolman. Everyone on the street watched him as he struggled into the car and fumbled for some crumpled-up napkins to wipe his streaming eyes. Tony leaned on the car door.

"You okay?"

"Yeah, dammit. I feel like a fool."

"No, don't. You knew the guy. You liked him."

"I feel guilty I didn't call him last night."

"You couldn't have known it'd go like this. Hell, who has a motive to kill him? Listen. The officers haven't canvassed the neighborhood or taken statements. I'll start with the funeral guy who saw some doctors over here last night, but we need a couple of others to help out. You want to radio back to the station?"

"And get myself under control? Thanks, Tony. I mean it."

"We're partners. Got your back."

CHAPTER TWENTY-SIX

The two guys sent by the PD couldn't have been out of basic law enforcement training for long. They confirmed for Tony that this was their first time out on an investigation. At least they seemed eager and started right in by dividing people up in the kitchen and beginning on the interviews. Two more officers arrived and started going door to door, looking for exterior cameras and any potential witnesses. Large oaks filtered the sunlight onto the uneven sidewalks and brick walkways.

Bob and Tony sat the funeral director down in the back seat of their car. As a precaution, Bob read him his rights prior to asking him any questions. The funeral director kept smoothing back the patches of brown hair that still clung steadfastly to his mostly bald pate.

"What did you tell the detective that you saw over here at the rectory last night?" Bob asked.

"Like I said, I saw doctors come at two different times. I could see them out my window, and each walked under the streetlamp here on the street. I saw Dr. Graham, and I don't know the other guy. I saw them go in, but I didn't see either leave. I was watching my Downton Abbey re-runs and got pretty caught up in those. You know the episode where—"

"No, I don't," Bob said. "How can you be sure who these people were or how both were doctors?"

"I've been around a lot of medical people in my career, heh-heh, and each of the guys had a black medical bag with them."

"Could've been a gym bag or suitcase," Bob said.

"No," he crossed his arms defensively. His oily sideburns glinted where the sun hit them. "The hospital emblem was on each bag. It's got that fancy light blue and red insignia. You know, it's on the ambulance parked right there."

Bob and Tony looked at the ambulance and took note of the emblem.

"Was there an ambulance with either of them?"

"No. I just thought the poor old guy had another case of heartburn. He's prone to it, but his congregation keeps bringing him fatty casseroles and artery-hardening desserts. They love him over there at the church. Probably loved him to death. Poor fellow."

"What time did these folks visit with him?"

"Oh gosh, it'd have to be around eleven or twelve? I don't know. I was watching my Downton Abbey reruns, so I didn't check the clock. You know the one where Matthew—"

"No, I don't," said Bob. Tony rolled his eyes so only Bob could see.

The funeral director huffed and recrossed his arms.

"If I get a sketch artist up here, do you think you can give her some details of both men? One you said was Dr. Graham?"

"Yes, of course, I'll try. But one did look like Graham, you know, that curling dark hair, aquiline nose, strong shoulders…"

"Is that the rector's regular doctor? I thought Graham was a surgeon?"

"Well, Graham's betrothed was buried earlier today, so I thought maybe he was going to thank the rector."

"At eleven o'clock at night?"

"Now that you mention it, that does seem strange."

"Anything else?"

"No, not really."

"Is there something?"

"I never saw anybody leave the house. And the rector's little dog is missing. I haven't seen or heard her. And she barks non-stop if there's a visitor. The rector can't, or couldn't half hear, so it didn't really bother him. I had to turn my TV up louder to listen to my program. You know it's a complete travesty that Dame Maggie Smith didn't win awards for every one of the Downton shows."

They sat in silence, each lost in their own thoughts, for a few minutes.

"Thank you," Bob said. "We'll send the artist over. Contact us if you remember anything else."

"I will. You know, this reminds me of the episode—" Bob quietly closed the car door after the funeral director got out. He radioed for the sketch artist to get with the funeral director as soon as possible.

Bob took out his phone and called Gus. "Hey, what's happening there?" he asked.

"A whole lot of nothing," she replied. "We've gone through about a fourth of Fulcher's list and got zero, *nada*."

"What about the others? They give anything? Any leads?"

"Nope," Gus said. "Well, actually, they did, but not the kind you mean. One of the groups of officers walked in on a big drug deal with a guy Fulcher had flagged. The guy's on probation, and a heck of a fight broke out. Your boys are okay. A couple of black eyes and loose teeth."

"You serious?" Bob asked.

"It ended up that one of the other guys on our list was also on probation and had the Sheriff's stolen weed and pistols, and the guy and his friends were selling it to the guys from Henderson, you know, the guys that are in one of those home-grown gangs over there. The boys from Henderson got pissed off when officers pointed it out to them that the garbage bag was stamped "Sheriff" in gold letters, and all hell broke loose. The good news is that everybody who was in the house for the deal is a felon, and everybody got tagged with possession of a firearm by a felon. Your new boys made solid arrests. After a few broken windows and a short shoot-out, it all worked out just fine. Oh, and the Sheriff is happy."

"Well, damn. That sounds like a lot more fun than my morning," Bob said. "You all still out talking to the rest of Fulcher's guys? Or did you have to stop?

"We're heading back to the station in a few and can help out with the few remaining after I type up my report."

"Not yet," Gus said. "We have to get the weed and guns processed back in and find places for the arrestees to go. Can't house them together since some of them are in rival gangs. I'll meet you there in about an hour."

"Can Katie and Johnson help out now?" Bob asked.

"Yep. Katie's got bruises. Johnson hurt his hand busting one guy's head after the guy pulled a pistol on him. Dropped the guy like a load of bricks. Never seen anything like it," she laughed. Gus changed the subject and turned serious. "You like our guy for the rector's killer? It's not the usual target."

"I don't know. It's not the same MO, but the cruelty and knife work? It's possible. All I know is that we've got to find the person who's behind these killings and fast," Bob said.

"Damn. Okay. We'll see you at the PD unless something else turns up."

"Buckle up. Let's head over to the hospital," Bob said to Tony.

"Why?"

"Let's find out if there's a record of doctors who responded to any calls last night from the rector's house and find out where Dr. Graham is. We need to talk to him again."

"Okay. I'll call Sternberg and tell him we're on the way there."

* * * * *

Dr. Graham flew into the hospital's conference room with his white lab coat flapping. He whispered instructions to the two surgery residents following him and then closed the door in their faces. He looked from Bob to Tony. "You've found Cassie's killer? Who is it?" Dr. Graham asked.

"Doc," Tony said. "Calm down. No. We just need to talk to you."

"Again?" he said as he sank wearily into a burgundy leather chair. His hair stood up where he'd shoved it back in frustration.

"Why were you at the rectory last night? Why did you take a medical bag?" Bob asked.

"Patient confidentiality. I can't tell you. You know that!" Graham snapped.

"Oh no? What about if the patient is dead?"

Dr. Graham's face turned white. "What do you mean, dead? He was fine when I left him."

Sternberg, the hospital lawyer, stirred to life in the corner of the room.

"Don't say anything else until we get you a lawyer, doctor," he said.

"You're a lawyer. And you're sitting right there," said Graham, his eyes blazing in contempt.

Graham turned back to Bob and said, "I don't know what kind of sick game you're playing, but the rector was fine when I saw him. And, no, patient confidentiality does not allow me to speak even if he is dead. And you can go…" Graham let the words linger and left the room.

"That went well," Tony murmured.

"Sternberg, Dr. Graham is coming to the station with or without a lawyer. Better go tell him," Bob said. "Also, did your staff have any luck finding a call out for another doctor to the rector's place last night? Do I have to go and bother Judge Jones for another subpoena or court order to get your cooperation?"

"No, you don't. I'll check in with the administration now and then go talk to Dr. Graham. Give me a few minutes," Sternberg said.

The detectives waited in silence.

"We need a break," Tony moaned.

"From your lips to God's ears," Bob said.

"What are we missing? I say we get out everything we've got and go back over it again. Get Gus, Johnson, and Katie and comb back through it all?"

"You're right. Let's go back over it all once we get Graham's statement."

* * * * *

Later, Graham and his high-priced lawyer sat with dueling crossed arms in the PD's conference room. Graham had left his white coat at the hospital. Each sported a similar dark suit and a dark look. Neither volunteered anything.

The lawyer kept chanting "patient confidentiality," and Bob kept saying "obstruction." Tony continued to check his phone for Emma Jean's email with Buck's promised receipts.

After a few more minutes of getting nowhere, Bob slammed his hand down on the table. His tie was askew, and he'd run his fingers through his hair so many times it was standing straight up. "That's it. We're done here. I'm getting an order for the doc's emails, texts, patient records, and the list will go on and on. You folks think you're funny, sitting over there silent, like a pharaoh in his tomb. We'll see how much you're laughing when you have to spend hours putting together what I want. And, Graham, we're working to solve your fiancée's murder, and you act as if you couldn't give a Goddamn."

Graham jumped up from his seat and shoved his finger into Bob's face. His attorney made a half-hearted effort to pull him back. "Then you're wasting *your* time, sitting here with me and asking the same questions over and over," Graham said. I've told you all I can tell you, and you won't bully me into saying something I shouldn't. Now, I'm running on about three hours of sleep and have a surgery schedule tomorrow. I'm leaving."

CHAPTER TWENTY-SEVEN

Tony escorted Dr. Graham and his lawyer back to the small public area of the precinct. The men avoided looking at one another.

A woman, Mia's mother, turned toward them as the group arrived. She froze. "You!" she shouted, pointing at Dr. Graham. "What's *he* doing here?" she asked Tony through clenched teeth.

"We've just been talking to Dr. Graham for a few minutes. He and his attorney are on their way out.

"Why?" Tony asked.

Graham and his lawyer picked up their pace heading for the door.

"Because he's Mia's 'sometimes boyfriend' and we haven't seen him since…" Mia's mother wailed and broke down in tears.

Looking at a young, uniformed officer standing by the front desk, Tony jerked his head toward the two men who quickly exited, but they'd high-tailed it out of the parking lot before the officer could stop them.

Tony led Mia's mother over to the chair with the fewest cracks in its green faux leather. He mouthed to Sarge to get water, but Sarge was already coming around with a box of tissues.

The big man knelt in front of Mia's mother and talked to her in a low voice. He held both of her small hands in his large ones.

Tony headed to the back to get Bob.

After a few minutes, Mia's mom quieted and agreed to go to the interview room. Sarge rested a protective hand on her shoulders for a minute and glared at Tony.

"Be gentle in there, or…" he hissed. Tony started sweating and placed his hand on the small of her back to guide her to the room.

By this time, Bob had combed his hair and straightened his tie. Tony was surprised when Bob asked him to talk to Mia's mother, but he felt a rush of pride to be given the opportunity to interview her. "Ma'am, thank you for coming down here. Did you have something you thought of that might be important to the investigation?"

"Yes, I think so," she said. She continued to look down at the tissue balled up in her hands. "It's just thinking about Mia and then seeing Dr. Graham brought it all back. Mia and I had quarreled over him. It got pretty heated, and it was one of the last times I spoke to her. Then, Graham hasn't even called or anything, and I just don't understand how he could be so callous," she wailed.

Tony looked nervously at the half-open door. He didn't need Sarge busting in.

"I'm so sorry," he said, handing her another box of tissues. "Do you think he could somehow be involved in her disappearance?"

She nodded. "I think he, or one of his so-called friends, had something to do with Mia going missing."

"How so?"

She straightened her spine and looked deep into Tony's eyes. "Because I heard him and his friends talking over at our house last week. They were out in the yard while Mia had gone inside to get her jacket. The door was open, and the screen door was latched. They were talking about operations—I think they were all surgeons—and they were laughing about cutting people open. I didn't like it and was walking into the other room when I heard one of them say he had a collection of special knives."

Tony stopped taking notes.

"Was it Graham?" he asked.

"I don't know. It was hard for me to pick out the voices, and I didn't know him well. I called him Mia's boyfriend, but they seemed pretty casual about getting together. Maybe once a week, they'd go out somewhere. His friends were over at our place because they were meeting before heading over to a concert in Durham."

Tony rearranged his pad and pen, giving her time to collect herself.

"I've been up most nights," she said. "Then I remembered those guys and I thought you should know what they were talking about."

Bob looked at Tony and nodded encouragingly, for him to keep pursuing this line.

"Did you or your husband or anyone else see these guys? Could anyone provide a description?"

"No," her shoulders slumped, and she rested her forehead on her hand. "My husband was in the kitchen, and Mia's brothers were all out. Nobody else saw them."

"Okay," Bob said. "I'd still like to send in a sketch artist just in case you remember more than you think you do. Would that be okay?"

"Fine. But do you think it could be Dr. Graham? Can't you make him come in here and make him tell me where my baby is?"

Sarge, obviously hovering outside the door, strode into the room. He glared first at Tony and then at Bob.

"Give her a break," he said. "I've called her husband to come sit with her, and he's on his way."

Bob and Tony quickly stood up.

"Sarge. We'll go and get the sketch artist. Take all the time you need," Bob said to Mia's mother.

"We promise we'll talk to Dr. Graham again," Tony said.

CHAPTER TWENTY-EIGHT

He busied himself by cleaning his knives. He lined them up precisely one inch apart on the pristine linen towel. He kept the lights low, preferring candlelight to electric light.

Days off were the hardest days for him. Controlling his… compulsions was easier when he was working, busy. Idle hands and all that.

He used a chamois cloth to tenderly wipe down each sharp blade. Each stroke brought him intense pleasure. His assortment of sharpening stones stood nearby.

His audience watched mutely and unblinking. The eyes on the table burned a hole in the back of his head. He whisked them away into a nearby drawer.

It had taken him a lot of time to arrange the tableau to his satisfaction. An arm here, a head there, and various pieces here and there. The hardest part was getting them out of and putting them back into the freezer.

In one chair "sat" Mia. In another chair, sat Cassie, who was across from Michelle, or parts of them anyway. He'd discarded the parts he didn't need where the local yokels could find them and wonder.

There was only one empty chair left—but not for long. He hummed quietly, savoring the near silence.

They all reminded him, in one way or another, of his bitch sister. The know-it-all lawyer who treated him like dirt on the bottom of her shoe. The one that went missing ten years ago. The one they'd never ever find.

CHAPTER TWENTY-NINE

etween Mia's mother and the funeral director, who'd been very descriptive, the sketch artist on loan to Oxford had two fairly detailed sketches. Bob stared morosely at them, seeing only a few similarities in the eyes and chin.

Bob wasn't convinced that the rector's murder was related, but he couldn't rule it out either. He yawned and stretched his arms. He was tired: tired of this case, tired of finding body parts, and tired of the grief—his own and others.

Tony sat slumped across from him. He'd pulled over a chair and propped up his feet on it. He looked worn out. His usual pristine shirt sported cuffs splotched with blue ink and a shirt collar bent in two different directions. Tony pulled the sketches over to his side of the table. After a few minutes, he shoved them back. "I can't say I remember coming across some guy that looks like this."

Bob heaved himself up from his chair. The Chick-fil-A wrapper stuck to his arm, and he shook it off.

"I'm getting Fulcher in here. And Gus, Katie, and Johnson, if they're around. You and I are just spinning wheels."

Tony leaned back and closed his eyes, just for a minute.

A few minutes later, Johnson shoved Tony's feet off the chair, and Tony came to with a jerk. "Nice work, Tony. You catching the killer in your dreams?" Johnson asked.

"Fuck you doing, Johnson?" Tony shot to his feet and stood chest to chest with the older deputy.

"Don't blow up at me unless you plan on following through," Johnson snarled.

"Hey, hey, hey," Bob said, pushing in between the two men as the other officers assembled in the room. "C'mon, let's sit down. We've got some sketches I want you all to look at here on the table."

Everyone sat in silence and passed the sketches around. Dr. Fulcher came in and picked up both of them. He took out a jeweler's loupe and bent closer. "Hmmm, hmmm," he murmured.

Johnson and Katie looked over at Bob and shook their heads.

"Nope. Ain't seen either guy. Where'd you get these?" Johnson asked.

"Two separate witnesses worked on these," Bob said. "One was from Mia's family, and one was a witness to a possible suspect who went to the rector's house the night before we found him dead in his house. I think these two sorta look alike," Bob said.

Gus interrupted. "Don't think they look like any of the sex offenders we've got on our list."

"Right. No resemblance to anyone we know," Katie said.

Fulcher left the room, humming to himself.

Bob looked at Gus.

"What's up with that?" he asked.

"No idea. Let's see, we got nothing as of now, right?" Gus asked.

Before he could answer, Fulcher strode back in carrying his computer. Typing furiously, he hit the "enter" key hard a couple of times and then turned the computer screen toward the officers.

"There," he said triumphantly. One of the sketches stared back at them from a photograph.

"Well, I'll be," said Johnson.

Bob squinted at the display.

"What's this site?"

"It's the state medical board's site. Here's some candid shots from a hospital gala a few years ago." Fulcher tapped on the screen. "This looks like he's your man, or pretty close to it."

The agent and officers leaned all over each other, trying to get a closer look.

"You think this doctor, next to Graham, is our guy? What's his background?" Katie asked Fulcher. Katie reached up and pulled the band holding her ponytail out, scraped her hair back, and wound it into the holder. Sweat stains snaked out underneath her shirt sleeves.

Fulcher shoved his thick, black-framed glasses back up his nose. "Look, I can't say for sure because I don't know the name of the man in the picture. What I did come across was the *curriculum vitae* of one Jared Gruber. The CV lists three articles about the precision of certain surgical implements and his own preferences, and one is about his hobby of knife collecting in general. I'll print out copies for all of you. So, if the guy in the picture is Jared Gruber, then yes, he's your guy."

Before anyone could comment, Fulcher scooted out, feet tapping down the hall.

"I'll be damned," Johnson said, looking at Katie. "Dr. Who Knows may just be onto something."

"If he's right, the FBI can hire him full-time now. He'll be off probation," Gus said.

Everyone's head snapped in her direction.

"Oh, forget I said that," Gus said.

"Gee-*zuz*," Johnson said. "Not only do they send us a socially awkward dude, but he's on probation?"

"Shhh! Here he comes," Gus whispered.

Dr. Fulcher gave each of the detectives a different article. For a while, the only sound in the room was the ticking of the city-issued black clock. Tony went out once and brought back paper cups of coffee and fake creamer.

"Damn," Tony said. "This is messed up as hell. He talks about his knives like they're living things. What a sicko."

"Agreed," Johnson said. "He really likes to describe what happens to people's flesh when it's pierced by the blade. Disgusting."

Bob looked over his half-glasses. "Tony, how are we gonna match the photo to the CV?"

Tony looked at the clock, which read 8:00 p.m. "After we finish up here. I want to read all of these articles first, or if y'all will take some notes, make a list of questions we should ask, that'd help too."

"Let's run a criminal history on Jared Gruber, then find out if a doctor by that name was either working here or assigned to the hospital during the days the ladies went missing. Since the guy resembling the sketches is in photos, we could see if Dr. Graham knows what his name is. It's gonna be a long night," Tony said.

"Good work, Fulcher," said Gus. "How'd you get onto him?"

Fulcher preened in the warmth of her smile. He smiled back, using muscles that seemed rarely used.

"I started looking at local state medical board sites earlier when y'all kept talking about the surgical nature of the cuts on the body parts. Just a guess, really. Well, I added doctors to my search requests in North Carolina, Virginia, and South Carolina, and kept scrolling around. The sketches there got me thinking about pictures I'd seen with Dr. Graham in them, along with a guy who looked like the one in the sketch. I'll keep looking for other pictures on other sites after dinner." He dropped the laptop into his computer bag.

"I need to get over to Mamie's promptly. She's cooking Chateaubriand and serving a lovely Chateauneuf-du-Pape."

Bob looked at Tony. "Chateau who?" Bob asked.

Dr. Fulcher enunciated the red wine's French name again for him.

"Okay then, Happy eating, you deserve it," Bob said.

* * * * *

Tony and Bob were the last to leave. Even Sarge had closed up his battered Tolstoy paperback and straightened up his desk for the next day. He'd left a single light burning in the front of the precinct.

"Think we should call Graham in to see if he can ID the guy in the photo, or how do you want to do it? We have to go through his lawyer to get him back," Tony said, hanging his jacket on a hanger on the back of the door.

"I can barely string two thoughts together," Bob said. "Plus, I want to read everything first before we start on him again."

"I feel better now that we've got deputies and officers patrolling the lawyers' and judges' houses at night. The law enforcement cars should deter anything from happening for the next few hours.

"Let's sleep on it and decide early tomorrow how to go about getting the Doc back in with his attorney and finding this guy from the photo. Heck, it's almost tomorrow."

* * * * *

A broad-shouldered man with an even larger hunting rifle in his big mitts stood in the shadows, waiting for the detectives. Lustrous auburn and brown hair spilled from the bag at the man's huge, booted feet. The muffled sound of dogs whining rode the dawn air. The man made a hand gesture, and the dogs quieted. The lot was otherwise deserted. One city light lit up the area closest to the precinct.

Bob spotted him as Tony was locking the precinct door.

"Hey, man," Bob said. "Easy now. Can you put down that rifle?"

The man didn't move. His sideways look at his bag was the only indication that he might have heard the command. A large knife's handle rode on his belt. His pants looked soaked with blood—or something else.

Tony squinted into the still-dark lot. Behind Bob, Tony quietly removed his service weapon from his holster and held it down by his thigh.

"I need you to put down your rifle, son. You can't have that out here in the city," Bob cajoled.

"Young patrolman told me to get up here. You wanted to talk to me?" the man asked without making a move to set down the rifle.

"Well, I'm happy to talk to you, son, but I'd like it a lot better if you'd put down your gun. You're making me too nervous to talk."

As if he were almost surprised by the fact that he was holding it, the man opened his truck door and put it inside.

"I'm out walking these woods around here most days, as you can see," the man said, gesturing to the bag as Bob moved closer.

"Ain't seen nobody acting weird while they's huntin' or no girls out where they shouldn't be. I don't study them that breaks the huntin' rules, and I can't abide somebody hurting girls. It ain't right. I'd a called that trooper-man if I'd seen anything bad. He lives beside my mama, and he's nice to me. I brought you what I did find today—an hour ago. Trooper-man said you'd want to know. He's parked on the street, making sure I brung it to you."

Seeing the men meet, the trooper beeped his horn and drove off.

As the large man walked toward them with the bag, Bob saw that he was a lot younger than Bob had first thought. He moved lightly on his feet. He looked like nothing more than a boy trying on the unfamiliar trappings of a man. His curly reddish-brown hair cascaded over his shoulders, but looked clean. His face was round and smooth. It held a perpetual expression of wonder. Proudly, he handed over his bag to Bob.

Bob gingerly accepted the offering. "Can you tell me what's in here? I need to know if it's something sharp, or something that will hurt me, and whether I need to get some gloves," Bob asked. Tony quietly re-holstered his weapon.

"Yes, sir. I mean no, sir. It's mostly hair. A lot of what I think is lady hair," the boy said. "I found it over at that dumpster at Food Mart a few days ago. It looked like it'd been kicked up under the dumpster. I go over there to the Food Mart at least once a week to get bones they save for me that they'd otherwise throw out, for my huntin' dogs. Although, now that they know me over at Food Mart, they'll save me a few at the first register," he explained.

Tony pulled out a pair of latex gloves and opened the bag wider. Bob held the flashlight feature on Tony's phone over it.

"Anyways, I'd been using this hair in here to help train my dogs to track, and, well, this is embarrassing." The man trailed off. He looked down at his feet for a few seconds.

"What's that?" Bob asked.

"Well, I found something I oughta turned in and I didn't. Now, honestly, I thought it was one of them bones for my dogs. I didn't understand what it was until them dogs grabbed it today after sniffing the lady hair. They got ahold of the bag and this thing just fell out."

The hair color matched Cassie's tresses.

Tony then pulled a finger out of the bag. He whistled. The hunting dogs started barking.

Several minutes later, the man, David Kellam, finished painstakingly writing out his statement. He'd kept his tongue in the corner of his mouth while slowly sounding out and forming the letters. He audibly breathed through his mouth.

Bob and Tony found some old paper bowls for the boy's dogs. They put fresh water in them, and the dogs gulped it down. A few leftover stale biscuits satisfied them. The hunting dogs now quietly sat under Kellam's chair at his feet.

CHAPTER THIRTY

My mind is all over the place, spinning and darting from one thought to another. My adrenaline pumps, and I've started sweating. The smell of rubbing alcohol, liniment, and bandages brings me back to the present.

It's hard to decide who's next-not so many choices for my next-er-muse. A small town is more of a challenge than big cities. Small-town people aren't satisfied with a word or two. I constantly get asked for my name, who my people are, where I live, and who with—the list is endless.

The voices are always the same: eager, prying, excited to dig and dig until they find out all of your secrets—or try to. The rural folks' curiosity is insatiable. But I understand appetites...

It's harder to blend into a small town, too. Maybe I've picked the wrong setting this time for my house of horrors. The townspeople's eyes follow me everywhere I go; the hands reach out and grab my sleeve to gently stop me to just ask a question; the heads nodding as I show up to church with my book of Common Prayer in my hand and my shoes shined but not too well because I've given out that there's no wife at home.

I've managed it because, well, I'm good at what I do. I also fake sympathy pretty well. I paste a sickly smile to my face and keep my eyes downcast as if in deprecation. Even when I feel like ripping out my colleagues' throats with my sharp teeth and watching their blood spray into the air and run in thick rivulets down their wizened necks and onto their white coats.

I feel myself engorge. I lean into the feeling.

The best time to strike would be during surgery, when everyone's concentrating on the poor patient—his vitals, his oxygen, and so on.

Instead, I just continue to do my job. I do it well. I look down and there's a scalpel in my hand. I've rubbed it up and down so hard on my pants that it sparkles. It is sharp and familiar. I take a deep breath and wait for quitting time when I can go back to the hunt, and everything that makes me, me.

CHAPTER THIRTY-ONE

Early the next morning, Tony and Bob snagged Gus on their way out of the police department's doors. She shrugged into her shoulder holster on the way out to the cruiser before putting on her duty jacket. "Where're we headed?" she asked, climbing into the backseat of Bob's car.

"There's a guy across the street from the rectory that just got home from a late night at the hospital and called the Crime Stoppers tip line. He thinks he remembers seeing a guy with a medical bag going into the rectory. The guy thinks he saw someone skulking around the preacher's house," Tony said.

Bob grunted and produced a bag of pork rinds from his wrinkled gray jacket. He handed them over the seat to Gus. "Gross, no," she said. "I didn't even know they still made those vile things. They smell to high heaven." She stabbed fruitlessly at the back seat window controls.

Bob shrugged and stuffed some into his mouth. Tony rolled down his window. "Damn, Bob. Smells like a pig went and died up in here," Tony said.

Bob laughed and kept crunching away.

"What's the neighbor got to add? Did you guys get to talk to him?" Gus asked, rolling down her window once Bob released the locks.

"He thinks he knows the type of person who carries the same medical bag and wants us to detail it for him. He got a quick look at someone the other night and thinks the person may be somebody he works with at the hospital. He's just getting back from having a kidney stone pulverized, so he didn't hear about the preacher right away."

"Is your sketch artist on the way?" Gus asked, edging her head closer to the fresh air streaming into the back seat.

Bob stopped crunching to turn around and look at her. He rolled his eyes. "You think we have a sketch artist with our budget? Did you get a load of the guns we carry? I think they're from World War II. Hell, we barely have an officer to man the phones. We'd have a better chance of getting a K-9 officer than a sketch artist. The Chief likes dogs. We've been using the artist that the SBI pays for the last couple of days."

They pulled up in front of a two-story, stately Georgian house. The dark red brick and white columns shone glossy with new paint, and the dark green shutters and door contrasted nicely with them. English boxwoods softened the stately home. A young man opened the door and stepped out.

"I think I know the guy who went into the rector's house," he said.

* * * * *

Gus, Bob, and Tony sat uncomfortably shoulder to shoulder on the brushed green velvet settee in the living room, holding dainty cups of aromatic tea. To keep their witness calm and rambling on, they'd let themselves get talked into organic herbal teas. Each cup arrived featuring the smallest ginger cookie sitting on the saucer. There was nowhere to put the cups down except for a spindly tea table in front of them. Every time one of them bent to slide it onto the table, the homeowner, Mr. Sturgill, frowned at them, and they took it back to balance awkwardly on their lap. Tony was the only one beside a small walnut chest who'd slid his eggshell-thin teacup into the forest of bric-a-brac that completely covered its top. He wrote in his notebook while Sturgill talked.

The scent of verbena mixed with cat urine wafted through the overheated room. Sturgill explained that he kept the heat up for his deceased aunt's elderly cat, Mr. Pickles. Mr. Pickles glared malevolently at the officers from the safety of his nearby perch on the built-in bookcase at Tony's elbow. Sturgill explained that the vet wanted the cat inside because he was fast losing his fur in clumps due to some unknown allergy. Mr. Pickles, he explained, came as part of his aunt's legacy along with the beautiful home. Every time Tony discreetly fanned himself, another ball of fur fell off of Mr. Pickles and onto the already matted red oriental rug.

Sturgill worked in the emergency room as a contract orderly at the hospital. He'd been at the hospital for several years after he left a career in the armed services. He felt he knew most of the hospital employees by sight. He'd also had the colossal bad luck to develop three kidney stones, one each month, for the last three months.

"Yeah, I seen Dr. Graham and them other doctors with these small medic bags a while back. I think it was some kinda promo from a drug company. I even seen Michelle and that Sternberg with one. Now, none of us orderlies got one. We never get the swag. That's reserved for the big shots." Sturgill trailed off, looking into space or into the face of the ormolu clock on the mantle. Tony couldn't be sure.

Sturgill had one eye that stared straight ahead and another that did its own thing. Tony thought the wandering one moved in time to the clock's ticking. It was hard to tell in the dimly lit and smoky room. Tony waved away Sturgill's cigarette smoke when it wafted toward him.

Sturgill lived alone in the house he'd inherited from his aunt Louise Penn Sturgill. He kept the lights inside dim for "atmosphere" but had solar lights, motion sensor lights, and streetlights outside to give him a good view of the houses across the street, including the rector's house.

"So, I kinda think it was Graham that I saw going over there a couple of times this month. The guy walked like Graham."

"What do you mean?" Tony asked.

"He kinda walked like a football player, arms out to the side, kinda on his toes."

"Did you see his face?"

"Naw. I went inside to get my dinner. I start a crock pot before I go into work most days and I was hungry. He didn't wave if it was Graham. You know, if it was Graham, I think he'd wave if he saw me outside."

Tony sat back in his corner of the couch and put his notebook down. "You and Graham are friends?"

"No, not friends, really. We don't eat lunch together or go the high school ball games or nothing. But he's really nice if we meet up in the hall. I think we talked about the UNC/State game the last time I saw him. He's like that. He'll talk to me like I'm a person. Not like some of them other docs. They're assholes. They act like I'm invisible, or they'll set together at their lunch table in the cafeteria and make fun of who walks by. I can be into the last foot of the hall, mopping away, and one of them will step right onto my clean floor with them big tread black shoes. Assholes."

Sturgill took a big slurp of his yellow mellow orange summertime tea blend and snorted. "So, yeah. I'm not really sure it was Graham, but it could've been him."

Tony wiped his sweating head with the sleeve of his shirt. It was broiling in the musty house. Stagnant air simmered over the stale shortbread that Sturgill had placed on a chipped floral cake plate in front of them. "Okay. So basically, you saw a person with a medical bag go into the rectory. And you have no idea if it was Graham or who it was?"

"So, yeah. Basically."

Tony hid his frustration.

"Thanks for the refreshments. And, thank you for talking with us. Call us if you remember anything else," Bob said.

The three struggled to rise together from the dainty couch without spilling their tea. Sturgill rose with the officers.

"Hey, can I get your card?" Sturgill asked Tony, standing a little too close to him.

"I just ran out of them yesterday," Tony said.

"Hey, Bob. Give Mr. Sturgill one of your cards, okay?"

Bob pulled out his worn leather wallet from his back pocket and fished out a card. "Here ya go, Mr. Sturgill. You call this number and ask for Tony, okay?"

"Yeah. I will. I'll keep thinking about it. I sure will."

After the big door closed and they were opening the car doors, Bob turned to Tony and said, "The medic bag is an angle we haven't thought about."

"I'm on it," Gus said. "Drop me at the hospital and I'll get a ride back from security if no one else is around. Hope to goodness this leads somewhere. I'm worried that this sicko is out there plotting about the next victim."

"I know," Tony nodded.

"This running around, chasing leads, feels like we're just marking time until the next murder. I don't like it," Bob said with a frown before adding, "The Chief met with members of the community and heads of churches all day today. The people are getting frantic. They're buying up guns left and right. The pawn shops had record pistol sales yesterday. Somebody's going to have a bad accident with all this fear and frustration of not knowing who to trust.. It's hard to blame them."

Tony and Bob dropped Gus off at the hospital and headed back to the PD.

Bob broke the silence first. "It's a damn shame that lead didn't work out last night. I thought we had him," Bob said.

"Yeah, me too," Tony said. "But that doctor in the picture's been dead for two years. Hard to pin him with the murders.

"I say we go back and talk to Graham. His name keeps coming up. Maybe he knows more than he's saying, or maybe he knows something he doesn't know he knows," Tony said.

"That doesn't make a damn bit of sense," Bob said, "but I get what you're saying. Let's go see Graham again. Call his lawyer and tell him we need to talk. We'll meet over at Graham and Cassie's condo. Maybe that'll get him talking."

CHAPTER THIRTY-TWO

"Who the damned fuck do you two think you are? I have surgery in one hour this morning, and here you guys are banging down my damn door!" Graham shouted in Bob's face. "Who's going to tell the poor patient and his family? He's been on the waiting list for over a month. Who's going to pay for this?"

Bob took a step back and put his hands out to placate him. "Look, Doctor, we're trying to run down all the leads—we have to stop this monster from striking again. We need your help," Bob said.

Graham blocked the entrance to his apartment, but Bob could see a portion of the living area with its sofa and coffee table where they'd been talking to him only a few days before.

Graham shifted angrily, obscuring Bob's view. "I've told you everything I know, but you're harassing me now. You're interfering with my job and my home. I'm calling the Chief and telling him to tell you guys to back the hell off!" The door slammed in their faces.

"Huh," Bob said.

"What?" Tony snapped.

"I saw into the living room. There was a medic bag on the coffee table."

"Yeah, so what?"

"Beside the medic bag was what looked like a lot of knives or scalpels on a tray. The tray was facing the door."

"So what. The man's a surgeon."

"These scalpels didn't look clean. In fact, they looked used. I think there was blood on them."

Tony looked at Bob. "Let's go get a search warrant."

"You read my mind."

* * * * *

Graham called the Chief. He screamed so loudly that Tony and Bob could hear him even with the handset held up to the Chief's ear. The Chief interspersed an "um hum" and a "is that so" at the beginning of the call.

A few minutes later, the Chief quietly put the phone in the cradle and stared off into space.

Neither Tony nor Bob spoke.

With a big sigh, the Chief turned his gaze to them. "Go get the search warrant. That prick isn't gonna tell me how to do my job. If you need to search his place, you're gonna search it. We don't play favorites or give guys a pass just 'cause they yell or throw around the Governor's name. I'll be damned if I let that guy or anybody else tell me how it's gonna go down." The Chief rifled in his desk drawer and came up with the much-depleted bottle of Scotch. "Now, close the door on your way out. Call me and his expensive lawyer when you get the warrant."

"Yes, sir," Bob said. "And, thanks for having our backs, Chief."

"Go on, get out of here."

* * * * *

Tony and Bob let out twin-held breaths they'd been holding when they got into their car. A few minutes earlier, they'd parked it in front of Judge Jones' house. They'd rapped on Judge Jones' door to get him to sign their search warrant after being assured by the deputy assistant DA that he'd already cleared their visit and the search warrant with Jones.

Jones's house looked positively medieval in the watery sunlight filtered through storm clouds. It featured turrets, stone fences, and a paddock with what they swore was a jousting arena on the side. The judge wasn't assigned to court, so he was taking a day at home to work on some court orders. The ADA had forgotten to call Jones, and the Judge was pissed.

"I've never been called a mawworm, o fish pancreas or what else?" Bob asked Tony, still dazed from the dressing down the old judge gave them for disturbing his rest, just to sign a search warrant. Spittle flew off the jurist's lips, coming to within an inch of Bob's wrinkled jacket lapels. He'd scooted back from the judge's desk, bowing nonstop as he kept his eyes front and center on the irate judge.

"Yeah. I don't know. I think he insulted my family if that's what a 'lineage' is…" Tony reflected. "I'm pretty sure 'son of a blighted goat' and 'muck on my shoe' were fairly derogatory."

They sat in silence for a few minutes, musing over the new vocabulary the old guy had spit out at them like machine gun fire.

"Did you get a load of the judge's dressing gown? I'm pretty sure my Aunt Agatha up in Quincey has one just like it. She's ninety-six," Bob said.

"I think the color is crimson," Tony mused, then shook himself. Neither mentioned the pin curlers in the judge's grizzled gray hair.

"But we got the search warrant, and that's all that matters. Let's put the blue light on and go see the good doctor." Bob grinned as he flipped the switch in the car. "Hope the judge has his earplugs in," he said as they whoop-whooped down the street toward Graham's apartment, playing the Stones at top volume.

Graham was no less incensed than Jones. He slammed the door in the detectives' faces. A few minutes later, he came back to the door holding his cell phone. He shoved it in Bob's face. "Talk to my lawyer. I refuse to talk to you two bozos."

Tony heard Bob explain, twice, that the detectives didn't need the lawyer's permission to execute the search warrant on Graham's apartment. Bob handed the phone back to Graham. Graham's face turned puce while he listened, then jabbed the off button. "He says I gotta let you in, but don't touch anything until he gets here to make an inventory of anything you take. I'm gonna take pictures of everything you put your grubby hands on." He'd walked closer and closer to Bob with each word until he was breathing on top of his head.

"Yeah, you do what you want," Bob shrugged, unfazed. "We've got a search warrant, here's your copy and, ah, Sergeant Johnson with the Granville County Sheriff's Office has kindly left his bed to come and sit with you while we proceed."

Johnson had walked up to the door from the parking lot and was staring at Graham. Johnson outweighed Graham by fifty pounds and was three inches taller. Graham turned and headed to the sofa, where he sat down with a huff. "Fine. I'm suing you, this lug, that moron, and the entire Police Department and Sheriff's Office," Graham said, thumbing through a magazine as if he couldn't be bothered.

Johnson turned toward Bob. "I got this, detective. You and Tony go ahead. The doctor won't give me any trouble."

By the time Graham's lawyer arrived, Tony and Bob had almost finished the search. They took the Medic bag they'd found in the hall closet and marked it as evidence. Inside the bag was an assortment of what looked like surgical instruments. They'd also found some handwritten letters from Cassie. They tagged and bagged these, too. The laptops were also put into evidence bags, and Graham and his lawyer were given a copy of the inventory.

"Jordan, tell these idiots they can't have my laptop. I need that for work. Make them put it back," Graham snapped at his attorney.

Jordan McNamara was the youngest member of a prestigious and venerable old Oxford law firm featuring his granddad's name on it. With his tie askew and shirt partially hanging out of his suit pants, he tried to calm his client.

"Look, doctor, I'll speak to them, but we're not supposed to get in their way while they're executing a search warrant."

"What the fuck I pay you for? You just going to let them waltz in here and take whatever the hell they want like, like I'm a criminal, for God's sake?"

Johnson stepped closer and peered at the two men. "We got a problem here, counselor?" he asked.

"No, no… um, Sergeant. Just give me a few minutes, a few feet away with my client. I'm sure we can resolve this," McNamara said.

Johnson turned to Graham. "Listen to your attorney. The boy makes sense."

The two scream-whispered at each other for five minutes, returning to the sofa at the same time Bob came back into the small room. "I called the tech folks to come in," he said. "They'll be here in about five."

Graham erupted, climbing over his attorney, stepping on his hand, and vaulting over the back of the sofa toward Bob. Johnson hurtled toward Graham and got him on the floor with his arms pinned behind his back.

Over Graham's moans, curses, and threats, Bob told the young attorney that he could meet with his client down at the PD after he'd been processed at the magistrate's office and bond was set. Or not.

Johnson picked Graham up off the floor like he was a sack of flour and marched him out of the apartment. McNamara stood with his mouth gaping open. One eye squinted behind a cracked pair of tortoise-shell glasses. "Well, darn," the attorney said. "Guess I'm going to have to call in the senior partner. He isn't going to like this, not one little bit. This is why I like working on estates and real estate cases. No mess, no fuss," he muttered to himself.

Bob patted him on the back and helped him put his papers back in his thin leather briefcase. The handle hung off where Graham had stepped on it and the attorney's hand. "You tried, son. Not much you can do for someone who won't take your advice. Tell your daddy that Bob said you did okay."

"Thanks, Bob. See ya 'round," McNamara said, already pulling out his cell phone to call his father, the senior partner.

* * * * *

"The pharmaceutical company brought fifty Medic bags to the hospital," Gus told Bob when he got to the PD. "The company dropped them off a few weeks ago on the morning of the big hospital conference. Two of the reps handed them out during the day, but they didn't keep good notes of who got them, where they went, or what department, except surgery. The only real requirement to get one was to be a doctor." She sighed. "There's no way to account for all of them. The drug representatives' cursory notes are in here." She held up a slim buff-colored folder. "General Surgery received ten of them."

"Could the hospital's Admin Department send out an email asking employees to turn in their bags or to acknowledge receipt?" Tony asked.

"Maybe worth a try," Bob said.

"But the killer won't and there's no way to make him, unless…"

"Unless what?" Tony asked.

"You'd need to word it to say there's a prize for turning in the bags, or maybe someone put illegal drugs in them by accident, and Admin doesn't want anyone to get into trouble."

"That's the dumbest thing I've heard," Gus said. "No offense, but we're no better off than we were before."

They stared tiredly at each other across the table. On the snack table and on the coffee table a few feet away, there were only crumbs where the night shift had devoured the volunteers' cookies and brownies like piranhas. Even the coffee urn stood empty.

At the far end of the table sat Johnson, who was sifting through photographs of hospital employees. He'd sorted most into stacks and said the shortest stack was pictures of people matching the profile sketch developed earlier by Dr. Fulcher. "Why don't you put the surgeons under surveillance? We got Graham in there," he said, jerking his head in the direction of the holding cells. "How many more can there be? Besides, the Sheriff sent over two auxiliary officers to help out. They've just been here eating snacks and flirting with the ladies in 911 Emergency. Send them over to stake out the hospital."

Gus stood after Bob nodded. "I'll go get them so we can brief 'em. Good idea, Johnson."

Johnson kept sifting through the photos and spread a few of them around like he was playing a match game. He grunted as Gus walked off to grab the two deputies.

* * * * *

"Bob!" Tony shouted.

Bob's head hit the conference table with a loud *thunk*. Tony winced but shook Bob's shoulder. Totally exhausted, Bob had made a nest of old files and discarded uniforms to get a few minutes of sleep.

"C'mon! Gus has some live ones down at the hospital. We need to get down there to interview a couple of doctors."

Bob scrubbed at his face with one hand and grabbed his rumpled blue jacket with the other. His knees cracked when he stood up.

"What've you got?" Bob asked as they headed down College Street to the Oxford Medical Plaza.

Tony almost hit old lady Royster, who was wobbling her way across the crosswalk in front of the elementary school. The large oak trees lining College Street made it more difficult to see pedestrians. "Damn. She gets shorter and wider every day," Tony mumbled while Bob waved to the irate widow screeching at them.

Tony thumped a beat on the steering wheel and waited impatiently for the widow to finish crossing. "Gus said she has two docs in the conference room. Each has a Medic bag and got them as part of the pharmaceutical swag. They seem super nervous about it. The hospital attorney is raising hell, but Gus posted one deputy inside and one outside the room until we get there."

"Know anything about them or how long they've been working there?" Bob asked.

"Naw. She's running their records and will have them by the time we get there. If we ever get there."

One door up from the school, the funeral home's high-gloss black hearse had eased out into the wide road and was headed down Highway 15 at a glacial pace. Bob leaned out of the passenger window and unsuccessfully tried to get the eye of the young deputy directing funeral traffic.

Suddenly realizing that a police car with lights lit was bearing down on him, the deputy stopped the funeral traffic so Tony could squeeze by down the middle of the road.

Gus met them at the hospital door, hastily putting out a cigarette.

"What the hell, Gus?" Tony asked, pointing at her crushed cigarette.

"Shut it. I smoke ten a year. That was number eight and if we don't get this guy, I'm upping the quota to twenty."

Turning to Bob, Gus said, "Here's the rap sheets for each of the doctors, Dr. Shaw and Dr. Blaine. Neither one really has anything, as you'd guess, but both are about the same height as Dr. Graham. Shaw is a male, and Blaine is a female. That being said, both have about the same girth."

She stopped outside the conference room door and nodded to the officer standing guard.

"Ready? I'll let you guys handle the interviews. Unless you want me to do it?"

"No," Bob said. "Thanks. Just sit in and write a note to us if we miss anything." Bob opened the door and confronted an apoplectic Sternberg.

"What the hell are you playing at?" Sternberg demanded with spittle flying from his fleshy lips. "You're totally disrupting this hospital and interfering with patient care. These doctors are highly valued employees. I've advised them not to say anything to you until you tell us what this is all about."

Bob took the toothpick out of his mouth and pointed it at the lawyer. "Look here, Sternberg, you're interfering with a murder investigation, and you need to stand down."

Sternberg's already puce face flushed dangerously darker.

Alarmed, Dr. Shaw placed a hand on the attorney's sleeve and guided him into a chair. He unobtrusively began taking his pulse while checking the hands on his watch.

Dr. Blaine interrupted. "We don't mind a few questions if it will help you track down the animal that's killing these young women."

Dr. Shaw nodded at the investigators and pronounced the attorney out of danger. Sternberg wiped his face with his handkerchief and wheezed into it.

If there could be a more cheerless room in the hospital, I can't imagine it, Tony mused while taking his seat across from the doctor. Yellowed prints of the town as it was one hundred years ago hung crookedly at uneven spaces on the walls around the table. The chairs themselves were rickety, with brown leather and brass studs.

Bob poured water from the cracked pitcher into the glass in front of him and began with introductions. He instructed Dr. Blaine to wait in the hall with the officer for a few minutes. She left without a word.

"Dr. Shaw, where did you get your medical bag?"

"As I explained to FBI Agent Augusta over there, it was given to me by my department several weeks ago. I mostly put my workout clothes in there and—given my schedule—don't use it a lot. I don't know the Episcopal priest and none of the young ladies that were, that were..." he trailed off.

"What department?" Bob asked.

"I'm a general surgeon. I started here about six months ago on a contract basis. I have two other hospitals where I'm sent periodically. Surgeons are in high demand, especially in rural areas, and I work most days and some nights."

Tony sat across the table from Dr. Shaw and continued taking notes on a small notepad while observing the doctor. He judged him to be about Dr. Graham's age and height, but not his equal in width or fitness. Dr. Shaw's grip had been perfunctory, and he'd struggled to help Sternberg into the chair. *But, in fairness, Sternberg is a big guy.* Bob continued to stare at Dr. Shaw.

"Uh, I can get you a receipt from the restaurant I ate in late on the night the old rector was killed. I, uh, what else do you need?" Dr. Shaw asked, shifting in his seat, trying to find a comfortable spot in the chair where the bottom was all stuffing and pieces of cracked upholstery fabric.

"I need you to be truthful. And that's not happening here. Do I need to take you down to the station? I have all day and all night," Bob said unblinking.

Dr. Shaw loosened his tie and looked sideways at the lawyer. "Okay, here's the thing, man to man," he said, looking nervously at Gus. "I was at the restaurant, but I wasn't with my family. I was with a friend. A friend my wife knows nothing about."

"Oh, Jesus," murmured Sternberg. He scribbled furiously on his yellow legal pad.

"Yeah, well. I don't want her involved in any of this."

Bob just looked at the doctor for several minutes. Dr. Shaw opened his mouth to speak, thought better of it, and snapped his mouth shut.

"Let me get this straight," Bob said. "You don't want your friend spoken to, you'd rather go down for murder than for adultery."

"No! That's not what I'm saying, you idiot. I'm saying I need you to keep this quiet!" Shaw shouted.

"And I need you to go down to the station and wait for me," Bob said, gently holding Dr. Shaw by the elbow and steering him out into the hall.

"Officer, take Dr. Shaw to the police department and get him settled into Interview Room one."

The officer nodded and left with Dr. Shaw. Bob could hear him snickering down the hall. The police department only had one interview room.

Bob ushered in a wary Dr. Blaine. He studied the doctor. She was attractive, of above-average height, and muscular. She wore her strawberry-blond hair in a loose bun on top of her head and had milky, unlined skin except around her eyes. He guessed her age to be about forty. She wore a short-sleeved t-shirt under her open white doctor's coat and long Lycra shorts.

Dr. Blaine looked nervously at Bob. She looked down at her shorts in embarrassment. "Sorry about the clothes. I was on a dinner break and headed over to the soccer field to jog. It's pretty nice outside…" she trailed off.

"Tell me about your bag."

"Okay," she said. "I got mine at a pharmaceutical promo event at the hospital. I didn't know the preacher, um, rector. I'm a contract doctor with the surgery department."

Bob studied her for a minute. She looked away and intensely focused on the black-inked map of the hospital grounds behind him.

"Let me guess. You're Dr. Shaw's *friend*," Bob said.

Her shoulders sagged as she started crying. "Yes, I'm the friend. It was a stupid, stupid mistake. He's not even that good of a surgeon," she sniffled.

Sternberg unexpectedly reached out and softly patted her hand. He snatched it back when Tony raised his eyebrows at him.

Bob sighed. "I need a timeline of where you've been, including time spent with Shaw, over the last week. We're going to check into every place you list and the time you fix. Can you do that?"

She nodded. "I can do that. I have a pretty good memory. I guess I shouldn't say it, but I'm also the better surgeon."

"That's the truth," Sternberg nodded. "She's been highly recommended. She also was in the last surgery class I taught at our old medical school before it was unaccredited."

"That's right," Dr. Blaine brightened. "Now, this one here was a surgeon's dream. Very meticulous and skilled. His surgery patients used to love him."

"You're a surgeon too?" Bob asked Sternberg.

Sternberg sat up straighter in his rickety chair. "Used to be. Then I had an accident and couldn't operate anymore. There are a lot of lawyers in my family, so I went to law school. I went so I could defend doctors and the work that they do. Protect them from piranha like, well, like you." He finished.

"Yeah. Okay," Bob said, adding, "You're welcome to sit in with Dr. Shaw. Good hire there."

Bob passed his card over to Dr. Blaine. "Get your timeline to me or to Mr. Sternberg as soon as possible. Here's my email." Bob motioned over to Gus and Tony.

"C'mon, Tony. Let's go see what Dr. Shaw remembers."

* * * * *

Bob got home after midnight to catch a few hours of sleep. The next morning, he woke up to chocolate brown eyes gazing into his. Dark brown hair with golden highlights draped over the adjoining pillow. Rancid breath wafted over him, and he jerked up.

"Bella! I told you, no sleeping on the bed!" he shouted.

His dog just thumped her tail and licked the hand still on the bed. Bella gingerly gripped her favorite stuffed bunny in her teeth and nudged it over to Bob.

Bob sat on the edge of the bed, absently petting the dog. His five o'clock shadow had turned into long, dark bristles dotted with gray.

"Let's go make breakfast, Bella," he said. Bella bounded off the bed and click-clacked down the hall to the kitchen. Bob followed more slowly.

His cell phone buzzed. He reached out and pushed the button to answer. "Bob," he answered. "What's up?" He moved around on autopilot, making his drip coffee from his favorite coffee maker. A Keurig stood on the counter, gathering dust. He usually hung his dish towel on it.

"Bob? This is Gloria. How are you?" she asked.

"Tired. We're no closer to solving the murder case—cases—than we were on day one." His voice softened. "I miss you. I really do."

"I miss you, too," Gloria whispered back. "Why don't I come up there and take you to dinner tonight? You have to eat sometime, and I'll just bring my laptop and get some work done while I wait for you, or I could cook."

"You know it could be late. I don't have a specific time to give you."

"That's alright. I'll bring my overnight bag, okay?"

"That's more than okay, that's... Thanks, Gloria. I'll leave the key under the old flowerpot. You know, the one without flowers on the porch. Bella will be in the kitchen or out in the back yard."

"Be safe," she said.

"Love you," he said after she'd hung up.

Bella clanged her metal bowl. "I know, I know," Bob said, grabbing the big sack of dog food. He stopped and went back to the pantry. "Here's some of the wet food you like. Gloria's coming. Let's celebrate a little." His dance steps petered out as he surveyed the kitchen. *Oh damn. Gloria's coming, and the house looks like a hurricane hit it.*

CHAPTER THIRTY-THREE

Gus pulled the gauzy pink organza away from her neck for the third time. The stiff fabric scratched. The ruffles at the neck rubbed a red spot under her chin. She was beginning to regret agreeing to be Katie's bridesmaid, but how she could say no?

"Hold still," the seamstress snapped. She was pulling pins out of the old-fashioned pin cushion she wore on her wrist, even though she had a few in her mouth. She'd been trying to get the dress's hem pinned up on the diminutive Gus.

"This frou-frou itches," Gus shot back.

Katie looked on and tried not to laugh while her bridesmaid had her final fitting.

Gus narrowed her eyes at Katie and muttered to herself.

Mrs. Davis was on cloud nine. The "girls" had invited her along for the final fittings, and she couldn't sit still. She went from the front of the store, bringing back ludicrous hats and bags, to the back where she kept up a running monologue on the virtues of peonies over roses and irises over gardenias.

Katie's mother had generously ceded her place at the wedding dress and bridesmaid's dress fitting in favor of working in her garden, trying to get the aforementioned peonies to cooperate in time for the wedding. She and Katie had their own moment a few weeks earlier when Katie first tried on wedding dresses.

Mrs. Davis put a hand over her heart and mercifully stopped talking when it was Katie's turn for her fitting.

Katie's dress was white with lace at the throat and sleeves. The train was short, but the matching veil was long and matched the dress's lace. Katie's long brown tresses were caught up underneath the veil in diamond clips that her mother had worn on her own wedding day.

Tears spilled down Buck's mother's cheeks. She clasped the much shorter Gus to her ample bosom because she couldn't crush Katie's dress. Even Gus stood still for a minute, admiring Katie.

Gus was the first to break the spell. "Girl, Buck is gonna cry like a baby when he sees you walking down the aisle."

Mrs. Davis nodded and wiped her tears with the tissue she'd been handed by the seamstress. "You've made it the perfect dress, Terry Lou," Mrs. Davis said to the young seamstress who was beaming like a proud new mother.

Katie gave her a one-armed hug, careful not to crush the white fabric. "Terry Lou, you're a miracle worker. You've made me look like a real bride," Katie added with a watery smile.

"Okay, girls. Somebody come get me outta this gown. I can't breathe with all of this fabric, and I feel naked without my gun," Gus said from inside the pink confection.

Terry Lou frowned at Gus but helped her out of the long fuchsia gown.

"Whew," Gus said. "I hope I remember how to walk in heels."

"You've got a couple of weeks to practice," Katie said. "I bet that hunk you're married to will take you to a fancy dinner just to see you in a dress."

Gus laughed. "Yeah, probably."

Mrs. Davis took the pile of hats and bags she'd accumulated back to the front of the store, still sniffing into her tissue.

Terry Lou looked at Katie, then jerked her head toward Mrs. Davis's back. "Is she going to make it through the ceremony?"

"Yes. She'll be in her element, and she'll have her two boys, Buck and Jeb, there to lend support. She didn't have any daughters to raise, and her only sister had boys. I think she's just a little emotional today." Katie started toward the fitting room but turned to Gus at the last minute. "How about pouring us some of the champagne? I'm off for the rest of the day, and Mrs. Davis should enjoy some too."

"I can do that," said Gus, moving toward the chilled bottle in a silver champagne bucket. "I'm officially off duty, too. The Bureau owes me, and it's time to celebrate," she said, clinking her glass with Katie's. They sipped in silence a few minutes. "Can't wait to see ol' Buck and Jeb in tuxedos. They probably clean up pretty good," Gus said.

"Oh, now I'll be the one getting teary," Katie sniffed.

"Go and get out of that dress before you ruin it," Gus said. "I'm pouring the bubbly. Here, Mrs. Davis, have a glass."

* * * * *

Meanwhile, in the Oxford Formal House, Buck and Jeb eyed each other suspiciously.

"Jeb, I don't think that's what Katie had in mind for formal wear," Buck said, gesturing to his brother's deep purple tails and top hat.

"What's wrong with it?" Jeb asked, trying to see the back of his ensemble in the three-sided mirror. "I saw some Duke wearing this outfit at the last coronation. I think Katie would like it," Jeb said, frowning.

The little old tailor rolled his eyes. They'd been at it for an hour.

The tailor had taught math in middle school to both boys before he quit teaching and bought the Oxford Formal Wear Shop. The two were like his own—but more irritating—children.

"Look, Buck. I know you've been busy with your law practice and all, but we're getting down to the wire to order something—with expedited shipping—for your wedding," the tailor said to Buck and then turned to Jeb. In frustration, he was starting to lose the faux British accent he'd adopted once he'd opened the clothing store.

"Jeb, I don't know what you've been doing other than obsessing over the king's coronation, but I've known Katie and her family for a long time. She won't like the purple. Trust me."

Jeb sighed. "But I look good in this color." Jeb had pulled back his long curly hair and tied it with a matching purple ribbon. He tied a lavender ribbon on the ebony cane he was brandishing, too. "I gotta look good walking Katie down the aisle," Jeb insisted.

"No one's going to be looking at you," the tailor snapped. "Wear a purple suit to the rehearsal dinner. You'll be fine."

Jeb stared open-mouthed at the man. Buck tried not to laugh at Jeb's wounded face.

The tailor clapped his hands. "Great. It's decided. You'll both wear morning suits. Jeb, you'll have the tails that you wanted, and Katie can hold her head up in this town when you all are dressed up to look like somebody and not a carnival side show." The old man smiled at them. "Now, where are the other idiots I need to measure for this wedding party? We're running out of time."

Johnson walked through the door while the owner was ringing up the rentals. "Sorry, guys. Got caught up at the Sheriff's Office."

"No problem. Here's the morning suit we'll be wearing. You just need to get measured." Buck said, holding up the sample.

Buck turned to the owner. "Meet Sergeant Johnson, the Man of Honor."

The owner groaned, eying Johnson's formidable girth. "You didn't tell me one of the suits would be special order," he said peevishly while circling Johnson and looking at his broad back and biceps.

"You're gonna need to get his from the Big and Badass shop," Jeb said.

Johnson laughed and slapped Jeb on the back, nearly sending him flying. You've got a weird sense of humor," he said. "That's why I like you. And Katie seems to like you. She has a soft spot for all kinds of stray animals. We have a cat that she brought to the Sheriff's office that we can't get rid of. Reminds me of you: cute face but totally vacant in the brain box."

* * * * *

Bob spent over an hour cleaning up the house for Gloria's visit. He'd even put the dog bed in the washer and was waiting for it to come out of the dryer. Bella was guarding the dryer in case someone tried to snatch the bed. "So, what do you think, Bella? I should ask her, right?" Bob said.

He'd spent the last twenty minutes debating the merits of asking Gloria to go with him to Buck and Katie's wedding with Bella. Bella had been a good listener, but not much help in the advice department.

"Damn," Bob muttered, looking at the time on his cell phone. He was already fifteen minutes late for the meeting he'd set up with Tony. They'd agreed to meet at Donna's Donuts to spread out their notes and talk through everything. This time of morning, everyone else would be at work. The older retired guys might be nursing a second cup of coffee, but they couldn't hear anything. He texted Tony and pulled the warm dog bed out of the dryer. Bella lay down and put her head on her paws with a satisfied sigh.

When Bob arrived at the drugstore and Donut shop, there was a table of retirees he nodded to, and in the back, he caught a glimpse of Tony and Dr. Patterson. Bob slowed his steps a little when he saw that they were holding hands.

Seeing Bob, Dr. Patterson took his hand from Tony's. He stood up and said, "Well, see you guys later. I'm heading to Chapel Hill. Hope you guys have more success today."

Bob wished him a good morning and slipped into the chair vacated by the big Texan. "When were you going to tell me?" Bob asked.

"Tell you what?" Tony said.

"That you and the good doc are more than friends."

"Oh, for God's sake, Bob. You sound like my virgin aunt. And, for your information, we're taking things slowly. We're 'more than friends' as you put it, but I don't know exactly what we are yet. I'm afraid to put a label on it." Tony kept his eyes on Patterson's wide back as he strode from the drug store.

"Hmm," Bob grunted while Doris poured his coffee into a large cup sitting on a partially discolored saucer which had probably once been white. Maybe before Sherman came through Oxford on his way to Richmond. "How are you doing, Doris?" Bob asked.

"Poorly, Bob," she answered, putting her hand on her ample polyester-clad hip. "My back's acting up and the bunions on my feet are big enough to sink the Titanic." She pointed to her ace bandaged and sandal-clad feet, which Bob dutifully studied.

"Sorry to hear it, Doris."

Tony shuddered out of her eyesight. Bob glared at him once Doris left. "That's no way to treat people, Tony," Bob growled.

"I'm sorry for her ailments," Tony said, "But really, those shoes, they should have been burned years ago. I think the last time they were in fashion, the priests at the Inquisition were wearing them."

Bob sighed. "Let's get to it."

Tony pointed to the folders stacked on the heavy table. "We've talked to everyone on shift at the hospital. Doctor Graham has an okay alibi. The rector's murder doesn't match up with the murder of the women, so we don't know if it's the same perp or not. And the rector wasn't really left in pieces. And his is the only pet that was taken, if it was taken. We're running out of leads," he said morosely. "And, to make it all worse, the Chief wants to do a press conference. What in the hell do we have to say?"

Bob smiled his thanks at Doris, who had handed him his "usual." He bit into the soft, buttery biscuit and savored the bite of mayonnaise and fried bologna.

Tony eyed him in disgust. "That's not good for your waistline," Tony began.

"Criticizing people before their first cup of coffee isn't good for your health," Bob said. "We need to go back over the statements of the hospital staff. The perp is skilled with a knife. Where is anyone better skilled with a knife located other than at a surgery or a taxidermist?"

"Maybe a hunter?" Tony added.

"I'm worried we're not going to be able to stop this killer before he strikes again. Sarge can't keep up with the calls and people coming by the station who think they have seen or heard something suspicious. Can't blame 'em."

A high-pitched scraping noise interrupted their conversation. Both looked up as Judge Jones hauled one of the ancient ice cream parlor chairs up to their table. The jurist and the black wrought iron chair shook in unison.

"Good morning, your Honor," Bob began.

"Is it? You boys need to find that killer and fast. My assistant and law clerk are refusing to come with me to court in this district until this killer is caught. My law clerk won't leave the office. Only gets takeout at lunch. She's scared witless."

Tony looked at Bob. The judge's law clerk was witless. She could type and answer a phone, but that was about it. The old judge could hardly see what she typed, so he wasn't too picky.

"We're working on it, sir. The Sheriff sent staff over to help us out," Bob said while moving the files out of the judge's way.

"What's that you're eating, boy?" the judge asked Bob, eying his biscuit.

"Bologna biscuit."

The judge narrowed his rheumy blue eyes, then turned around to beckon to Doris. "I'll have me one of those," he said, pointing to the biscuit, "And a black coffee. Put mine on the Detective's tab."

Bob smiled at Tony's affronted expression, which he hid from the judge.

"Now, what's happening in court today?" Bob asked.

"Well," said the judge, "We've got us a love story. Ol' boy broke up with ol' girl, then ol' boy wanted her back, and to show her his undying love and devotion, he beat the tar out of her."

"That's terrible," Tony said.

"Yup, it is. Because ol' girl went and got her a double aught shotgun and cleaned ol' boy's clock."

"Did he die?" Tony gaped at him.

"Naw, he didn't. But he wishes he had of."

A few minutes later, after spreading biscuit crumbs all down his suit coat and across the table, the judge shuffled out toward the courthouse.

"That guy is a character," Tony said.

"He's been on the bench a long time. Since God was a little boy. You should meet his twin brother," Bob said.

"No way there are two of them."

"Oh, yeah. And the other one has no filter."

The two got up and Bob paid Doris at the relic of a cash register. A couple of the buttons stuck, but she wrestled them out and finished the transaction. The two headed to the department to re-read the witness statements and to try to talk the Chief out of a noon press conference.

* * * * *

The Oxford police responded to the anonymous caller's complaint about a dog barking. The landlord met Officers Alston and Muhammed downstairs. Wiping tomato juice off his pants from his lunch, the landlord pushed aside bikes and a few boxes to let them in the tiny office. A window unit barely cooled the stagnant air which was redolent of soy sauce and some sour smell. Take out containers overflowed the trash can.

"What's going on?" Officer Alston asked.

The landlord shrugged and lit a cigarette. "I got someone calling about a dog barking all day, and we don't allow no dogs on the premises. Dogs dirty everything up," he said, not meeting their eyes.

Alston looked pointedly at the disheveled reception desk and papers scattered on the floor.

The landlord continued undeterred. "Near as I can tell, it's coming from the second floor. Only apartment let up there is leased to a doctor. Lemme see," he said, consulting a worn index card. "Yeah, Doctor Klonsky. One of them foreign dudes." He snuck a glance over to Officer Muhammed, who stared back. "Uh, not like, you know, foreign dudes are bad or anything…" he trailed off.

Officer Alston turned away from him in disgust, and both officers headed for the second floor.

The stoop outside the apartment, next to the apartment's entrance, had a small dog crate occupied by one scraggly mutt who whined and pawed at the officers. The dog had pushed his water bowl and dog food bowl through a few broken slats.

"Oh, for Pete's sake," Alston muttered.

Muhammed opened the door and handed the dog to Alston while he put the bowls back into the crate.

Alston scratched behind the dog's ears, which blissfully stopped his high-pitched whine. White dog hair clung to his blue uniform. "Damn," he said.

"What?" Muhammed asked, getting to his feet.

"I thought this mutt looked familiar," he said. "It's got the rector's name and phone number on the collar."

"The rector that was killed?" Muhammed asked.

"One and the same. Better radio it in," Alston said.

CHAPTER THIRTY-FOUR

I stop on my way to work when I see her through the large window. The gauzy curtains are only partially closed. I see her trying on her wedding gown. I hear her laughter. I recognize that voice.

She'll make a beautiful bride. Her long, shiny brown hair caught up in beautiful combs that wink in the morning light. Her lithe form is surprisingly curvy in the clinging wedding gown. Ah, what a vision.

I want to linger, to drink in the sight of her, but I wouldn't be able to explain away my interest if someone stops to chat. And someone always stops to chat. Maybe a small town wasn't the brightest idea for a place to hunt, but I've been tired of the big city life.

Here come those two bumbling Oxford detectives headed, no doubt, to the police station where they'll continue to scratch their heads.

They don't even look at me. They're talking and laughing about something else.

I'm even carrying my bag. The one with the sharp, sharp knives.

CHAPTER THIRTY-FIVE

Bob and Gloria savored perfectly grilled steaks and a salad Gloria had made with goat cheese, pecans, and strawberries. Gloria even whipped together a citrusy salad dressing. Bob hardly tasted anything because he was drinking in his fill of Gloria.

They'd laughed over some of their family vacations when things hadn't always gone smoothly, like the camping trip in torrential rain and the beach trip complete with jellyfish swarming the ocean waters.

"Bob, you need to try this stuffed baked potato. It's delicious," Gloria said.

Bob started, feeling his phone vibrate. He listened as dispatch replayed the 911 call for him. "Oh, damn," he said.

"Get it. Don't worry about me. I've got Bella to entertain me." Bella continued to stare at her soulfully.

Bella parked herself at the edge of Gloria's chair, hoping for a dropped morsel, and wagged her tail when she heard her name.

Bob called Tony, who replayed the call for him, and went to get his holster and jacket. He bent down and kissed Gloria. "Hope I'm back soon."

"I'll keep your dinner warm," she said.

* * * * *

Bob and Tony met at the vacant lot described by the caller in the 911 call.

"What exactly did they say?" Bob asked Tony.

"I think it was a woman's voice saying that her boyfriend had a knife and she needed help out here at the ball field." Tony scanned the empty field, which was dimly lit by streetlights.

"I don't see anyone," Bob said, peering into the dark. The patrol officers who had arrived ahead of the detectives were just coming back from searching the area with high-powered flashlights. "It seems odd, doesn't it?"

"How so?" Tony asked.

"We don't get many prank calls. Not here. No colleges in the town for college kids to yank our chains. The nursing homes don't let their residents use the phone unsupervised."

"We couldn't find anyone, sir," the first patrolman said.

His partner piped up. "Nothing out there except mosquitoes and mites." He scratched vigorously at his arms.

Bob turned to the first officer. "Get 911 on the phone and ask them to replay that call for us on speaker phone."

The four stood over the patrol car listening to the call. The 911 caller sounded muffled, but the caller also sounded scared and described her boyfriend and the knife.

"It sounds like a female, but you can't be sure," Tony said.

"I don't know," Bob began.

A third patrolman began running back to the cars.

"Sir, sir, I found something!" he shouted while waving a piece of paper. He'd had the foresight to put gloves on before he picked up the paper.

Everyone gathered around Bob as he read the note out loud.

"You've come on a fool's errand. The real target is one of yours! Who is the fool now?"

"What the hell does that mean?" Tony asked.

"It means he's going after somebody else, and this was a distraction."

"What is *one of ours*?"

Bob and Tony looked at each other.

"Katie!" they said at the same time. Everyone scrambled for their cars and turned blue lights on, headed to Katie's house.

Bob pushed Tony away from the driver's door, and Tony barely got seated in the passenger seat before Bob sped off. "Call Buck," Bob snapped.

"That's not protocol," Tony said.

"Damn protocol. That's his fiancée. Maybe, please to God, she's with him."

Tony hit a button and got Buck. "Hey, Buck. Is Katie there? I needed to speak to her," Tony said, trying to keep the tremor out of his voice.

"Hey, Tony. No, Katie's at her house. She said she needed time to organize her trousseau and that she didn't need me standing around to do it. Everything okay?"

"Yeah, yeah. Fine. Okay. Thanks."

Bob turned his head to glare at Tony. "You call that boy back and tell him what we suspect. Tell him we're sending a patrol car over to her house and to his house. Then do it."

"Okay, boss." Tony redialed Buck's number.

"Um, Buck? We think someone may be targeting Katie. Yeah, we've got a patrol car headed out to her house and to you. Hopefully, it's just a crank message that someone left us. Whoa, whoa.

No, don't go anywhere, just stay tight. We're on the way to her place now."

Bob could hear Jeb's voice coming from Buck's phone.

"Jeb, hey, yeah, we think someone's playing a mean joke. Well, we're hoping that's what it is. No, damn it, don't load up your guns and go over. Let us handle it. Keep off the phone until we call back," Tony shouted. He was sweating. "That crazy Jeb is gonna go over to Katie's armed to the hilt," he said.

Bob glanced over. "No, he won't. Buck'll talk him out of it. Jeb's a mean shot, though. He can knock a hummingbird out of a tree from a hundred yards away."

"Why would someone do that?"

"Just an expression, Tony. Calm down. We're a minute away."

They heard on the radio that the patrol car had arrived at Buck's and Jeb's house on Main Street.

Bob slid the car into park as dirt spewed from the tires where he'd half missed Katie's driveway. The historic farmhouse was dark except for one light burning in the back.

"I wonder if Charles is here with Katie," Bob muttered.

"Who's Charles?" Tony asked.

"Buck's dog. Named after Charles Barkley. I should've had you ask him about the dog. That dog adores Katie. He'll rip up anyone who tries to get near her, though."

Guns out and at the low ready, they crouched down and silently approached the house. One motion sensor light illuminated a good-sized wraparound porch in the front. It was pitch black dark on the sides of the house. They paused a few seconds each time after going about ten feet to listen. Nothing except crickets and the low moan of a far-off owl.

Bob waved Tony around to the back of the house.

Tony whisper-screamed: "Shouldn't we wait for backup?"

Bob shook his head and motioned for Tony to get ready.

"Okay. I'm going," Tony said.

Three minutes later, the two breached the front and back doors. The doors splintered. No yelling or gunshots. Nothing.

A huge yellow Lab lay unmoving on the den floor at Tony's feet. As Tony crouched closer to the dog, he saw the animal taking shallow breaths. Tony let out the breath he didn't know he'd been holding.

Bob cleared the kitchen and then, with dread, approached the bedroom. He scrubbed the sweat off his face with his sleeve.

The bedroom was empty, and so was Katie's holster, which was hanging on a quaint four-poster bed. Her uniform was neatly folded on a nearby chair. There were signs of a struggle—broken glass, ripped clothing, blood spatter—and what looked like a pool of blood on the knotty pine wood floor. The smell of chloroform permeated the air.

Bob called in for backup and the crime scene techs, stressing it was for one of theirs and to "goddamn hurry if you know what's good for you." He walked out to the den. "Tony. The bastard's got her. He's taken Katie."

Tony gently scooped up the heavy Lab. He opened what was left of the old door wordlessly with his shoulder and took Charles to the back seat of their patrol car. He covered Charles in a soft blanket and cracked the window for him.

* * * * *

Bob dreaded making the call but knew he had to, protocol be damned. The boy had a right to know what was happening. "Buck?"

"Yeah, hey, Bob. I've tried Katie on her cell. She doesn't answer. Okay. Look. We think there's a situation here."

"Quit the damn police talk. Where's Katie?!"

"We're at her house out on Tar River Road. She's not here. There's been a struggle. Stay where you are. And for God's sake, don't let Jeb loose with his shotgun or rifle. Y'all got to be interviewed first. Sit still for two seconds and keep Jeb inside. I'm sending a detective out to you to take your statements. Stay put."

Silence.

"We're staying here until your detective rolls up and we make a statement. Then we're going to go find Katie, and you can stick your procedure up your ass," Buck growled.

Jeb, who'd been standing inches away, grabbed Buck's phone. "Bastard's got Katie. He's a dead bastard," Jeb shouted at Bob through his tears and hung up before Bob could say anything more.

"Damnit!" Bob yelled in frustration. "Yep. One dead bastard if he's touched Katie." Bob muttered to himself. He wiped his suddenly moist eyes on his sleeve. He needed to keep it together. He needed his wits to help find her.

He'd completely forgotten Gloria. He sent her a quick text. She sent back a heart emoji, and he smiled. His smile disappeared while he waited for the slow crime scene techs to get to Katie's house. He called his contact at the FBI, told him it was an emergency, and asked them to send an agent. Once he'd explained it and told them it was one of their Task Force Officers, the Bureau promised him three agents and an hour's turnaround.

He dreaded calling Gus because she was so close to Katie. She'd want to be in on it and they couldn't let her. He also had to call Johnson. That call was going to be even worse.

Tony sure is taking a long time getting the dog settled. Gotta give the boy some time to get his feelings under control, he admonished himself.

CHAPTER THIRTY-SIX

Katie spat blood at her abductor through the hole he'd left when he'd struck her so hard in the jaw that her tooth shot out. The pain was excruciating.

"You're a worthless piece of crap. Preying on defenseless women and setting up this, this gruesome…" Katie stopped, at a loss for words as to what "this" was.

Fortunately, the light inside was low, and she could only glance at the room through the slits where her eyes were puffed up. He'd smacked her there first, while she slept, so that each eye was almost swollen shut. Then he'd put the chloroform pad over her mouth and nose. She'd gotten in some jabs trying to get it off. That's the last thing she remembered.

She started crying, not for herself, but for Charles. The bastard laughed as he told her how he'd killed Charles and cut his limbs off. Buck's beautiful, sweet dog, which would never hurt a fly, no matter how many training classes Buck took him to, hoping for a fierce guard dog.

She couldn't even wipe her eyes. Her hands and arms were bound behind her with duct tape, and she was starting to lose feeling in them.

He stayed in the shadows, taunting her, not letting her see his face.

Unwillingly, her eyes kept returning to "this."

She was seated at a long mahogany table inlaid with another wood. The massive table could easily accommodate twelve. Most of the chairs were full.

One chair held a woman's head set on several cushions. One chair held another woman's leg. Each chair, except hers, held a different body part. She shuddered. Katie couldn't let herself think about it, or she'd lose her mind. She consciously steadied her breathing.

The room was permeated by the smell of rotting flesh and formaldehyde. A silver candelabra adorned the table, and the white candles' flames wavered in the stale air. A cut crystal bowl held pride of place in the center. Each "guest" had a place setting of formal china, sterling silver cutlery, and empty goblets.

Oh, my God. That's Michelle, she screamed inside, staring at the closest chair with the head. The long hair draped over the armrests appeared to be curled and styled. And the smell—the smell was some combination of decay and disinfectant.

I can't be sick, I can't be sick, she repeated like a mantra.

"Not so tough now, are you, Lieutenant?" he said from the shadows. "You're just a scared little bitch—like the rest of my guests." He gestured to the macabre scene at the table.

"You'll be joining them soon, permanently," he whispered.

She squinted to try to see better through her half-shut eyes. He was only a shape in the gloom. Using the door frame behind him as a point of reference, she estimated his height to be around six feet, and that's as much as she could see. The voice was unidentifiable. He was using a voice synthesizer to scramble it.

"I think you'll be my last in this town. My *piece de resistance* as it were..."

Whatever he'd given her in the glass of water was starting to work. She felt woozy and so, so tired.

"That's right, princess, sleep, sleep now," she heard him say in a disembodied voice from far away. She felt like she was sliding into a deep, dark hole.

"Wouldn't want you to go to pieces just yet," he added with a long laugh.

CHAPTER THIRTY-SEVEN

Jeb jumped into the passenger seat of their dilapidated old Mustang. Buck slid in and cranked it. He'd looked in the back and saw three long guns, one of which was an assault rifle. Jeb shrugged and held on to his Beretta. In a bag at his feet were the extra rounds Buck had stuffed in along with his pistols, an old Browning Hi-Power, a Luger, and a M1911.

Neither man said anything. They didn't have to. Their thoughts were focused on finding Katie and getting her away from whatever mad person had her. That person wouldn't have long to live once they extricated her.

After the officers had taken their statements separately, both men dressed hurriedly in dark clothing and smeared eye black on their faces.

Jeb had spent all winter on the old car so that its muffler didn't make a sound. It had a lot of horsepower, which Buck took advantage of to get to Katie's house in record time. He parked on the road so no one would look in and see their arsenal. They met Bob a few feet up the drive. "What's going on? What're y'all doing to find Katie," Buck demanded.

Bob looked at the younger man for a second, noting his blood-shot eyes and swollen lids. "I told you and your crazy brother to stay out of this. You need to leave," Bob said, using his most serious voice.

Buck used all of his six-feet-five-inches frame to crowd the detective. "Fuck that, Bob. My fiancée's missing. We're staying with you, or we're going out to hunt for her ourselves."

Bob stood his ground and glared up at him and Jeb. Before Bob could respond, three men wearing black shirts with FBI emblazoned in gold on them stepped up. The one in front put his hand out, trying to diffuse the argument. "Whoa, now. Take it easy. We're here to work together with the police and the Sheriff's Office. No civilians," the agent started.

Buck glared at him, then spotted Dr. Fulcher cowering behind the three. "Fulcher! You're a goddamned idiot! You couldn't lead a dog to a pile of shit! You need to fucking tell us who has Katie!" Buck screamed.

Jeb put his arm gently around Buck and drew him backward a little, watching the agents' hands move toward their firearms. "C'mon, man. Let's go over and get Charles. Tony says he's in the back of the cruiser over there," Jeb said, turning Buck toward the car and eyeing each agent in turn, letting them know this was just a brief reprieve.

When the two walked away, Bob looked at the agents who, to be fair, had arrived in record time from Raleigh. The Henderson police officers, who picked up the alert on the scanner, were talking quietly amongst themselves a little further up, closer to the house, and looking over a Granville County map with the Sheriff's deputies. They'd kept their heads down after Jeb and Buck leaned in the doorway of the cruiser to pick up a sleeping Charles.

The Sheriff looked beat. He was almost sixty-five and heavy with a good-sized gut, and just two months from retirement. He had hoped to ease his way quietly through to the goal line. He'd bought a small fishing boat and promised his wife of thirty years a nice vacation. He was holding it together pretty good and getting ready to leave with a detective to visit Katie's mother in person.

Bob didn't envy the Sheriff. Katie's mom was just as likely to get her firearm and join Buck and Jeb as to stay quietly at home, worrying about her daughter.

"Tony!" Bob bellowed, scanning the groups of men.

"Right here," Tony answered a few feet behind him.

"Call the hospital. See if they're missing any staff—a doctor or surgeon—tonight."

"Got it," Tony said on the run to get his cell phone from the police car.

Dr. Fulcher cleared his throat to get the detectives' attention.

"What is it?" Bob said to the man cowering behind an agent.

"I think I can be of service." Dr. Fulcher said, pushing up the square black glasses sliding down his pointed nose. His shirt was rumpled, and his tie was sticking out of his shirt pocket.

"Well, you sure haven't been so far. What is it?" Bob glared.

"Yeah, um, well, I got these things on Amazon and I went over to the hospital a couple of days ago, and…" he trailed off, realizing he had an audience.

Dr. Fulcher looked at the FBI agents leaning closer with every word.

"Um, detective, might I have a word with you alone?" he asked.

Bob sighed. "Yeah, okay, but hurry it up."

When the agents walked over to the group of crime scene techs coming out of Katie's house, Dr. Fulcher continued. "Yes, well, see, I um…"

"Jesus, Mary, and Joseph," Bob screamed, his Boston accent thickening with his mounting frustration. "Get it out already, Fulcher!"

"I put trackers on all of the surgeons' cars. I can track them on my computer, which I brought with me."

Bob glanced over at the agents to make sure they weren't listening. "No shit?"

"No, detective. I know it's a little out of the ordinary realm of procedure," Fulcher started.

"Fulcher, it's in another fucking universe, but I could kiss you for it. Bring up that screen."

* * * * *

Jeb crouched low in the brush and shrubs a few feet away and overheard the exchange between law enforcement. No one was looking in his direction as everyone was hunched over maps and holding flashlights. In this part of the county, the roads were devoid of streetlights, and neighbors were several acres apart.

He stayed down and crab-walked back to where Buck was sitting on the ground. Before he could tell his brother what he'd overheard, he hit something hard. "Ouch, what the—" Jeb said, rubbing his shoulder.

"Jeb, it's me, Emma Jean," he heard a soft female voice say. Jeb looked over at Buck, who just shrugged, acting as if it was entirely normal for his legal assistant to be sitting with them at the bottom of the front yard in the pitch dark.

"Emma Jean. What the hell you doin' out here?" Jeb asked.

"I heard from my cousin Gracey Mae, who heard from her neighbor, who's a deputy goin' on now for about two months, and he really likes it there at the Sheriff's Office, and the girl who does my aunt's hair said—" Emma Jean began.

Catching the glint off her shotgun, which Emma Jean was waving while she talked, Jeb reached out a hand and gently eased the barrel away, so it didn't point in his or Buck's direction.

Buck intervened. "Emma Jean. I appreciate you wanting to be here, but why don't you go on home, and I'll call you just as soon as we know anything."

"Nope. I'm gonna help find Katie and these boys here," she said, nodding toward the FBI agents standing a few feet away, "don't know the county like I do.

"Besides, my neighbor up the road said that the FBI profiler right there," pointing to Dr. Fulcher, "don't know his ass from first base, and so I figure you all could use some help," she finished for a minute.

"But look, Buck, we gotta find her fast," Emma Jean continued. "That butcher has hurt these young women mighty bad, and we don't want that for our Katie. I got a list from my aunt-in-law, Myrtle, what works at the hospital, and it's got all the surgeons with addresses and telephone numbers, and even the contract surgeons are on it. We should start there. Following up on who's home and all."

"Yeah. Fulcher said he put trackers on every surgeon's car and they're loading up his computer program to find them," Jeb interjected when she paused for breath.

"Well, he ain't a complete dumbass, then," Emma Jean sniffed. Her strawberry-blond curls were tied up in a bandana, but one side was half off. Pine needles were stuck in her hair.

"Yes, he is. That's not FBI procedure, but fuck it, we need to be in on what they find."

Emma Jean laid her shotgun down and began walking toward the group of officers and deputies. They could see the back of Emma Jean's white short-shorts swishing from side to side. The group of officers parted at her approach.

"She could get information out of a turnip," Jeb observed.

"She's a really great legal assistant. Everyone loves her—the clients, the lawyers, even the court staff, but we gotta unload this shotgun of hers pretty quick. She's already broken half of my office furniture by falling into or over it," Buck said. "I don't want her shooting us by mistake."

"Good idea," Jeb said, cracking open the long gun and sliding out the shells. "While you hide her shells, I'll crawl back over to Bob and Fulcher."

"Thanks, Jeb. I mean it. Thanks for everything," Buck said.

"I want her back, Buck. I love her, too," Jeb said with a small smile.

His smile disappeared looking over Buck's shoulder. Johnson was striding toward the group of officers fast, and he looked pissed.

Johnson poked one agent in the chest. The FBI agent stood his ground and stared stonily at Johnson. "Why the hell didn't you cowboys call me about Katie? I had to hear it from the Sheriff. You bastards are going to get her killed advertising yourselves in these candy ass SUVs that scream *Feds*. Everybody knew who you were two minutes after you rolled into town," Johnson snarled.

"Look, deputy," the agent began.

"Sergeant," Johnson spat out.

"Sergeant. I don't know who you are, but you're interfering with an important operation," the agent continued.

"You'll need an operation to remove my foot from your ass, Agent," Johnson said.

"Oh, for the love of God," Bob murmured, then stood up and jogged over to try to prevent any violence.

Johnson rounded on him. "Why didn't you call me? It would've taken you fifteen seconds," he started in on Bob. "You know Katie's my boss and partner at work. I have to be in on this and help try to find her."

"I'm really sorry," Bob said. "I should have given you a call, but you're here now to give us a hand. Come over here with me and Jeb. We're wasting time."

"Buck's brother's here? I can't believe this shit," Johnson said.

CHAPTER THIRTY-EIGHT

They were spitting mad, every last one of them. Shouts of "I'll call my lawyer!" and "I'll sue your ass!" were repeated over and over. The two-man teams made up of Oxford and Henderson officers made quick work of the short list of surgeons and doctors working under contract at the hospital. They found most at home at dinner time. One or two were located at the local watering hole, Williamson's Brews and Booze, or at the one local non-fast-food restaurant, The Oak Room.

The surgeons had a point. Nowhere in the police, sheriff, or FBI procedure manual did it give directions for rounding up a group of people solely based on their profession or specialties, but they were running out of time to find Katie, and the FBI didn't know what the locals were doing, at least not yet.

Bob walked to the front of the conference room and addressed the angry group. When they ignored him, he shouted: "Shut up!"

The group of five men and four women shut up. They were in various stages of dress. Some were in workout clothes, some still in suits, and one was in his robe and pajamas. Each one glared at Bob.

The oldest among them, a silver-haired gentleman, still in his dark suit, trembled with rage. "This is outrageous!" he squawked. "You can't hold us here. What kind of ramshackle business is this?" His plummy accent placed him as a Harvard or Yale graduate.

Bob hated both schools equally. "Sir, respectfully, sit down!"

Stunned, without a word, the man folded into his seat.

Bob continued, "We have a situation. A female officer has been abducted. We need short statements from each of you."

"Alibis?" one young female surgeon spoke up.

"Yeah, something like that. We have enough officers here to take your statements, so you should be home within fifteen or thirty minutes, tops. Unless, of course, you want your lawyer. We'll get 'em here, but hey, it's Friday night. They're probably home for the day. They've probably had that first glass of bourbon. That's gonna cost you."

Harvard doc put his hand up.

"Yes, sir?"

"I'm glad to write out or give a statement. I'm guessing, though, you want to know who among us is missing? The general surgeons?"

Bob had to give it to the old guy. He was smart and had cut to the chase. "Sir, step over here to this corner desk and I'll take your statement myself."

* * * * *

Tony and Dr. Fulcher were in the hospital's parking lot checking all of the trackers on Fulcher's computer against the cars parked and elsewhere. All but two trackers were accounted for, with some in the lot and others at the doctors' confirmed residences.

"Two are parked a few miles away," Dr. Fulcher started. Dark purple circles had appeared under his eyes.

"Are the trackers together?" Tony asked.

"No, they are apart and stationary."

249

A bright light hit Tony in the eyes. At the other end of the flashlight was Gus. She was dressed all in black and had a gun in a holster on her side. Her FBI badge was clipped to her belt. "What the hell are you two doing here? What are you up to?" she asked, her tone quiet and more menacing with each question.

Tony started in on an update on the search for Katie. He briefed her on the trackers and the deployment of the backup FBI agents to the county.

Gus stared wordlessly at Tony, which made it worse than if she'd shouted at him. Fulcher shrank back against his seat.

She shone her light into the car and spotted Fulcher. "Fulcher! What the hell are you doing?"

"Um, er, well…" he stammered.

Gus opened the back door of the car and climbed in. Tony knew he should've locked the car.

"Give it to me," she demanded. Her clenched fists were the only things that betrayed her emotions.

Tony swallowed and laid out Fulcher's tracking plan and where the trackers were now.

Gus smacked the back of Fulcher's head. "You're an idiot, Ful-cher," she said.

"Well, I know, but—"

"But this may be genius," she added. "Text Bob about the two stationary ones, and let's go see the missing doctors or surgeons."

"You shouldn't be here," Tony started.

Gus could've bored a hole through him with just a look. "Neither should you nor Fulcher, with this tracker bullshit, but here you are. Let's go," she said, pulling on her seatbelt.

Tony texted Bob and then ignored the calls that Bob frantically placed to him. He finally entered the word *Gus*, and the calls stopped.

"I hope we don't get fired over this, going off on our own without backup, but Katie is more important than any job," Tony said.

"Yes, she is," Gus said. "And her time may be running out if she's with that knife-happy piece of crap."

The three rode on in silence.

* * * * *

Bob was going to kill Tony when he showed his face. Going off with Fulcher on a half- cocked plan? He felt a little better once he knew Gus was with them, but only a little. God only knew where Buck and Jeb had gotten to tonight. He couldn't worry about that now. He had a couple more interviews to do.

Sternberg showed up halfway through the interviews, all bluster and shouting at Bob. His suit coat was covered in animal hair and food stains. "I'm gonna have your badge, your retirement, and everything you own over this, detective!" he'd shouted in Bob's face.

"Sternberg, if we don't find our officer in the next few minutes, you can fucking have them," Bob shouted back, pushing the attorney away from him.

The doctors all looked up in surprise, but no one said anything.

Three names kept coming up in his and his colleagues' interviews with the group of doctors as potentially suspicious: Dr. Graham, Dr. Klonsky, and Dr. Sullivan.

Apparently, Dr. Graham imagined himself as a real "ladies' man," without regard for his engaged status, and the doctors eagerly made sure law enforcement knew about his misbehavior. As a brilliant surgeon who brought in major money, he'd only received a few mildly worded letters of caution from the hospital. Two of the women doctors in the room tonight had filed complaints against him for inappropriately grabbing them or their nurses.

Dr. Klonsky was foreign, vehemently hated the United States, and daily talked about returning to Eastern Europe when his contract was up, in a few days. That's about all it took to make his colleagues suspicious of him. They talked about how the patients hated Klonsky primarily because they couldn't understand a word he said, and he made no effort to try to communicate. He made no efforts to participate in the community. He biked everywhere and didn't have a car that anyone knew of.

Dr. Sullivan was a newer doctor to the staff, a contract surgeon who had graduated from med school up north in the last ten years. Sullivan had come in recently as part of a rural share program or something like that. Getting federal funding for his position was a real coup for the hospital.

Bob went over the list of hospital employees who had been interviewed with Sternberg. Bob furiously texted Tony: PICK ME UP IN FIVE.

Tony glanced down at the message on his cell phone and told Fulcher and Gus that they needed to head back to the hospital to pick up Bob.

They'd ridden past Dr. Graham's apartment complex and didn't see his vintage Saab in the parking lot. That was strange. Fulcher's tracker was showing that his car was in the lot. They kept circling and finally found the tracker stuck to an old Prius that was sitting in its parking spot on three wheels and a jack.

"Damn," Tony and Gus said at the same time. Tony immediately called the police station and told them to put out a BOLO or "be on the lookout" for Dr. Graham.

They rode back to the hospital in silence. When they arrived at the hospital's front entrance, Bob opened the back door. "Get out," he said to Gus.

"Nope. Not happening. Get in," she said, scooting over. "Better hurry," she said.

"Why's that?" Bob said, huffing and folding up his big frame to roll into the back seat.

Gus pointed to two black SUVs rolling up to the entrance.

"Because those contain some pretty angry FBI agents," she observed.

"Drive!" Bob yelled.

Buck and Jeb were in the dark Mustang in a corner of the hospital parking lot, away from the lights. Buck put the Mustang in gear to follow Bob and Tony's car again. They tailed it all over town, but no one had gotten out of the unmarked car, so they hung back. They finally talked Emma Jean into going back to the police station and organizing the large number of volunteers and Katie's mother into setting up a coffee and food station for the police officers, deputies, highway patrol, and FBI agents involved in the hunt for Katie.

Tony's Dad and Granddad texted Tony periodic updates as to what the word on the street was. Tony's Dad loved Katie because, about once a month, she'd bring over dinner for the two old men, and for Tony, if he was staying over. Charles and Buck came with her most of the time. Charles loved Pops because he kept treats on hand for the big Lab.

Katie also tried to convince Tony's dad to enter rehab in that nice soft way she had of talking. She hadn't given up on his dad like so many others had.

His father called Tony a minute later. "Tony," his dad said. "You gotta look hard for Katie. She's a good soul and she's been mighty kind to me and your Pops."

"I know, Dad—" Tony started,

"Your Pops and I are gonna do our part to try to find her. I'll call you if we hear anything."

"Dad, we've got this. Don't you and Pops go out where you shouldn't be to look for her. Bob and I are doing that right now."

There was a long silence on the phone. "Tony, I'm sorry… for everything," his dad said gruffly. "I haven't been easy on you. I didn't make it easy for you to be, well, yourself."

"I know you are Dad. We'll talk once we find Katie, okay? I have to go."

"Love you, son," Tony heard his father say after he'd partially pulled the cell phone away from his ear.

Bob couldn't see Tony's face from the back seat, but he heard part of the exchange. He awkwardly patted Tony on the shoulder. "Sounds like your old man is trying to meet you halfway," he started.

"Later," Tony said, staring straight ahead.

Regardless of Tony's warnings for his relatives to stay at home, the two older men were out shaking down the area drug dealers and their acquaintances for any information about Katie. Granddad was using his electric scooter to visit the elderly folks who were still part of the neighborhood. Those elderly ladies he visited used their churches as grapevines for information. No one had heard anything or knew where Katie was, but the dealers and their mules stopped business for the night and jumped into their cars to help. They patrolled the highways and main thoroughfares. Of all of the law enforcement officers and deputies in town, Katie had always treated everyone fairly, even those she was arresting, and had been polite to the dealers, the mules, and their families.

The pool halls and bars closed up early. Wait staff, dishwashers, and cooks all over the county also left work early, got on their motorcycles or into their borrowed cars, riding up and down the country roads. A few of the area's pastors started prayer chains for the missing lieutenant. Everyone was out either looking for Katie or praying for her safe return.

* * * * *

"Is the fair in town?" Bob asked after they'd passed another set of cars cruising down the road.

Tony mumbled something from the front seat.

"How's that?" Bob asked.

"I said, I heard some folks are out looking for Katie. They, uh, got wind of it on the scanner. A lot of folks like Katie," Tony trailed off. He was still looking at his cell phone.

"Tony. This is more than 'some folks.' Where the hell did all these people come from?"

Gus interrupted. "Bob, concentrate on what you're gonna say when we get to Dr. Klonsky's place. You need to focus. You and Tony go talk to him, and Fulcher and I will watch the trackers on the laptop."

The car pulled up in front of Klonsky's apartment. One streetlight weakly lit the parking lot, which was full of potholes and weeds where the pavement had cracked. A few cars and a few bicycles were parked outside.

Tony and Bob headed for apartment 2A, which was on the right side of the second floor. They side-stepped tricycles, empty boxes, and garbage. Most of the other exterior doors they'd passed had wreaths or decorations, but not Dr. Klonsky's door.

They listened for a minute. They could hear some talking, but couldn't tell if it was the doctor or the TV.

Tony knocked on the gray front door, which was smeared with red clay at the bottom, then yelled, "Police! Open up!"

The sound inside stopped. Heavy footsteps approached the door. They could hear the metallic rasp of a chain. A few seconds later, the door cracked open. The muzzle of a gun appeared.

"Down, down," yelled Tony.

"Gun!" Bob yelled.

Gus flew out of the car with her gun drawn and screamed, "I got you covered, I got you covered!"

A slender brown man slowly eased out of the door. He was wearing loose long pants and bedroom shoes. He looked at the three and shrugged, lowering the gun. "What? This is bad neighborhood. I not know if you really police. Why you come here?"

Everyone lowered their guns. Tony, Bob, and Dr. Klonsky talked quietly on the porch. He allowed them inside and invited them to look around. It was a no-frills one-bedroom apartment. The den had one sofa and one TV, which was playing a true crime show. They looked in every closet and under the bed.

Tony examined the knives in the kitchen and found some that might match the one used on the women. He quietly bagged them up to the sound of Dr. Klonsky's vigorous complaints. They found nothing else of interest to take or to convince them that a search warrant was needed.

"Nowhere to stash woman or women," he said, shrugging. "Plus, I am going home. See my boxes?"

They went through the partially packed moving boxes and found nothing of interest. Tony wrote a receipt for the knives they'd collected and handed it to the doctor. Dr. Klonsky balled it up and shoved it in his pants' pocket.

"You know," Klonsky said. "Dr. Sullivan, he is not *right*, as you all say."

"What do you mean by that?" Bob asked.

"He is creepy. He is loner and does not sit with doctors at lunch or break. He is always off polishing his pocketknife or Bowie knife. Looks like a machete."

Bob and Tony looked at him. Bob nodded for him to continue.

"I have a life," he said defensively. "My life is at home where my wife and young child are. I am giving up this fancy life for home. I save lot of money by living in this dump. Me and my family will be fine." He smiled in deprecation.

When they got to the parking lot, they saw Gus talking to Buck.

"Oh no," Bob said. "No. You guys go home. We'll call you as soon as we know something. I promise. This looks like a dead end here."

Tony agreed. "Klonsky's in a hurry to leave the country, but he doesn't have anything inside to incriminate himself. Just standard kitchen knives. We'll get them processed for prints or DNA, but I don't figure him for it."

"Yeah. Right. We wait for you two to cover the county by yourselves. We're wasting time talking," Buck said, slamming the car door.

Bob slammed the back passenger door of the unmarked car. "Damn it. He's right. We are spinning tires out here."

"Boss?" Tony said.

"What, Tony?"

"I got a lead on Dr. Graham. He's holed up at the Holiday Inn now with a nurse—actually two nurses. She's posted a video of the three of them partying, and it's time-stamped. Her roommate texted me and confirmed it's posted in real time. She's there too. Hold on. She's sending photos. A lot of booze, a lot of what appears to be cocaine, and a whole lot of Dr. Graham that I didn't need to see."

"Well, that drops him to the bottom of our list. Send a patrol over to take some statements and download that video. Wait, get one of the detectives to do it and have them take a patrolman as well. Let's go pay a visit to Dr. Sullivan. And, Tony?"

"Yeah?"

"See if you can lose the 'wanna be' NASCAR boys driving behind us in that Mustang on our way," Bob said, jerking his right thumb back over his shoulder.

"What about the feds?" Gus asked.

"Once we get out of town on the road to Sullivan's house, it shouldn't be hard to lose them, too. If we can't, it won't be much of a problem. At least they're trained to use a firearm."

* * * * *

"Uh oh," Fulcher and Gus said at the same time. Gus continued, "You're not going to like this. We just got some intel on our phones from the other agents."

"What?" Bob asked. He'd taken over driving, telling Tony he knew the county roads better. Tony slid into the front passenger seat without comment.

"This Dr. Sullivan? He isn't a doctor. Or, rather, he was a doctor, but he hasn't been for some time," Gus said.

"How did he show up here? How could the hospital hire him if he isn't a doctor?" Tony asked.

"I'm reading from an FBI communication. It says here, from the medical society records, that Dr. Sullivan's medical license was suspended three years ago. There's a summary about a civil suit he brought to get it back when the licensing board wouldn't reinstate him. Apparently, he lost that and was then charged with communicating threats and cyberstalking. The threats case was brought on behalf of his civil attorney, and the cyber stalking was charged by the investigators on behalf of the judge hearing the civil case. Both the attorney and the judge were female."

"So, he hates women attorneys," Tony mused.

"I'd say so. The report goes on: He brought a knife into the courthouse for his contempt hearing, which was related to the civil suit. He hid it in a metal scooter. He lied and said he had to have the scooter because he'd had a knee replacement. When they found the knife on him, he fought law enforcement and was jailed for forty-eight hours."

"I still don't get it. How did the hospital even hire him? Don't they check out their doctors?" Tony asked.

"I'm going to find out right now. Am texting the agent in charge to see if he can get the intel on how the doctor was hired and when, and anything else about him," Gus said.

Fulcher busily typed on his computer.

"I'm checking a few sites for more information myself," he said. "Usually, hospitals are very picky about their hires, but rural counties are medical deserts. Maybe they took whoever they could get to come to the hospital."

CHAPTER THIRTY-NINE

There was silence in the car while Bob searched for Sullivan's house number. Gus had pulled up a Google map, which showed the sprawling house, detached garage, and outbuildings sitting way off the county road by a small pond. She talked quietly to the federal agents, asking for any better intel on the house.

Bob had tried to drop Gus off earlier, but she refused to get out of the car. She also refused to join the new group of FBI agents. "I'm helping you find Katie so I can wear the goddamn ugly pink bridesmaid dress she picked out and see her and Buck married," she sniffed. "I'm going with you."

Bob had lost Buck and Jeb a few miles out of town. Bob was almost more worried that he didn't know where Buck and Jeb were than having them on his tail. He shoved that thought to the back of his mind, squinting in the dark at the dented and rusty black mailboxes on wooden stakes lining the road. Kudzu and Queen Anne's lace choked the drainage areas near the boxes. Honeysuckle filled in among the young deciduous trees and pines dotting the lots.

The FBI had peeled off to follow up on their emergency order for Katie's cell phone records and the cell phone records of the three suspects. The assistant US attorney promised he was committed to working all night to help out law enforcement in any way that he could. He'd wake up the federal magistrate on duty if something was needed. It was easier than involving the District Attorney since his office would disqualify their staff from prosecuting any crimes against a member of the Sheriff's Office.

After finally locating the house number, Bob slowed the car down to a crawl and shut off all but the parking lights.

"We need a plan," Bob said.

"What about—" Dr. Fulcher began.

"Any plan we make has you sitting your ass down in the car," Bob interrupted. He half-turned to Gus. "I'm worried that if Katie's even here, she could be in the garage or the outbuildings that show up on that map. There's only three of us to cover the ground. How do you want to handle it?" he asked.

"How about I go around on the far left, to the outbuildings, and work my way over to the house," said Gus. "You guys go to the main house and keep the Doctor occupied. We'll need some kind of signal in case I find her, or if you do."

"I think we should wait for backup," Tony started.

"Katie may not have time for us to wait," Bob interrupted.

Car lights lit up the back of the car, and the four hit the floorboards as best they could. The car drove slowly by and disappeared into the night.

"Tony, you're right," Bob said. "Call 911 for police backup and tell them no lights or sirens. Ask them to send two cars and wait for our signal before heading up the driveway. Gus, go ahead and start looking into the buildings. If you find anything, text Tony. Don't take any chances. Katie would have my hide if anything happens to you. We'll give you a five-minute head start, then we'll go up the drive.

"Tony, put your phone on silent and let's go up and talk to the doctor. Fulcher, you sit in the car and wait for the search warrant.

Sarge texted that he woke up Judge Jones and is getting him to sign one for Dr. Sullivan's house, property, and various buildings. Text Tony when you have it in your hand. Absent that or Armageddon, don't text him. Tell backup officers or agents where we are and tell them to approach the house cautiously. Assume he is armed and dangerous until we say he isn't. And assume he has a hostage."

Fulcher nodded vigorously, and Gus slipped out into the darkness. Despite the gravel road, she didn't make a sound. An owl hooted in the night, and the stars were dimmed by the cloud cover.

Bob and Tony waited a few minutes until she'd faded into the dark. They started up on either side of the drive, avoiding the gravel. The ground softened the sound of their footsteps. Without warning, hands clamped down over their mouths simultaneously, and each struggled until they heard Buck and Jeb whisper: "Stop it, it's us!"

"Well, this is my worst nightmare, finding you two out here," Bob seethed. "You better not mess this up."

"Goddamn it, Jeb, you scared the shit out of me," Tony growled.

"We'll go around back while you all talk to the doc out front. We'll sneak into the kitchen and wait for your signal to come into the house," Jeb said.

"You will not wait on my anything, you idiot," Bob said.

"We're staying," Buck said.

"Fantastic. I'll tell the Chief I got two civilians killed tonight," Bob said. "And you smell like the backside of a mule. What the hell is that?"

"That's the eye black we found in our sports stuff. We used it when we played football in high school. It's kinda old," Jeb said.

"Gross," Bob said.

"We're wasting time," Tony said.

Bob fumed for a minute, then turned to Buck and Jeb. "Okay. Go to the back. You got your cells?"

Buck nodded yes.

"Tony or I will text you one letter: G for go or S for stop. Got it? Don't move without my say so."

"Got it."

"Wait a minute. Are you armed?"

Buck and Jeb looked at each other.

"Not really," Jeb said.

"What the fuck is *not really*? Don't jerk my chain. You know what? No. I don't want to know. Do not get us or Katie killed. That's all I ask."

The brothers gave thumbs-up signs and moved off quietly toward the side of the house where they'd stashed an arsenal of firepower.

"If we get out of this alive and get Katie home, I'm going on vacation. A very long vacation. I might even retire. I am too old for this stuff," Bob said.

"I get it," Tony said. "This whole case has made me old."

* * * * *

The Sullivan house was a large, three-story stone and stucco home painted white with black shutters and a wide wraparound porch. A few wicker rockers moved in the slight breeze. There was an old coir welcome mat, and an umbrella stand in chipped blue pottery to the right of the door. The smell of freshly mown grass wafted on the breeze.

They waited just outside the light shining from the carriage lamp fixed on the side of the door. Hearing nothing from Gus for a few minutes, they mounted the steps and knocked on the door.

Almost immediately, they heard footsteps. Tony kept his firearm at the low ready, using Bob to block his position in case the visit proved fruitless.

"What a pleasant surprise," Dr. Sullivan said, opening the front door. A minute ago, he thought he'd heard something out front but figured it was the pack of raccoons that stole the cat food on a nightly basis, even though he didn't have a cat. Since everyone in the big neighborhood had one, he didn't want to stand out. So, he continued to fill the feeder, and the raccoons.

He looked like someone's favorite uncle in a blue button-down shirt, gray vest, and old navy cardigan. His reading glasses were propped up on his head, and he smelled faintly of cough syrup.

Fulcher texted Tony: "Search warrant here."

Tony turned a little to the side to text Fulcher to send Sarge up to the front and to bring both his gun and the search warrant.

"Well, now," Bob started, using his friendliest fake southern voice. "Hate to bother you, Doctor. May we come inside?"

Dr. Sullivan shifted his weight a little to block Bob's probing eyes.

Dr. Sullivan finally responded, "I'm so sorry, but this isn't a good time. Last week, I donated online to the police officers' association. I appreciate the men in blue. You boys have a nice night now."

"And women," Bob drawled.

"Yes, well, we can't all be as progressive and enlightened as you, I expect," Dr. Sullivan said. "Really, gentleman, I've just gotten a call. I'm needed at the hospital. I was getting ready to pick up my bag and head out when you knocked."

The doctor pointed down at the black bag by his feet. The Medic bag was one the pharmaceutical company had given out.

Bob stared pointedly at the doctor's slippers. "Glad to walk you to your car," Bob said. "I didn't see it. Is it around back?"

I don't have time for this bullshit, Sullivan thought. "Oh, please don't bother. I usually go out the back to the garage. No worries. Good night," he said, closing the front door.

Sarge ran up the driveway, barely stopping until he threw his large hands on the doctor's front door, trying to catch it before it closed.

"Open up," he yelled. They heard him bolt the door and turn the lock.

"Goddamnit!" Bob swore.

Sarge looked ready to bust an artery. "I'm opening that asshole's door, now," Sarge seethed.

"Okay, okay. Give me the search warrant. You bust down the door. The guy's not stupid, I'll give him that. You got your bullet-proof vest on, Sarge?"

Sarge thumped his chest in response and backed up to take the door down.

He rammed it with his meaty shoulder, and the wood split in two. All three men stepped cautiously around the wood fragments and into the entry, letting Sarge lead the way.

Silence.

Tony texted Buck that the officers were in and told him to hold tight.

"Doctor lied about the emergency," Tony whispered. He'd stepped off the porch a few minutes ago to call the hospital. "The hospital operator said no one there had issued an emergency order for Dr. Sullivan to return to the hospital."

"What a lying sack," Sarge mumbled.

He led the way and cleared two rooms between the front door and the kitchen at the back of the house, trying to locate Dr. Sullivan. He stopped short of the kitchen.

Tony and Bob drew up behind him. The burled wood and brass grandfather clock in the living room ticked in the corner. The air was stagnant, heavy with the musty scent of old books and damp.

The longer the men stood at the entrance to the small kitchen, the more the overwhelming odor of decay overlaid with something sweet wafted over them.

Bob felt increasingly uneasy and hissed at Tony. Bob held his service revolver in his right hand. "Use your cell to give Gus and Johnson the heads up that we're in. Tell Buck and Jeb, too, and tell them not to shoot anybody. I'll cover you."

Tony shoved his firearm back into his holster so he could use both thumbs to text. The cell screen lit up his face with an eerie glow.

Bob heard a low sound. "What was that?" Bob whispered.

Sarge took one step toward the kitchen.

Bwam! A shotgun went off, nearly decapitating Sarge. He had tripped a wire that pulled the shotgun's trigger. Because he'd stumbled first over the threshold, only his head was grazed by the shotgun blast. Blood trickled down his face from the \shotgun shell, scoring a path down his face.

On the floor, Bob and Tony kept shaking their heads, trying to get their ears to work. Neither could hear the other whispering.

"Sarge, you okay?" Bob asked, looking at Sarge's face.

"Damn, that was close!" Sarge yelled. He shook his big head, dislodging splinters of wood and paint chips that had sprayed him when the blast hit the doorframe.

They waited in silence a few seconds. The back door blew open. Jed and Buck rolled across the ripped linoleum.

"What the fuck?" Jeb shouted.

"Don't stand up!" Bob yelled. "He booby trapped the kitchen. Be careful coming across the floor. We don't know what else is in here."

"Where's Katie?" Buck yelled.

"We're looking—stay in here. Don't touch anything. I mean it," Bob shouted.

He pointed to Sarge, who leaned up against the door jamb to stay on his feet.

"Don't let these two morons move a muscle. Tony and I will check out the rest of the house. You got your phone?"

Sarge nodded. He'd wadded up the search warrant to put pressure on his head wound to stop the blood flow.

"Text Gus and Johnson, tell them to look for Sullivan but to use extreme caution. Tell them everyone in here is mostly okay. I'm worried they didn't come to the house. Let me know if they don't respond to you."

Bob and Tony crept back the way they'd come into the house. Every few feet, they paused to listen.

They heard a whimper coming from the door to the right of the living room. The thick wood-paneled door was closed and locked.

"Where the hell is backup?" Bob muttered.

"They should be on the grounds by now," Tony said. He checked his phone. Nothing from patrol, and nothing from Gus and Johnson.

"If Katie's in there, we gotta get to her," Bob said.

"I agree. We can't wait," Tony said.

"Okay, but if shit goes down, it was my call and mine alone," Bob said. "You got it?"

"Yeah, but—" Tony started.

"Zip it. We're going in. Sarge is out of commission. We can't use him as a battering ram. As much as I hate to ask them, we need Jeb or Buck to help us get the door down. Guess their football-playing years are worth something now. Go get Jeb, and get Sarge's bulletproof vest. If I'm going to lose my gold watch and pension, at least it'll be for a good cause," Bob said.

Tony left, and Bob heard some murmurs from the kitchen. In no time, he returned with Jeb wearing the vest.

"Need the door kicked in? No problem," Jeb said.

Bob grabbed him before Jeb could rush the door.

"Whoa, whoa, we don't know what or who is on the other side of this door. You break it down, roll to the side, and stay on the ground and out of the way. I don't care what you see or hear, you don't fuck with the plan, got it?"

"Yes," Jeb said. He gripped his shotgun tightly.

"I mean it, Jeb. No wild ass stuff in there. Don't touch anything or anyone. I don't want you or anybody else hurt tonight. Am I clear?"

"Yes, Detective, you are more than clear," Jeb said.

"Let's go, Katie may be in there and…" he faltered, "and hurt. On my count. Tony, you get behind me and cover Jeb and me."

"I got you," Tony said.

CHAPTER FORTY

Gus and Johnson quietly opened the door to the first out-building after waiting what seemed like years. Not hearing anything, after several minutes, Gus twisted the door handle and slowly eased the door open. The smell of damp and rodent droppings hit them first. Gus gagged and used her shirt collar to block the worst of the smells. They waited a few minutes, then stepped inside and dropped to a crouch.

A humming noise underlay the outdoor sounds of crickets and cicadas. As their eyes adjusted to the dark, Gus motioned for Johnson to go left as she went right.

Johnson nodded and quietly moved off. Gus stayed at a low crouch and felt along the walls for a door or cabinet, anything that could conceal Katie.

She jerked up at the sound of a loud *thump* and "Dammit!" from Johnson.

Screw this. She fumbled on the wall looking for a light switch. A solitary bulb lit up the room. Johnson was leaning on the table he'd bumped into and rubbing his shin.

"Don't touch anything," Gus growled.

They surveyed the room in silence. Other than the table, a couple of freezers, and a refrigerator, the room was empty.

Gus widened her eyes at Johnson, but his head was down. He was examining the dark stains and gouge marks on the wooden table. He snapped a few photos of the table and the room.

"We've got to open the freezers and the fridge," she said.

"I know it," Johnson snapped back.

"Let me see if Tony has texted me before we get started," Gus said. "Nope, nothing."

Johnson stood still with his head down.

"Look, Johnson, I can do this, open all of them up, and call out if I find anything," Gus started.

"No. I owe it to Katie to find her no matter what," he said.

"Okay. I'll start here with the fridge, and you open the freezer on the far side," she said. "Take photos of the outside first and then the inside."

Johnson squared his shoulders, took the photo of the freezer and opened it up.

"Thank God, just bags of ice and a few quarts of ice cream," he said, snapping another photo of the insides.

Gus took a deep breath and swung the fridge door open. The smell of formaldehyde wafted out.

"Hell," she said softly.

Johnson peered over her shoulder.

"Mother fucker," he choked out.

Glassine bags on each shelf of the fridge held what appeared to be various cuts of meat, but the eyes in the bag on the second shelf and the hands in bags on the first shelf belonged to humans. The parts were brown and gray in color.

Gus started taking photos of the shelves while Johnson stepped out to call for the crime scene techs. The cool outdoors helped to restore Johnson's racing heart.

"Hey, we need backup," he began in a whisper. "We're out here off Highway 15, and we've found something. You guys need to get out here and bring all of your gear. You're gonna need it."

The other man groaned into the phone.

"I don't care what time it is, this is some sick shit out here. You need to tag it and bag it and process a big table that looks like it's been used to butcher something, probably humans. Get Feinstein on this one. That dude'll go over it with a magnifying glass. It'll take him two damn days, but he's good. Don't roll up the driveway. We're still looking for Katie and the owner. You'll see the fed SUV down a bit. I'll meet you there. I'll tote your gear. Yeah, yeah. Quit complaining," Johnson said, ending the call.

Gus felt sickened by the smells from the open fridge door. She photographed as much as she could without moving anything. Her gloves were on, which made it harder to maneuver the phone, but they needed a clean crime scene.

She waited for Johnson to get back before opening the last freezer.

Johnson walked in and said, "Crime techs are on their way. I'm gonna meet them down the road so they don't get lost. Thompson can get lost in his own office. Ready to open the last one?"

"Yeah, let's get it over with," Gus said.

"Femurs," Johnson muttered. "Arms, pelvis, shit, it just gets worse and worse."

Gus snapped the photos while Johnson held the door open. She affixed biohazard stickers and exhibit numbers to the outside of each unit.

"The police department is gonna have to store all this," Johnson said.

"Sarge is going to be pissed. He's going to have to keep these things running. Come to think of it, so will the techs," Gus acknowledged.

"Come on, we still have the garage to check. Tony still hasn't texted about the house or Katie, so we need to keep moving."

"Let's do it," Johnson said.

Tony's text for assistance popped up on their phones the next second, and they sprinted for the house.

* * * * *

Jeb rammed the dining room door with all of his 230 pounds. The door popped off its hinges and fell into the room.

Dr. Sullivan sighted down his firearm and fired at Bob.

"Dad!" Matthew yelled. Bob turned his body toward the sound of his son's voice. Searing pain bloomed from his shoulder, and he went down, blood pouring out of the wound. His eyes were barely open, and he moaned.

Before Sullivan could squeeze off another shot, Jeb was up and swung his shotgun like a bat, hitting Dr. Sullivan on the side of his head with enough force to send him flying. Buck ran in the back door, jumped on Sullivan, and pinned him down with his considerable weight.

Tony was kneeling near a dining room chair, untying Katie. He talked to her in a soothing tone but stopped after a minute and glanced over at Bob, who wasn't moving.

He'd already texted 911 emergency and then Johnson and Gus with the "officer down" code and struggled to untangle the knots. His hands were sweaty, and he wiped them on his pants.

Katie moaned. Her pallor contrasted with the streaks of blood down her neck and arms. Most of the blood was dried, but a few fresh rivulets ran down one side of her neck.

Buck jumped up, keeping one size fifteen boot on Sullivan. Sullivan grabbed weakly at Buck's leg with the intact hand.

"Get back down, Buck," Tony said. "I got this. Katie's going to be okay. You keep Sullivan restrained. Emergency is on the way."

"Switch places with me," Buck shouted. He stepped on Sullivan's good hand, and the doctor shrieked.

"No. It'll be just a minute," Tony shouted back.

Sullivan writhed on the floor and screamed obscenities at Buck. Buck continued to look at Katie and didn't see the small gun in Sullivan's hand.

"Boom!"

Tony's Glock 9mm thundered in the small room. Sullivan's gun, aimed at Buck's head, went flying, along with half of Sullivan's remaining fingers.

Johnson barreled into the room like the wide receiver he'd been. Empty chairs flew as he wrenched them aside to check on Katie. Gus followed, keeping her gun trained on Sullivan. Sullivan screamed for medical aid, and Johnson switched places with Buck. With Johnson's weight on him, Sullivan gasped for air. "Get the Doc a dish rag for his hand," Johnson said to Jeb, who headed to the kitchen.

Buck knelt by Katie and put his hand on hers. He tenderly removed the tape from her mouth.

"It'll be over soon, Katie," he said. "We'll get you out of this madhouse."

Tears trickled down Katie's cheeks. She gave a tremulous smile at the sound of Buck's voice.

Before she said anything, the Feds burst into the room. The lead agent took over, issuing orders to the emergency workers, crime scene techs, and local officers arriving on the scene. Officers stood ready to take Sullivan into custody.

"Always late to the party," Johnson mumbled in the direction of the lead agent.

Deep cuts bloomed from Katie's neck, chest, and down her arms. As the final knot was untangled, Buck eased her chair back from the table, careful not to dislodge the occupant or parts of the occupant beside her. He was doing his best not to look at anything but Katie.

Over the loud objections of Tony, Gus, and Johnson, Buck carried her outside to the waiting ambulance. The paramedic trailed behind them.

He gently set her on the tailgate of the ambulance and looked at her. Deep channels scored Katie's legs. Part of her ear was gone. She sobbed against Buck's chest. Buck gripped her tightly until Jeb hugged her gingerly from the side.

"Katie girl, you're going to be okay. You're a fighter. We're with you all the way," Jeb whispered to her. Buck, the paramedics want to take her to the hospital. The docs are waiting for her in the ER at the medical school hospital in the next town over. You need to let her go for a minute."

"I'm riding with her. She's not leaving my sight," Buck shouted.

"I know, but you need to let go of her so they can load her into the ambulance. I'll pick up her mama and our mama, and meet you in Durham," Jeb said. "We'll be right behind you."

Buck wiped his face with his sleeve and allowed the ER workers to load Katie onto a stretcher. She'd passed out from the pain.

Buck slid off the back of the ambulance. "I'm going to kill that bastard," he said, heading back toward the house.

Jeb grabbed him. "No, you're not. You're getting in that ambulance right now and letting the cops do their thing. Katie needs you."

Buck shrugged him off and punched him in the jaw.

Jeb got up slowly. He shook his head and brushed off the dirt and gravel from his pants. "That's a free one. I know you're hurting. But, hit me again, and you're going down."

Tony pushed in between the two big men who were squared off and breathing hard.

"You idiots! Save it for later. Katie needs to get to the hospital, stat. Buck, you either get in that ambulance or I will. Jeb, go get your car and follow after you get her mom and yours."

Buck silently hugged Jeb and climbed into the waiting ambulance.

"They loaded Bob into the other ambulance," Tony said. "I'm headed over to the Medical Center in Durham. I think he's going to need surgery where the bullet hit him. He's lost a lot of blood. See you over there."

Tony rushed off and jumped into the back of the waiting ambulance.

"Who's got Sullivan?" Jeb asked the last patrolman standing beside him.

"About fourteen officers and the feds. His ambulance will get here when it gets here."

* * * * *

Bob's head pounded like a hammer was hitting it every few seconds, and his shoulder, oh God, his shoulder burned. The morning light crept into his room. He'd been moved to the rehab unit from the hospital last night.

He moaned.

"Dad?" Matthew asked.

He opened his eyes to see his son sitting on his bed. Gloria was asleep in the fold-out chair that the hospital generously called a bed.

"Son. You saved my life. One inch to the left and he'd have shot me in the chest," Bob said.

Matthew smiled. "I'm glad I could help. I think that's why I was sent, the reason why I'm not, you know, gone." He looked over at Gloria. "I'm glad Mom's here with you. You two are good together. You should stay together." Matthew brushed his hand gently over Gloria's hair.

"Yeah. She's really something," Bob said with a smile. "I'd like her to stay, too."

Matthew turned serious. "It's my time to go, Dad. Don't be sad. I love you," Matthew said, his image wavering.

"I love you, too, son. You are the best," Bob whispered to his son, who dissolved in a shimmer.

Gloria stirred, then sat up across from Bob. "I thought I'd lost you," she said. She came over and squeezed into the space at his side.

"Not this time," Bob said. "Though it was a near thing." He tightened his grip on her waist. "I know you never thought you'd hear me say this, but I'm taking two weeks of vacation when I get out of here. Go with me?" he asked, smiling at her and awkwardly smoothing her hair away from her eyes.

"I'd like that," she said. "Somewhere warm or somewhere exotic?"

"You pick. I'll follow your lead."

"Bella, too?"

"Bella, too."

Under the bed, Bella whimpered, hearing her name. Violating all rehab rules, Gloria had snuck her in wrapped up in blankets and seated in a wheelchair.

EPILOGUE

It was a glorious day for a wedding. The robins and sparrows were singing. Dew sparkled on the freshly mown grass in Katie's mother's garden full of gardenias, cow parsley, peonies, and hydrangeas. The bees buzzed in the nearby shrubs and butterflies circled the yellow black-eyed Susans.

The bride's dress of white satin and lace was magnificent. No one but her mother and Gus knew that the seamstress had hastily added lengths of Belgian lace at the neck and sleeves. The fabric hid the worst of the physical scars. Katie was working hard on coming to grips with the internal ones. A long veil hid her shining visage.

The groom looked handsome in his morning suit. He stood up straighter when he saw Katie start down the aisle with his brother.

The bride had planned to walk down the aisle on Jeb's arm, but, at the last minute, Katie accepted Jeb's thoughtful offer to help her complete her journey without the use of a walker.

Jeb carried Katie down the aisle with her white dress billowing over his arms. Charles walked beside them with his huge head held high in his wedding finery of a black bow tie. He'd only sampled part of his boutonniere while waiting to begin. His doggy smile was infectious.

Gently, Jeb set Katie down next to Buck and kissed her tenderly on the cheek. He clapped his brother on the back and sat with their mom. The brothers' mom wore a loud jacket with yellow sequins that she'd purchased and snuck out from the bridal shop when the bride was distracted.

Johnson, Man of Honor, steadied Katie on her left by giving her his arm. She smiled up at him. He sniffed back tears.

Gus beamed at her husband in the audience while stoically wearing the awful fuchsia confection her friend had selected.

Tony smirked at the clearly uncomfortable agent and laughed when she mouthed an obscenity at him, taking care to turn away from the officiant. Dr. Patterson, seated on Tony's right, cleared his throat. Bob and Gloria, seated on Tony's left, spent as much time looking at each other as they spent looking at Katie and Buck.

The moms patted their wet cheeks with their lacy handkerchiefs and beamed at each other across the makeshift aisle.

Buck gazed, completely besotted, at Katie. The diamond clips in her hair sparkled in the sunlight. They were almost as radiant as the bride's smile. She had to call Buck's name twice before Buck realized he was supposed to start his vows.

Johnson glared at him while Charles pushed between Buck and Katie.

"Don't mess up Katie's wedding, you idiot," Johnson hissed.

Buck laughed, and the officiant rolled his eyes.

THE END

ACKNOWLEDGMENTS

My parents, Sally and David, committed themselves to providing me and my three siblings with an outstanding education. These wonderful schools supplied the rest: Wake Forest University (English and Politics departments), Wake Forest University School of Law and Queens University of Charlotte (MFA 2019). I cherish the lifelong friends made at each university.

Thank you to my wonderful and patient Beta readers: Teresa Blemings, Carole Griffin, and Ellen Thompson. The time, support, and encouragement you gave meant everything to me.

With gratitude to the fantastic weekly writers group led by novelist David Payne. Everyone gave such helpful feedback and encouraged me to move forward with the book.

Thank you to my excellent editor, Sherman Morrison, and to all of the dedicated people at Authors Unite.

Thank you to novelist Martin Clark for spurring me on to finish the book and for always generously answering my questions.

Thank you to all of the readers who read my books, short stories, and poetry. Your kind comments mean so much.

To the special people living in or from the counties of Granville and Vance in North Carolina: no, this book is not about your uncle Fred or your aunt Mae—it's fiction.

Finally, to my sweet husband who has (almost) controlled his eye rolls when I ask him to listen to me read a few pages, and to Lucy Jane, the perfect gray tabby.